WALL

A Post-Apocalyptic/Dystopian Adventure

The Traveler Series Book Three

Tom Abrahams

A PITON PRESS BOOK
WALL
The Traveler Series Book Three
© Tom Abrahams 2016. All Rights Reserved

Cover Design by Hristo Kovatliev
Edited by Felicia A. Sullivan
Proofread by Pauline Nolet
Formatted by Stef McDaid at WriteIntoPrint.com

PITON PRESS

JOIN TOM'S PREFERRED READERS CLUB

@

http://tomabrahamsbooks.com

WORKS BY TOM ABRAHAMS

SPACEMAN: A POST-APOCALYPTIC/DYSTOPIAN THRILLER
(coming November 2016)

THE TRAVELER POST-APOCALYPTIC/DYSTOPIAN SERIES
HOME
CANYON
WALL

POLITICAL CONSPIRACIES
SEDITION
INTENTION

JACKSON QUICK ADVENTURES
ALLEGIANCE
ALLEGIANCE BURNED
HIDDEN ALLEGIANCE

PERSEID COLLAPSE: PILGRIMAGE SERIES NOVELLAS
CROSSING
REFUGE
ADVENT

For Don
Ching Ching.

"We shall draw from the heart of suffering itself the means of inspiration and survival."

— Winston Churchill

CHAPTER ONE

OCTOBER 25, 2037, 2:00 AM
SCOURGE +5 YEARS
PALO DURO CANYON, TEXAS

Dragging a fresh corpse across the canyon's floor wasn't part of the plan. Not much that had happened in the week since he'd arrived had gone as Charlie Pierce expected, but there was a job to do.

Regardless of the obstacles or the unforeseen circumstances, Pierce had to deliver. General Roof was relying on his surveillance for the coming assault.

Pierce was bent over at the waist, slogging backwards on his heels as he pulled the body through brush, over rock, and across dry creek beds. He didn't know how far he'd have to go to find the right spot to dump the man he was forced to execute. He'd know it when he found it.

Lightning flashed in the sky above, illuminating the steep, jagged walls of the canyon. Thunder followed and reverberated as it traveled the wide valley of Palo Duro. Pierce stopped and dropped the body. He stood erect and put his hands on his hips. He was winded and, despite near freezing temperatures, was sweating through his shirt. He could feel the perspiration chill as it dripped from the nape of his neck down his back.

Another fork of light jabbed the black sky, pulsing as the thunder cracked and rumbled before the afterglow was gone. The storm was getting closer.

Pierce wondered if the turn in the weather was a good thing. A heavy rain would wash away the impression of the body from having pulled it through the dirt.

He'd snapped the man's neck during a brief struggle. The man, a sentry for the Dwellers, had asked too many questions. He'd pressed too hard about Pierce's intentions. Although Pierce had tried to talk his way out of the predicament, it hadn't worked.

Pierce had found a communications bunker on the canyon's floor. It was two miles from the Dwellers' central encampment.

The bunker wasn't much more than a grotto nature had carved into the mesa walls. There were several two-way radio base stations, their orange displays casting a warm, fire-like glow on the cave's pale walls. It was the rumble and hum of a generator that had led Pierce to the grotto. Sound traveled in the desert night, and the rumble was unmistakable from a half mile away.

A thin, camouflaged wire serving as an antenna extension ran up the steep wall as far as Pierce had been able to see in the dark. The Dwellers' communication system was a fortunate but critical find for the spy. If he couldn't disable the two-way system as the attack occurred, he could at the very least relay frequencies to the Cartel so they could monitor the Dwellers' tactical positions. The sentry had surprised him as he was checking those frequencies.

"Hey," the sentry had called out from beyond the bunker's entrance, his voice echoing inside the small cave. "What are you doing? You're not supposed to be in there."

"I just stumbled in here," Pierce had lied. "I was out for a walk…"

The sentry had stepped into the cave, aiming a penlight at Pierce's face. It had been otherwise dark save the glowing green and blue lights on the two-way transmitters. "It's two o'clock in the morning."

"Yeah." Pierce had shrugged before making his deadly move. Now he found himself dragging a body along the canyon floor.

The canyon was immense in size. It ran seventy miles long and, at its widest, twenty miles across. Its walls stretched skyward close to nine hundred feet from the floor. Pierce had learned in his brief stay that the Dwellers were experts at navigating and protecting it. Pierce had done everything he could to soak in as much information as possible. He'd listened to conversations, observed patterns of movement and behavior, and he'd absorbed the bizarre philosophical bent of the bellicose pacifists who gave themselves Hindi names in a freakish ritual that, to Pierce's limited theological education, bore no resemblance to Hinduism.

Pierce had done his job invisibly until he'd killed the sentry. He'd performed exactly as the general had instructed.

"Be a fly on the wall," General Roof had said the night before he put him in the Jones. "Learn as much as you can about how they work. Then, when we attack, damage whatever defensive systems you can and run."

They were broad orders with little assurance of survival. Pierce gladly accepted the challenge. He had no family. He'd grown tired of his monotonous and sour post-scourge existence. This was an adventure with the promise of greater things to come should he succeed and live.

Pierce blinked against another flash of lightning and shivered at the first icy drops of rain that smacked against his head and shoulders. The storm was coming.

He was running out of time to dispose of the body in a way that made the sentry's death look like an accident. He needed to finish the job and return to the camp before anyone knew he was missing.

Pierce looked around at his surroundings. He couldn't see much beyond a few feet except when the lightning flashed. He decided this spot was as good as any. The ache in his lower back made the choice as much as his brain.

He lifted up his shirt and reached into his baggy, sweat- and dirt-stained pants. Strapped to his leg was a gift General Roof had given him. He flipped it open and pressed a series of numbers before pulling the satellite phone to his ear. It took a couple of minutes for the satellite to acquire his signal. When it did, he heard a series of warbling rings.

The general answered with a voice more gravelly than usual. "It's two in the morning," he said.

The rain was intensifying. The drops were heavier and equally as cold. Pierce wiped the water from his eyes. "I found their communications hub. They're working with two-way radios. I've got the frequencies."

"Go ahead," said the general. "Give them to me."

"Four sixty-seven point fifty-eight seventy-five," Pierce answered. "Four sixty-two fifty-eight seventy-five. Four four six zero zero and four forty-six five."

"Only four frequencies?"

"That I could tell."

"So they've got a two-mile range."

"I don't know."

"And they're operational?"

Pierce squatted, resting his weight on his heels. He shielded his face from the rain and tried to cup the phone tight to his ear. The rain was making it difficult to hear. "What?"

"They're operational?"

"They seem to be," said Pierce. "They've got a generator charging the batteries."

The signal was beginning to weaken. "Are they onto you?"

Pierce turned his back to the gusts of wind blowing through the canyon. "No."

"You sure?"

"I had to kill a guy," Pierce admitted. His body involuntarily trembled from the cold.

"That changes things."

"I'll be f-f-fine," Pierce stammered. His jaw was beginning to ache from his chattering teeth. The temperature had dropped what felt like fifteen degrees in a few seconds. The rain was beating down, slapping Pierce's neck and arms with a cold sting.

The general's voice was hollow and digitally distorted. "Hello?"

Pierce pulled the phone from his ear and looked at the signal. It was nonexistent. He pressed a button to end the call, wiped the screen with the tail of his shirt, and stood to stuff it back into his pants.

"Pierce?" a voice called from behind him.

Pierce spun as thunder shuddered through his shivering body. A flash of lightning revealed a dark figure standing a few feet from him. Pierce couldn't make out the man's features, but he knew who it was and saw the gun in his hand.

"What are you doing, Pierce?" Marcus Battle asked the question as if he already knew the answer.

Pierce balled his hands into fists. He set his feet shoulder width apart and braced himself for the coming confrontation. "What do you think I'm doing?" he asked, the rain spilling into his eyes as he tried to focus on Battle's right hand.

"Helping the Cartel."

Pierce laughed. "You're quick on the uptake," he said. "I've been helping the Cartel since you chose to take me from the Jones. You're not nearly as smart as you think you are."

"You were a plant."

"Something like that."

Battle waved his weapon at the body on the ground. "And you killed this Dweller here?"

Pierce had his eyes on the gun. "Something like that."

"Just killed him. No reason."

Pierce shuddered against the cold. Rain sprayed from his lips as he spat. "Who the hell are you to judge which side is right and which is wrong? You're a homeless vigilante. You —
"

The single shot from Battle's nine millimeter was hidden by the throaty roar of thunder rolling through the gypsum, shale, and sandstone walls, but it traveled straight into Pierce's open mouth and dropped him where he stood.

"Homeless vigilante?" asked Battle. He stepped toward the pair of bodies on the flooding canyon floor and crouched down. He looked into Pierce's eyes. "Something like that."

CHAPTER TWO

OCTOBER 25, 2037, 3:00 AM
SCOURGE +5 YEARS
PALO DURO CANYON, TEXAS

Battle tossed the satellite phone onto the wood-planked table in front of Juliana Paagal. It slid to the edge and came to a rest between her elbows. Paagal was leaning forward, her chin resting on the knuckles of her folded hands.

She was a regal woman who carried herself with quiet dignity. Her ink-black short hair gave her a youthful appearance that belied her age. Her coffee-colored skin blended with the light brown sleeveless top hanging on her narrow shoulders.

Paagal, as she'd asked Battle to call her, had welcomed the weary travelers without question. She trusted fellow Dweller Baadal's judgment as her own.

She and Battle were alone in her large ten-person tent. The rain was constant and deafening against the tent's red nylon walls. There was a lone light hanging from the center pitch of the large space Paagal called her home. A bare mattress and lumpy feather pillow sat atop a futon in one corner, a threadbare wool sofa in another. An orange extension cord snaked its way across the dirt floor and provided enough electricity to power the light and a hot plate perched on one side of the table.

"So you were right," she said, her ice blue eyes staring unblinkingly at Battle without lowering them to look at the satellite phone. "He was a spy."

"I apologize for bringing him here," said Battle. "It's my fault."

Paagal shook her head and smiled. Her eyes narrowed as she spoke. "It was not your fault, Marcus. I am the one who allowed you here. The blame rests with me."

"He killed one of your sentries," said Battle. "It happened inside a communications bunker a couple of miles from here. I wasn't trailing close enough to stop him."

"Ahhh," she said, lowering her arms and nodding. "That would be Sahaayak. He was a good helper. We will miss his kindness and his soul."

Battle nodded at the phone. "Take a look at that," he said. "Pierce used it to call the Cartel. I'm guessing he was giving them intelligence about your two-way radio system."

The smile evaporated from Paagal's face. "Where is Pierce?" she asked. "I can ask him directly what he was doing. I'd rather not make any assumptions."

Battle hesitated and bit the inside of his cheek. "He's dead."

Paagal cupped a hand behind her ear, catching the large wooden hoop hanging from the lobe. "He's what?"

The slap of the rain on the nylon made it hard to carry on a conversation, especially given that Battle didn't really want Paagal to hear him. "I killed him," he said above the din.

Paagal nodded. "I see."

"I shot him. His body is next to Saya—"

Paagal spoke slowly, a syllable at a time. "Sa-ha-a-yak."

"Sahaayak," Battle said. "They're maybe a quarter mile from the bunker."

"Well—" Paagal sighed "—I'll go ahead and make an assumption then. I'll assume your life was in danger and you had no choice but to defend yourself. Otherwise, killing Pierce would have been a reckless and cruel act unbefitting a man who, up until now, I've given great respect. You're former military. You know the value of a prisoner who has information to impart voluntarily…or involuntarily, especially given all of the extra Cartel patrols we've spotted nearing the rim."

Battle pulled out a chair and sat down at the table across from Paagal. He leaned in, his forearms resting on the rough-hewn wood. "My life wasn't in danger. I wish I could say it was self-defense. I think I lost that impulse-control mechanism a while ago."

Paagal leaned back in her chair and folded her long, lean arms across her chest. Her biceps flexed as she adjusted herself. "As you judged Pierce, I should not judge you," she said with more than a hint of irony. "We all learn to function, to cope in different ways. Yours is to kill at the hint of a threat. I see a man who struggles with his own darkness. You see the light. You want to live in the light. But the dark is more comfortable for you, so you slink into its embrace at every opportunity."

Battle laughed. "You were a shrink before the Scourge, weren't you?"

Paagal nodded. A smile spread across her face. "You might consider I am still a shrink," she said. "Being a leader requires the effective use of psychology."

Battle scowled. "So what now?"

"I suppose I should ask you that question," Paagal said. "You arrived here a week ago. You've recovered from your injuries. Your woman, Lola, is—"

"She's not my woman," said Battle.

Paagal's eyebrows arched with doubt. She raised her hands in surrender. "Whatever you say. Your friend Lola is again walking without a limp. Her son seems healthy."

"Your point?"

"We've not discussed your plans," she said. "You are our guests for as long as you like," her voice lilted.

"But…?"

"But," she continued, "there is a war coming. You are a soldier."

"I *was* a soldier."

"Semantics, Mr. Battle," she replied. "Do you plan to help us? Our common enemy is knocking at our door."

Battle squeezed his eyes shut and pinched the bridge of his nose. "I'll be honest," he said, "I need to get to the wall."

"The wall."

"The wall," he repeated. "Lola and Sawyer need a fresh start, as fresh as can be had in this wasteland."

"And you?"

Battle shrugged. "I don't know about me. But I need to get them there."

"It sounds to me as if you're looking for a quid pro quo," said Paagal. "You help us. We help you. I know Baadal discussed with you the wall and what may lie beyond."

"He didn't tell me what was on the other side," Battle said. "I know the Cartel doesn't exist north, east, or west of it."

Juliana Paagal stared at Battle without saying anything for several minutes. Battle felt as if she were taking some sort of psychic inventory, taking mental notes without permission. He sat there, staring back at her, trying not to give away anything.

"Here's what I want from you, Marcus Battle," she said. "You help us defeat the Cartel, or degrade them such that they dare not attack us again, and we will help you find your way beyond the wall."

Battle shook his head. "You can't beat them," he said. "They're not only here. They're everywhere. Abilene. Houston. Dallas. San Antonio. Austin. Galveston. You know that better than I."

"That man, Pierce, the one you brought here is not the only spy," she said. "We too have the ability to infiltrate."

"Really." It was less a question and more a doubtful dismissive.

"Ever since the truce," she said, "we've been dispatching cells. They've lived and worked amongst the Cartel in those cities you mention. They've painstakingly recruited allies. All of them are ready to pounce when we signal them. We can end the Cartel. You've come at the right time."

"Or the wrong time." He sighed. "You're talking about war."

Paagal pressed her lips together. She scratched her left bicep and nodded. "I prefer to call it an insurrection or a revolution."

"Semantics," he said.

"Touché."

"So you can beat the Cartel?"

"We believe so," she said. "The time is upon us."

"Then once the Cartel is beaten," Battle said, leaning in, "I won't need your help."

"Yes, you will," she said. "The Cartel is the largest, vilest of the organized groups to emerge after the Scourge. But they are not the only one. There are pockets of thieves and killers who live along the wall, who worm from one side of it to the other, feeding off of those who would cross it. You will need our help."

Battle leaned back. He nodded. He knew he had no choice in the matter. "For being such a proclaimed pacifist, you seem eager to fight," Battle observed. "Seems hypocritical."

"Does it?" Paagal asked, her expression unchanged.

"I'm violent for the sake of violence," he said. "Though I don't like it, I admit it. It's my cross to bear." Battle thought about how he hadn't prayed in days. He was losing his religion in the wilds of the untamed landscape that surrounded him. It wasn't that he'd forgotten to pray. He didn't feel like it.

"Interesting self-awareness," said Paagal. "I would counter your assertion by suggesting I am for violence only because nonviolence means we continue postponing a solution."

"Paraphrasing Malcolm X, are you?" Battle asked.

A sly grin crept across Paagal's face, her magically white teeth aglow in the red hue of the tent. "Be peaceful, be courteous, obey the law, respect everyone; but if someone puts his hand on you, send him to the cemetery," she said. "By any means necessary."

CHAPTER THREE

OCTOBER 25, 2037, 7:49 AM
SCOURGE +5 YEARS
HOUSTON, TEXAS

Ana Montes was late. She hurried down the frozen escalator, her right hand sliding along the rubber railing as she descended into the darkness, her feet clomping on the aluminum steps. Even in the blackness of the underground tunnel, she knew where she was and where she needed to be. Ana stepped off the escalator threshold twenty feet below what remained of downtown Houston, Texas, and took fifteen steps straight ahead before turning ninety degrees to the right. Her footsteps echoed against the walls of the six-mile-long tunnel system, and she made another ninety-degree turn.

She could hear the hushed voices of the others. They'd begun without her. She took a deep breath and pushed her way into the room. It was lit with LED flashlights illuminating the faces of the dozen men and women who crowded around a map on a table. All of them looked up at her when she slid into the room.

"You're late," growled the man at the center of the group. "We had to begin without you."

"I couldn't get away," she said breathlessly and found her spot at the table. From her perspective, the map was upside down. She was opposite the man in charge.

His name was Sidney Reilly. Everyone called him Sid. He was the one who'd recruited most of them to join the Dwellers' resistance.

His eyes lingered on Ana as he spoke. "As I was saying," he huffed, "we are getting close. Within a day, maybe two, we'll begin. Our job—"

"That soon?" Ana interrupted. "A day or two? I don't think—"

Sid's eyes narrowed; the shadows cast from the flashlight deepened across his furrowed brow. "I didn't ask what you think. We move when we move. You're either with us or you're not, Ana."

Ana shrank back from the table, trying to lessen the burn from the eyes glaring at her. She nodded and bit her lower lip. "I'm with you."

Sid nodded and continued the briefing. Ana wasn't listening. She was looking at the men and women flanking her to either side. One by one, Sid had convinced each of them the Cartel's rule was coming to an end. All it would take was enough people to rise up. The ones at the table bought what he was selling.

Each of them then recruited their own cadre of revolutionaries. Those people, in turn, recruited another group. It was an uprising's equivalent of multilevel marketing, and it provided for a stopgap plausible deniability should any one person flip or be discovered by the Cartel.

In all, Sid estimated they had as many as five thousand people on board. That number, they all knew, paled in comparison to Cartel loyalists. But under the right circumstances they were large enough to deliver crippling blows to the despots in charge of their city.

Next to Sid was Nancy Wake. She was a Cartel bookkeeper who had access to the locations and depth of their provisions, illicit drugs, weapons, transportation, and other holdings. Her husband, Wendell, was a disillusioned posse boss. Together, they were the deepest penetration into the Cartel's Houston structure.

The others around the table were a mixture of grunts, urban farmers, and shopkeepers. They offered a variety of skills and insight the revolutionaries would need if they had any chance of succeeding when the time came. The time was coming fast, too fast for Ana Montes.

Ana looked at the map of Texas. It was marked with intersecting blue and red lines. Arrows marked the direction of movements. Large and small circles indicated the revolutionaries' strength in numbers at various locations. Close to Ana, in an area near Amarillo, Palo Duro Canyon was highlighted in fluorescent yellow.

It all seemed to be too much. She'd signed on with the belief that the revolt against the Cartel was a nebulous pipe dream unlikely to ever come to fruition. She'd agreed to do things she never thought she'd actually have to do. Now she stared at the reality of the impending action and her pulse quickened. Her knees weakened. Beads of sweat bloomed on her forehead and above her upper lip.

"Are you okay, Ana?" Nancy Wake asked, interrupting Sid. "You don't look good."

Ana leaned on the table, locking her elbows for support, and she nodded. She felt the return of everyone's glare. "I'm okay," she said. "I…"

Nancy's eyes narrowed. "You what?"

Ana inhaled deeply and wiped her upper lip with the back of her hand. "I just…this is suicide, isn't it? I don't see how we can beat them. Their numbers are too great. They have too many weapons."

"What are you saying?" Sid asked, his head tilted to the side. Others mumbled their concerns about Ana's doubts. Sid raised his hand to quiet them.

"I think they'll slaughter us," she admitted. "I don't want to die or end up a slave."

Sid laughed condescendingly. "We're already slaves, Ana. They already control most aspects of our lives. We didn't choose them as masters."

"They robbed us of our liberty," said Nancy. "They duped us into believing they'd provide security and structure. And then they squeezed us of our rights. They lord over us like we're their minions. I can't live like that anymore. I'd rather be slaughtered."

Others voiced their agreement. A couple questioned Ana's loyalty, asking aloud if she could be trusted. Sid silenced them.

"You knew the stakes when I recruited you," he said. "You knew the end game. You agreed to your role, your vital role. None of this can be a surprise to you."

"No. Not really." She looked down at the map, her eyes blankly tracing the colored lines on the map. "I'm not surprised. I'm afraid." She looked up, tears stinging the corners of her eyes.

When Ana signed on, she didn't have a reason to fear death. She wasn't a mother yet. Now she had a nine-month-old daughter. What would happen to her child if she died? Who would raise her? What kind of woman would she grow to be if she lived to grow up at all?

Nancy spoke softly. "We're all afraid, Ana. I'm more fearful of what will happen to us if we do nothing. Our future is sketchy if we act, it's bleak if we don't."

Ana swallowed against the thick knot in her throat. Nancy was right. Sid was right. They had to act. They had to fight. They had to end the Cartel.

CHAPTER FOUR

OCTOBER 25, 2037, 8:02 AM
SCOURGE +5 YEARS
LUBBOCK, TEXAS

General Roof sat on the edge of his bed, staring out the large picture window of his temporary home. It faced east, and each morning as the sun rose, the bright orange light that filled his room forced him awake.

This morning, however, he'd been awaiting the sun. He couldn't sleep after his phone call with Pierce. The mole had given him valuable information, which he rolled over in his mind like sheep jumping a fence. It should have helped him relax and gain the needed hours of rest.

Instead, he found himself thinking about the man Pierce had killed. That was a lamentable mistake Roof knew would be Pierce's undoing. The general concluded that satellite call from Pierce was likely his last. The Dwellers were smart. They'd put two and two together and they'd end Pierce's usefulness one way or the other.

Roof rubbed his eyes and slid his feet to the cold concrete floor. He tested his weight on his bad leg and felt the dull familiar ache that forced his awkward limp. He measured the difference between his two legs. One was muscular and whole. It was hairy, as a man's leg should be, and its skin was an even creamy Caucasian tone. The other was thinner and sicklier in its appearance. Below his knee, large pinkish areas the color of a newborn's feet were devoid of hair. The patches of transplanted skin looked like a collection of former Soviet states decorating his leg.

There wasn't a day that passed where Roof didn't think about the day his leg was mutilated. It was etched in Technicolor, that singularly defining day of his life. Another man had sacrificed, had put his own survival in jeopardy for his sake. It was the kind of selfless action that should have forced Roof along another path upon his return from Syria. He should have paid it forward, helping others in their daily lives.

Instead, the guilt he felt at having survived the IED and resulting ambush that killed four others had consumed him. Roof, who'd dabbled with drugs and alcohol for much of his adult life, dove headfirst into addiction. He'd been in and out of VA hospitals and homeless shelters.

He'd somehow ended up in Houston and had found help at a halfway house for vets. They'd gotten him sober, taught him business skills, and had sent him on his way with a new confidence.

Unfortunately, a hobbled recovering addict wasn't atop employers' "to hire" list. So Roof had taken work where he'd been able to find it and slipped into the criminal underworld of the Bayou City. He'd dealt in drugs and women and had quickly made a name for himself as a ruthless purveyor of illicit goods and underage flesh. He rose to the top of the game in a city known for being the highway for trafficking from Latin America into the United States.

He'd always worn his dog tags on the outside of his skintight shirts and had earned the street handle General. His penchant for drugging unsuspecting women and his birth name Rufus had led some to call him Roofie. He'd shortened it, combined the two monikers, and adopted General Roof as his name. His life force grew stronger, his cult of personality irresistible.

The Scourge was his deliverance. He'd emerged from the shadows, joined forces with prior competitors, and after months of work, consolidated disparate gangs into the Cartel. He'd agreed to share power with two other men, but they knew he was stronger. He'd been as fearless as Pablo Emilio Escobar Gaviria and Jorge Luis Ochoa Vásquez, the men who half a century earlier had founded the Medellín Cartel, and had a reputation for being as ruthless as the Salvadoran Mara Salvatrucha gang that ravaged Central America and spread to the southwestern United States in the early years of the twenty-first century.

Through brute force and will, General Roof had engaged in a meeting of the minds with the Sureños, Sinaloa Cartel, Gulf Cartel, La Familia Michoacana, Mexican Mafia, Yakuza, and Los Zetas. It hadn't hurt his mother was Panamanian and his Spanish was impeccable.

As powerful as they had become, as much as they had struck fear into the surviving populous and had driven the government from their newly staked territory, Roof had always felt inferior somehow. Maybe it was the daily morning reminder of his external wounds. Maybe it was the internal ones, the truth that his life had been saved by a better man than he and that he'd chosen to waste that gift on the easier, darker path.

He rubbed his thighs with his palms and pushed to his feet. Roof balanced himself for a moment on his heels before rocking to his toes. He stepped to the window. The sun was lifting above the flat horizon of the southern end of the Llano Estacado. He bit his lower lip, considering whether letting Marcus Battle live was the right thing to do. It was a moment of weakness, he admitted to the imp on his shoulder. It was a payback: a life spared for a life saved. It was also probably a fatal mistake.

For as heartless as he'd become since earning his sobriety, he'd never been as tough, as relentless, as unwilling to quit as Marcus Battle. He knew that. A shiver ran along his neck and he trembled. He took a rubber band from his wrist and worked it into his hair, looping it twice to help shape a wiry, shoulder-length ponytail.

Roof scratched an itch in his thick beard and turned from the window, his feet scraping along the concrete as he moved to his clothing draped over the back of a desk chair. He'd slipped on his pants and an undershirt when there was a loud knock at his door.

"Just a minute," he called and slid one arm into the long-sleeved plaid cotton shirt. He walked to the door and peeked through the peephole. It was Cyrus Skinner.

Roof snapped the last of the pearl buttons on the shirt and pulled open the door. Skinner took off his white hat and held it against his chest.

"Sorry to bother you so early, General," he said, stepping into the room. "I wanted to give you a tactical update."

"It's not a problem," said Roof. "I was awake. I got a call at two o'clock this morning from Pierce." He looked over at the clock next to the bed. It was flashing. The power had gone out and come back.

"The mole?"

Roof limped back to the chair to retrieve his boots. "Yes."

"And?"

"He gave us good intel," said Roof. "He found their communications bunker and provided frequencies."

"That's in addition to their security setup, their weapons, and the position of their men around the canyon rim," said Skinner. An unlit cigarette was bouncing from his lips as he spoke. "You were genius to set that up. I gotta say, General, I had my doubts. But you were right."

Roof plopped into the chair. He winced as he slid on one of the boots. "Maybe."

"What do you mean?"

Roof exhaled and then sucked in a deep breath as he pulled on the other boot. "He killed a Dweller."

Skinner shrugged. "So?" he asked, standing across from the general with his arms folded. "Since when is killing someone a problem?"

Roof laughed. "I don't have a problem with killing," he said. "I wouldn't be where I am if I did. For the most part, I'd suggest a violent execution is the best way to maintain order and control, but not this time. Killing that Dweller exposed Pierce. He's done."

"We lose our eyes and ears in the canyon," said Skinner.

"It accelerates the timetable," said Roof, pushing himself to his feet. "That intel he gave us is going to be worthless. How fast can we move?"

Skinner pinched the cigarette with his fingers and plucked it from his dry lips. He used it as a pointer as he spoke. "That's why I knocked on your door so early," he explained. "I wanted to let you know we're ahead of schedule. I've got grunts and bosses heading toward the canyon from all over. San Antonio's men are already on their way. We could move on the canyon in a day and a half, maybe two days tops. We'll end the Dwellers once and for all."

"Good," said General Roof, "make it happen."

CHAPTER FIVE

OCTOBER 25, 2037, 11:45 AM
SCOURGE +5 YEARS
PALO DURO CANYON, TEXAS

Battle stopped short of the garden. He leaned against a cottonwood tree. Lola plucked cucumbers from their vines, dropping them into a basket she had cradled in the crook of her elbow.

The overnight storm had passed, leaving behind clear skies and an intermittent breeze that curled through the valley. Battle shivered against the chill and stuffed his hands into his pockets. He was impressed with the garden. It was maybe a quarter acre in size and irrigated with PVC pipe and drip hoses that ran from a metal cistern at the edge of the plot. The rain from the night before was a bounty.

Fall plantings were ready for harvest, and Lola had volunteered to help. She was working with three other Dwellers combing through the vines and stalks. Sawyer trailed behind her, looking for cucumbers she might have missed.

There was a brightness, a sparkle even, in her eyes Battle had never seen. She seemed happy. Her limp was gone, her red hair soaked up the bright overhead sunlight. Battle's eyes were magnetically drawn to her.

"You should tell her what you're thinking," Sylvia's voice whispered. "It would be good for you."

Battle closed his eyes and inhaled. "I'm not telling her anything," he told the voice in his head. He set his jaw; his shoulders tensed.

Sylvia wouldn't relent. "I've told you," she said, her voice filling Battle's head. "You need someone. You'll lose yourself otherwise."

"I've already lost myself. I killed an unarmed man for no good reason last night. I'm not praying. My faith…"

"My faith in you is as strong as it's ever been," Sylvia said, and another voice joined the conversation.

"Mine too." It was Wesson. "Dad," he said, "she's got a son. He needs a man like you to help him. He doesn't have a dad to show him things."

Battle shivered again. It wasn't the breeze running through him. It was his son's voice, as clear as if Wes were standing in front of him with his tiny arms wrapped around his legs. Battle could smell the baby shampoo in the wind.

His lips curled into an unexpected smile as he thought about Sylvia's insistence that Wes use baby shampoo even after he'd protested that it was for babies. She'd explained it was healthier than other chemical-laden shampoos. Both Wes and Marcus had known it was really because it was the only way she could hold on to the vestiges of their only child's infancy.

Battle chuckled and leaned into the cottonwood with his shoulder, his eyes focused on some nebulous distance. "You hated that shampoo," he said. "It did smell good, though."

A third voice entered the internal conversation. "Battle?" It was a woman's voice. "Battle? Are you okay?"

Battle shook his head into reality. Lola was standing inches from him, her eyes narrowed with concern.

He cleared his throat. "Uh, yeah," he said, blinking Lola into focus. "I'm fine. Why?" He stood up straight and folded his arms across his chest.

Lola took a half step toward him and switched the basket from one arm to the other. "You were doing that thing again," she said softly. "You were in another world, talking to yourself."

Battle looked at his boots. They were caked with the red mud of the canyon floor. His face flushed. He flinched at Lola's touch as she put her hand on his arm and squeezed gently.

"It's okay," she said. "It doesn't bother me, but the others were looking at you. I don't want them looking at you."

Battle looked up and over Lola's shoulder. The others had returned to their harvesting duties. Only Sawyer was staring back at him. Battle offered a weak smile at the boy and then caught Lola's gaze.

"I don't care what they think," he said. "We won't be here long."

Lola stepped back and shifted the basket, leaning it against her hip. "We won't? What is it you're not telling me?" She looked over her shoulder at the Dwellers and back again.

"A war is about to start," he said under his breath. "The Dwellers are ready to fight. I'm pretty sure the Cartel is too."

Lola's gaze intensified. "How do you know this?"

"A couple of ways," Battle said. "Paagal is hell-bent on getting rid of the Cartel. She's got spies in every major city who are ready to strike."

"And the Cartel?" she pressed, her eyes searching his for the answer. "How would you know what they're planning?"

Battle scratched his forehead. "Charlie Pierce was one of them," he said. "He was feeding information to them. He killed a Dweller last night. I killed him."

Lola's mouth dropped open, her arms fell to her sides, and the basket dropped to the ground. The cucumbers rolled out into the dirt. "Pierce?" Tears pooled in her eyes. Her lips quivered. "We can't escape. No matter where we go. We can't escape."

Battle wanted to throw his arms around her. He wanted to comfort her and promise her they would escape, they would find a place beyond the reach of the Cartel and the grip of the evil that had the world in its clutches. He tried to will himself to listen to Sylvia and Wesson and give in to his evaporating need for human contact, for an emotional connection.

Instead, he adjusted the Sig Sauer tucked into his waistband and offered her a choice. "We have options," he said and knelt down to help gather the vegetables back into the basket.

Lola pulled her lower lip behind her teeth and bit down as she joined him on the ground. She slid the basket toward her feet.

He tossed a trio of cucumbers into the basket and held up his index finger. "We can leave now," he said. "You, Sawyer, and me. We can find our way to the wall and get to the other side."

"Or?"

He held up a second finger. "We stay and fight. We beat back the Cartel. Paagal helps us get to the other side."

They both stood. Lola wiped the corners of her eyes with her knuckle and folded her arms across her chest. She'd closed her mouth and was chewing the inside of her lip.

"Paagal says there are scavengers out there along the wall," Battle added. "We could probably use her help."

Lola took in a deep breath and pushed it out through puffed cheeks. Her entire body appeared to deflate. "We need to fight," she said. "These people helped us. We fight; then we leave."

Battle imperceptibly tilted his head in surprise and then pulled his shoulders back. Her resolve was empowering. She wasn't the same defeated woman he'd met thirteen days earlier.

"I agree," Battle said. "We fight. Then we find the wall."

"What's on the other side of the wall?" Sawyer had snuck up on them. Battle hadn't seen the boy approach.

"That's a really good question," said Battle. "I don't know."

Sawyer took the basket from his mother and held it for her. "What if it's worse than this side of the wall?" he asked. "What if we have it better here than there?"

Lola bristled. "I don't know what could be worse than living under the Cartel," she snapped, her eyes flashing with a bolt of anger before filling with sadness. "You know the things I've done to keep us alive."

Sawyer recoiled and stepped back from Lola, seemingly surprised by her reaction. "I was just saying —"

"We know," said Battle softly. "It's a fair question, Sawyer. We could be jumping from the frying pan into the proverbial fire. We can't live here."

Sawyer's eyes darted between his mother and Battle. "Why not?"

Battle didn't have an answer for Sawyer. He couldn't rationalize to a thirteen-year-old why they couldn't stay in the canyon with the Dwellers. He knew instinctively this was not the place for them.

He'd lived in environments like this before: pockets of resistance trying to overthrow powerful despots. If the insurgency failed, they'd die or live in fear of dying under conditions worse than those in which they'd previously lived. If it succeeded, the insurgents would rule a fractured state. At best, they'd restore a wire-thin order to a lawless land. At worst, the power vacuum created by the fall of the suppressive dictator would give rise to new, more violently desperate factions fighting to control the new world. It was best not to be on the southern side of the wall when that happened.

Battle stepped to Sawyer and put his hands on the boy's shoulders. "We can't," he said. "We just can't."

CHAPTER SIX

OCTOBER 25, 2037, 1:45 PM
SCOURGE +5 YEARS
HOUSTON, TEXAS

Ana rocked in the chair, rolling her toes forward and back on the cold wood-planked floor as she comforted her daughter. Ana's blouse was unbuttoned from having breast fed, and the child gripped her open collar. The child cooed and burped into her mother's neck.

Ana closed her eyes as she rocked. Back and forth. Back and forth. The movement was soothing to the child. For her, it was the equivalent of anxiously pacing. Her mind was swimming with regret.

She never should have agreed to join the Dwellers. She never should have agreed to do the things they'd asked of her. She never should have had this child.

A wave of guilt washed over her as that last thought played itself over and again in her mind. She pulled her hand from the child's back and caressed her head. Her black hair was so soft. It was curly and had grown across the top of her head. Ana nuzzled the baby and inhaled her aroma before placing a kiss right behind her ear.

Penny was the child's name. She was beginning to socialize, to understand phrases, and babble. Ana knew it would only be a few weeks before Penny walked. She was already wobbling from table to table, chair to chair.

She was as striking a child as her mother was a woman. Large, inviting brown eyes, light brown skin. Anyone who saw her was drawn to her as if her aura invited them closer.

Ana was cursed with the same gift. It was why the Dwellers recruited her. They knew the task that they'd assigned was suited for her. She'd succeed, they'd told her.

So far, she had.

She shifted Penny from one shoulder to the other and gently rubbed her back until she sensed the baby falling asleep. Penny's head was resting in her mother's neck; a soft gurgle tickled her mother with each breath.

Ana stopped rocking and tried to button her blouse with one hand without waking Penny. She'd completed one of the three when a voice in the doorway startled her.

"You don't have to button up on account of me," said the tall, weathered man leaning against the frame. A smile snaked across his face and he winked.

Ana jumped at the sound of his voice, managing not to wake the baby. She pulled her finger to her lips. "When did you get home?" she whispered.

The man strode into the nursery as if he owned it, because he did. His boots thumped on the floor as he stepped toward Ana and Penny. He reached the rocker and stroked the baby's head.

"She's sleeping," said Ana. "It's not often I can get her to take a lunchtime nap. She's outgrowing them."

The man's hand moved to Ana's face and he gently touched her cheek. He towered above her, his chin at his chest as he looked down at her. He slid his hand inside her open blouse, trailing his fingers across her body. His unblinking eyes were affixed to hers.

"Why are you home?" Ana pressed. She didn't dare remove his hand.

The man pulled his hand from her skin and raised his finger to his lips. He motioned to the crib before reaching for the child. He took Penny, cradled her, kissed her forehead, and then slowly lowered her into the bed. He looked back at Ana and nodded toward the door.

Ana stood from the rocker and buttoned her blouse. She tiptoed from the room and met the man in what he liked to call "the settin' room." He'd already found the worn easy chair and had his feet up on the ottoman. His arms were perched on the chair's wide arms. She moved to the loveseat opposite him.

The decidedly masculine décor of the room, complete with a buck's head above the encased gas fireplace, preexisted their having moved into the large townhouse. It was among the nicer remaining homes near what used to be downtown Houston. It was an area north of the central business district called Midtown.

He'd picked the house, displacing another family, when Ana had agreed to move in with him. She didn't have a choice, really. She was carrying his child and cohabitation was part of the plan.

"What's for lunch?" he asked. "You cook me up something in the microwave?"

"The power's out again," she said. "When did you get home?"

"The gas should work," he said. "You could make some corn chowder."

Ana ran her fingers through her wavy black hair. "I already have some beef broth in the refrigerator," she said. "I should probably heat that up. It'll go bad if I don't."

He frowned. "Fine." He waved her to the kitchen.

Ana pushed herself to her feet. "When did you get home? I've asked you several—"

"When did you get home?" he called from the chair. His words followed her along the short hallway to the galley kitchen. "Answer me that one."

Ana chose to pretend she hadn't heard his question and opened the refrigerator. The chill was already dissipating. "What was that?" she called. "I couldn't hear you."

"When did you get home?"

Ana turned on the gas cooktop and flicked a lighter over the burner. It burst into a blue flame and she turned down the heat. "A while ago," she said. "Maybe eleven o'clock."

He appeared in the doorway to the kitchen, swinging himself into the galley. "Where'd you go?" He plucked an apple from the granite countertop and took a large bite. He chewed loudly and used the back of his sleeve to wipe the juice from his chin.

"Downtown," she said. Ana couldn't lie to him. She knew he had her followed when possible. She knew the nanny, a bar wench who was probably more than a nanny to him, would tell him exactly when she left and when she returned.

"What for?" he asked through a mouthful of Red Delicious.

"I'd planned on buying more fruit," she said, stirring the broth into the pot. "But the market was closed."

"It's a Sunday," he said and crunched another bite. "It's always closed on Sunday."

"I was thinking today was Saturday," she said. "You don't usually work outside the house on Sunday. So when you were gone when I woke up this morning, I thought it was Saturday."

"Huh." He tossed the core into the trash bin on the far side of the kitchen and spun to leave. "How long on the broth?" he called as he walked away. "I'm hungry."

"Just a few minutes," she said and peeked into the hall. He'd returned to his chair in the sitting room. She could see his boots on the ottoman.

Ana ladled herself a bowl of the broth and then opened the freezer. Behind a set of ice trays, she'd hidden the gift Sidney Reilly had given her at the end of their meeting.

She uncapped the bottle, and the smell of bitter almonds immediately hit her. She pulled the bottle away from her face, holding it at arm's length, and tapped the contents into the broth. The white crystals, which looked like sugar, dissolved into the liquid immediately.

She stirred the broth with a wooden spoon until the plain brown soup swirled on its own. She recapped the empty bottle and replaced it in the freezer behind the empty trays.

"A half a gram of potassium cyanide is likely to kill him within a few days," Sid had told her. "I gave you two grams. Give him all of it."

To mask the acidic taste of the poison, Ana added a healthy dose of chili powder to the broth and waited for it to reach a simmer. She washed her hands in the sink, her hands stiffening from the cold water, and she wiped them on the hand towel lying on the counter. She was careful not to inhale the steam from the broth. Sidney told her that heating the cyanide would create a dangerous gas.

"It's almost ready," she called to him. "You want a beer?"

"That would be great," he said. "Some beer, some broth, and then some you."

Ana swallowed the sting of bile in her throat as she envisioned giving herself to him again. She'd been able to detach for so long. Once the baby came, the plot thickened, and the rebellion grew closer, it became more difficult to play along. She was afraid he'd begun to sense it. To ward off his suspicions, she'd had to up the ante in ways she'd never enjoyed.

She found a serving tray in the generous pantry and set his bowl of soup, a bottle of room-temperature beer, a spoon, and a bottle opener on top of it. Ana took in a deep breath and, holding the tray at arm's length, carried his lunch into the sitting room.

General Harvey Logan rubbed his hands together and sat forward in the chair when he saw her. He rubbed his bald head and licked his lips.

"Enjoy," Ana said to her mark. She handed him the tray, which he set on the ottoman. "It's a bit spicy," she added. "If you want another beer, I'll get it for you."

He looked at her warily. "Aren't you gonna eat? I like it when you eat with me."

Ana nodded and spun on her bare heel to go back to the kitchen. "Yes," she said. "I poured myself a bowl. I'll go get it now."

"I'll wait for you," he said and snapped off the top of the beer bottle with the opener. He pointed the bottle at her and took a slug. "Hurry up."

Ana's heart was pounding. She could feel the cold dampness under her arms and at the nape of her neck under her hair. She picked up her bowl and dropped a spoon into it. She cradled it with both trembling hands and found her place on the love seat.

He swallowed a swig of beer and belched. "You're shaking," he said.

"I'm cold."

"Take a sip of the broth," he ordered. "I'm waiting on you. I gotta be a gentleman and all." He winked and took a final pull of the beer.

Ana pulled the spoon to her lips and sipped the warm, salty broth. She took another sip. And another. "It's good," she said and looked at his bowl.

General Logan set the empty bottle on the tray in front of him and cupped the bowl with both hands. He brought it to his lips, tilted the bowl, and downed the soup. The hot liquid streamed down the sides of his face as he drank it.

"Ahhh," he said. He plopped the empty bowl onto the tray and smacked his lips. "Whew," he said. "That's got a kick, don't it?" He shook his head like a wet dog and exhaled loudly, his lips flapping.

Ana sipped another spoonful. "Too much chili powder?"

"Whew," he said again and punched his sternum with the side of his fist. "Maybe. How much did you put in it?" Sweat bloomed on his bald head as he stood from the discomfort of his chair.

Ana took another sip. "Not more than usual," she said indifferently, unaware of the speed with which she'd killed the father of her child. "Do you want another beer?"

Harvey Logan, one of three living Cartel generals, stumbled forward. His eyes widened and he gasped. He fell forward, crashing against the wooden table that separated the chair from the love seat.

Ana shrieked and dropped her soup, splashing it into her lap. She curled her legs behind her, crawling into the back of the love seat.

General Logan landed on his side, facing Ana. He grabbed his throat and twitched. His arms and legs spasmed. He growled something as white foam frothed from his open mouth.

Inside Logan's body, the poison was preventing his ability to use oxygen. His central nervous system, his heart and blood vessels, and his lungs were shutting down as if someone had flipped the switch on an electrical generator. A cell at a time, he was suffocating from the inside out.

Ana screamed between gasps for air. Her chest heaved and she sobbed with the reality of what she'd done. Harvey Logan was a detestable, violent man. He was responsible for the misery of thousands, but he was human. His bulging eyes and bluish skin were images burned into her memory, an everlasting reminder of her betrayal.

Ana had done a lot of reprehensible things to survive post-Scourge. Most people had. She'd never killed anyone though. Not until now.

Her wails and her cries were not for Logan as he dove painfully headfirst into a coma and then died. They were for her own soul. She was a murderer.

From the nursery, she heard Penny crying. The baby's wail was piercing and angry. Ana covered her ears with the palms of her hands and squeezed. She pulled her knees to her chest and closed her eyes tight, pressing tears down her cheeks. She buried her head between her knees and rocked.

CHAPTER SEVEN

OCTOBER 25, 2037, 2:51 PM
SCOURGE +5 YEARS
LUBBOCK, TEXAS

Cyrus Skinner tapped the last cigarette from the pack and slid it between his lips. He crumpled the cellophane-wrapped cardboard in his hand and tossed it to the dirt in front of the Jones.

"Those things are gonna kill you," said General Roof. He was leaning against a Humvee.

"If something's gonna kill me," Skinner said, "it might as well be something I love."

Skinner tipped his white hat back on his head and looked at the general. Roof wasn't himself. He appeared preoccupied and unfocused.

They were on the precipice of a defining moment for the Cartel, and Roof seemed disinterested. Skinner lit the cigarette and sucked in the bitter taste of the tobacco as the paper crackled and burned.

He blew out the smoke from the corner of his mouth, careful not to direct it at Roof. "What's going on with you, if I can ask?" said Skinner.

Roof looked at Skinner sideways and combed his fingers through his beard. "You can ask."

Skinner sucked in his cheeks, pinched the smoke, and flicked the ashes onto the ground. He exhaled again. "So then?"

"I know Marcus Battle."

"Mad Max?"

"Yeah."

"I know him too," said Skinner. "He's an ornery cuss. True enough, he's a badass, but he don't know when he's beat."

Roof's eyes narrowed. He pouted and shook his head. "No," he said. "I've known him for a long time. Or I *knew* him is more like it."

Skinner played that over in his head. It didn't make sense. He dropped the cigarette to the ground and ground it into the dirt with the toe of his boot. "I don't get it."

Roof adjusted his shirt collar, pulling it up on the back of his neck. "What's not to get, Cyrus?" he asked incredulously, looking off into the distance. "I knew him. Marcus Battle. We served together in Syria. He…"

Roof drifted off, and Skinner wondered where the general's mind had taken him. He knew Roof had served in Syria. Everybody knew that. Everybody knew that was where he'd killed his first man, his first woman, his first child. They also knew Syria was where Roof almost died. Nobody knew how. That was all conjecture and campfire gossip on long posse rides.

"He what?" Skinner asked, snapping Roof to the present.

Roof's eyes fluttered and he looked over at Skinner. "He saved my life."

The look on Skinner's face must have conveyed the surprise he felt inside, because Roof took a step back and looked at the ground, as if he were ashamed of what he'd revealed.

Skinner motioned his head toward the stadium. "That why you let him live after the Jones?"

"Partially," he said. "I also saw an opportunity to gain access to the canyon."

"And he didn't recognize you?" asked Skinner. "Even after he saved your life and all?"

"Guess not," said Roof. "Maybe it's the hair or the beard. I've gained weight. I've aged. Who knows?"

A smirk spread across Skinner's face. "It makes sense now," he snarled, judgment oozing from his dry, cracked lips. "That's why you didn't want me to kill him. That's why you wanted him brought to you here." Skinner shook his head in disgust. He snorted as he inhaled through his nose then spat of thick glob of snot onto the ground. "I wonder what the other generals would think."

Roof's jaw tightened and his shoulders squared. He stepped to Skinner and stuck his finger into the captain's chest. "You best watch yourself, Cyrus." He poked. "Don't forget your place."

Skinner held his ground, forcing Roof's finger to bend against the weight. "I ain't forgot nothin', General. I ain't gonna forget neither." His eyes dove deep into Roof's, staring until it was uncomfortable. "You got a soft spot for Mad Max. It's gonna get a lot of people killed."

In a swift move Skinner didn't see coming, Roof snapped his wrist upward and wrapped his thick, muscular fingers around Skinner's neck. He squeezed the surprise onto the captain's purpled face. Skinner grappled with Roof's wrists and forearms, unsuccessfully trying to loosen the grip.

Although Skinner muscled against his general, attempting to leverage his exceptional strength, Rufus Buck was surprisingly strong in his adrenaline-fueled rage. Skinner was failing, and the dizzying buzz in his head, accentuated by the blurred vision of Roof's gritted teeth, only made it worse. Roof drove him backward, off his feet and onto the dirt.

His hat flew off when his head snapped back and slammed onto the ground with a sickening thud. Skinner bit clean into his tongue at impact and tasted the warm, coppery taste of his blood pouring into his mouth.

Roof was on top of him, straddling him as he pushed downward on Skinner's neck. With his free hand, he palmed Skinner's face and shoved it sideways into the gravelly dirt.

Skinner was losing consciousness. Before he blacked out, Roof released the pressure on his throat. Skinner gasped and choked on the blood draining into his throat. He rolled onto his side and coughed until his chest burned. He opened his eyes, his vision returning to focus, and saw dark red splatter on the dirt in front of him.

His tongue was thick and throbbing. He curled his knees up toward his chest and reached for his tender neck. His body couldn't decide which pain to focus on. Everything hurt.

"You don't know," growled Roof with a vitriolic tone Skinner had never before heard from him, "so you don't get to judge. Try it again, Cyrus. Try taking a tone with me. Try threatening me. I'll end you."

Roof delivered a forceful kick to Skinner's lower back, and he emitted a cry that sounded like a frog dying in the jaws of a copperhead. He didn't recognize it as his own voice, but knew the shrill cry must have come from him. The solid pulsating pain in his back told him so.

He didn't have the strength, the breath, or the tongue to speak. He could feel the weight of his body sinking into the ground, searching for some modicum of comfort. Still, Skinner thought to himself through the fog of pain, *That's the Roof I know.*

***

General Roof marched back to the stadium. He kept balling his hands into tight fists before releasing them and extending his fingers as far as they would stretch.

He pounded through the entry and back into the meeting room adjacent to where he'd bunked for the last week. His leg ached as if a storm were coming. His teeth were clenched vise tight until he spoke.

"Computer on," he said. The trio of wide screens flickered awake. "Conference generals. Live chat."

A series of numbers and letters moved across the center screen. It reset itself and Roof's face appeared on the fifty-inch-wide panel. The monitors to either side clicked and hummed to life.

The screen to the left, assigned to General Harvey Logan, flashed the words "Connection Offline". To the right, General Parrott Manuse's wizened face pixelated into focus.

"What is it, Roof?" Manuse asked, rubbing his Play-Doh chin. He was chewing something. "I'm eating lunch," he smacked. There was a man wearing red boots standing behind him, toward the back of the room. He was Manuse's head of security.

"I want to make sure everyone is on board with the plan of action," Roof said.

Manuse's tributary-mapped face grew larger in the monitor. His already almond-shaped eyes narrowed further. "Your face is red," he said. "You're sweating too. What's going on?"

"I want to wait for Harvey," said Roof. "He's not online yet."

Manuse stabbed something with a fork and shoveled it between his teeth. His eyes shifted to the right as he chewed with his mouth open. "I don't see him either. Where is he?" The man in the red boots brought him a bottled water and then returned to the back of the frame.

"I don't know," said Roof. "It's a Sunday. He doesn't usually leave the house."

"Huh." Manuse pulled a bottle to his lips and gulped audibly. His pronounced Adam's apple slid up and down as he chugged until the bottle was empty. He smacked his lips again and tongued the foamy liquid from his lips.

"You might as well tell me what's what and let General Logan figure it out later," Manuse said. "Maybe he's fussing with that baby of his. Or he's fiddling with that young wife. Either way, I'm not inclined to wait."

"Fine," Roof huffed. "This affects him more than you. One of his captains, Charlie Pierce, is either dead or will be."

Manuse licked the front of his teeth. "That the one you sent to the canyon? The spy?"

"Yes," said Roof. "He gave us some good intel, but he was compromised and had to take action. He's probably found out by now."

"That it?"

"No," Roof said. "I've got a couple more things to discuss. First, have you sent your posses from Dallas?"

"They leave in the morning," Manuse replied. "They'll be moving slow. Probably be a day before they get there. They'll hit the north edge of the rim like we planned. Last I talked to Logan, his men we're gonna come northwest and attack from the western side of the canyon. They're set to leave after dark tonight."

Roof nodded. "Good. San Antonio's already left. They're moving up through Skinner's territory and coming north through Abilene. They'll grab the southern rim. I've got one advance team from Wichita Falls that may hit them tonight. They're made up of good men, all posse bosses. They're moving up Highway 287, approaching from the southeast. They'll do a little reconnaissance, which will add to the real-time actionable intelligence we got from Pierce."

Manuse plunged a finger into his nostril and fished around as he talked. "And your men in Lubbock will make their way to the western edge from Amarillo?"

"Yes."

"We'll position ourselves at a good distance and then hit them in waves," said Manuse. "That canyon is a double-edged sword."

"How so?"

"They can hunker down inside its steep walls," Manuse said. He was talking with his hands. "They can make themselves nice and cozy there, but they can't see us coming from all angles. They don't have enough people to surround the place. When we hit them, they'll be surrounded. Sitting ducks."

"Maybe," said Roof. "All they've had to do in the past was guard part of the rim. They protected the easiest descents into the canyon and let the impassability of most of it do their work for them."

"We've never used this kind of manpower," said Manuse. "We've let them think they could hold their own, keep us at bay. Not anymore."

Roof folded his arms across his chest. He stared at the monitor without a connection and thought about what he'd done to Skinner. A wave of nausea washed over him when he considered Marcus Battle coordinating a defense of the canyon. He'd made a mistake letting Battle live. Even with the intelligence Pierce had gleaned, it wasn't worth it.

Battle might have slipped tactically and might have begun a solitary descent into madness, but he was a lucky man, a man who found fortune where there was none. And Skinner was right about one thing: Battle didn't know when he was beat.

Roof hadn't been afraid of anything or anyone since he'd survived the IED Elmo in Aleppo. He'd resolved to be fearless and reckless and immoral. He lost himself in the blank screen, thinking about the fear swimming under the uneasy rapid racing through his gut.

Marcus Battle frightened him. There it was. The truth for a man who'd lied to himself for so long. That was why he hadn't killed him or let Skinner do the deed. He was afraid.

Manuse tapped on his camera to get Roof's attention. "What else is there?" he asked. "You said there were a couple of things."

Nothing else," he said. "Let me know if you get a hold of Harvey."

"Yep." Manuse ended the call. His screen went blank.

There was a knock at the door. Roof turned to find a chubby grunt filling the gap between the open door and the frame. His eyes were wide and he had blood all over his tight-fitting shirt. He tugged on his pants at the empty belt loops.

Roof shrugged impatiently. "What?"

"Somebody beat up Captain Skinner pretty good," said the grunt. "I don't know who it was. I thought I should—"

Roof raised his hand to stop the grunt's mouth from moving. "Who are you?"

The grunt looked down, averting his eyes. "They call me Porky."

"I beat him up, Porky," said Roof. "He gonna live?"

Porky's eyes widened and then narrowed with confusion. He bobbed his head up and down. "Yes. I think so. His tongue, though."

"What about it?" Roof walked toward the grunt as he spoke.

"It's messed up," said Porky. "It's...he can't talk."

"Get him some ice from the mess hall," said Roof. "He'll be fine by the time we move out tomorrow."

"Sir, General, sir, I don't know if—"

"He'll be fine," said Roof. "We're gonna need every last man on this run. He better be fine. If he's not—" Roof stepped to within six inches of the grunt and leaned in "—I'm holding you responsible."

CHAPTER EIGHT

OCTOBER 25, 2037, 3:43 PM
SCOURGE +5 YEARS
PALO DURO CANYON, TEXAS

Felipe Baadal stood outside the entry flap of Juliana Paagal's tent. He looked up at the sun and noticed it had dropped maybe fifteen degrees since he'd started waiting. He guessed an hour had passed. When he'd left her, she was communicating on a satellite phone with someone in Houston. She'd asked him politely to give her privacy. It was what she called a "high-level conversation".

The cool, dry October air made the wait palatable. It was a far cry from desert patrols in mid-July. Baadal put his hands on his hips and twisted to stretch his back. He put one hand on the opposite elbow and pulled. He purred from the relief.

"Sore?" Paagal emerged from the tent and moved into the sunlight, her hand lingering on the red flap.

Baadal stopped midtwist and turned with a smile. A torrent of warmth flooded his body. His cheeks flushed. "It's the mattress."

"Ah," said Paagal. "The mattress."

Baadal's eyes widened as he remembered his fingers trailing along her toned arms, his olive skin a faint contrast with her smooth brown complexion. His pulse quickened when he thought about what else had happened before he fell asleep on the lumpy mattress. Before he'd had to leave when Battle appeared in the middle of the night with urgent news.

"You know," she said, stepping closer to him, "you are the first man in a long time to…" She smiled. Her eyebrows curled into an arch, finishing her sentence for her.

Baadal wanted to push her inside the tent. He knew it would have to wait. There was work to do.

"And you're the first woman in I don't know how long."

She touched his chest with the flat of her hand. Her eyes told him she was as eager as he to lose herself.

The smile drained from Baadal's face. "I have to remind you," he said earnestly, "I'm not a good man."

Juliana Paagal pulled her hand from his chest and raised it to Baadal's smooth cheek. "I'm not a good woman," she said. "But we're both survivors. That's a place to start. I wish I'd gotten to know you more intimately before now."

Her eyes shifted from his and she looked over his shoulder. Baadal turned to see what had caught her attention.

"I'm interrupting again," said Marcus Battle, Lola and Sawyer in tow. "Sorry. I don't mean to be a buzz kill."

Paagal dropped her hand to her side and shook her head. "It's fine."

"It's not," said Battle. "You shook your head no while you were telling me it was okay. Subconsciously, you'd rather I not have interrupted."

Paagal smirked. "A dose of my own medicine, as it were?"

Battle shrugged. "Maybe. I think you're going to want to hear what we've got to say."

Lola sidled up to Battle. She reached for Sawyer's hand and held it, lacing her fingers between her son's. Paagal folded her arms across her chest.

"What is it?" asked Baadal when nobody else took the lead. He sensed Battle, Lola, and Sawyer had something important, something urgent to tell them. He could see it on their faces.

Battle, he'd learned, was aptly named. It wasn't only because of his survival skills or tenacity. It was also because the man always wore the face of someone in pain, trouble brewing beneath the surface and ready to erupt in the right conditions.

Lola, Baadal had come to believe in the short time he'd known her, was like reading an open book written in large bold print for kindergartners. Her emotions were sprawled on her face, in the way she stood, in the tone of her voice.

Lola squeezed her son's hand and cleared her throat. "Battle told us you're about to go to war with the Cartel. You been planning it, he said."

Paagal nodded. Her eyes bounced between Lola and Battle. "Yes. That's true."

"He said you would offer help getting past the wall if we agreed to stay and fight," said Lola.

"Yes. That is also true."

"You'll be able to get us to the other side?"

"Yes."

Lola took a step toward Paagal, bringing Sawyer with her, and offered her free hand to the leader of the Dwellers. Paagal looked down at the offer and took Lola's hand. She shook it firmly.

"We'll fight," said Lola resolutely. "Whatever we need to do to put an end to them, we'll do."

Paagal let go of Lola's hand and nodded. "Good," she said. "We'll meet tonight to discuss what we do here in the canyon. The plan itself is already under way."

Battle's eyes went hard and his shoulders squared. "What do you mean already under way?"

Baadal had deduced the high-level conversation that forced him from the confines of the tent was specifically about whatever effort Paagal had initiated. He looked at her as she pressed her lips together, seemingly weighing the pros and cons of divulging too much information to relative outsiders.

"C'mon," Battle pushed. "We agreed to fight for you, to give our lives for your cause. You can tell us what's happening."

Paagal crossed her arms and snickered condescendingly. "Let's not confuse our mutually beneficial arrangement with benevolence on either of our parts."

"What is that supposed to mean?" asked Lola.

Paagal opened her mouth to speak but paused. She took a deep breath and let it out. "It means," she said, "this is a quid pro quo. I said as much when we spoke early this morning. You do for us and we do for you. You're not helping us out of the kindness of your hearts, Lola. And we're not taking you to the wall because we're offering a free taxi service."

Battle looked at Lola and then back at Paagal. He pointed his finger at her as he spoke in a measured but forceful tone. "Nobody said anything about benevolence or a free ride other than you. My point was that you need to trust us with information if we're going to fight for your cause. Regardless of the motivation behind our help, you owe us that much."

"I don't owe you anything," said Paagal. "You came here as a guest. You can leave whenever you want." She pointed back at Battle, her finger wagging amongst Lola, Sawyer, and him.

Paagal stepped closer to Battle, her arms straight at her sides. Her hands were squeezed into fists. Any hint of a smile had melted from the fiery gaze she shot at Battle. "The whole secret lies in confusing the enemy so that he cannot fathom our real intent," she seethed. "Whoever is first in the field and awaits the coming of the enemy will be fresh for the fight."

"So you can quote Sun Tzu," said Battle, his eyes searching hers as he spoke. "That doesn't make you a general."

"Neither does being a soldier," she spat, her muscular arms flexing with the intensity of her words. "Nor does being a man on the brink of insanity. You speak of trust? Trust me when I tell you we are already winning the war. You either join us tonight to learn what comes next or you don't."

Paagal spun on her heel and turned back to her tent. She slapped at the entry flap and ducked inside. Baadal looked at Battle, offered an unspoken apology, and ducked into the tent behind his lover.

"What the hell happened?" asked Lola.

"She let me know who is in control," he said, "and it's not us."

***

Battle motioned for Lola and Sawyer to follow him back toward their tents. Theirs were about one hundred yards from Paagal's command center, tucked amidst a dozen rows of similar four-person tents. Lola had offered to share with Battle, telling him they were only three. A four-person tent, she'd suggested, would be enough. Battle had declined, using the excuse that tents actually only comfortably accommodated half the number of those advertised. He'd told her she should be happy to have her own space.

They reached their row, their tents adjacent to each other, and Battle suggested they get some rest. Once the fighting started, it could be days before anybody got any real sleep.

Sawyer ducked inside and left Lola and Battle standing in the alley between the tents. It was quiet other than the flapping of the nylon pitches against the swirling breeze and the rustle of thirsty, dying leaves on the nearby outcrop of soapberry trees.

"You might have crossed a line with her," Lola said softly.

Battle cocked his head. "How so?"

"The trust thing," she said. "Everyone is entitled to skepticism without judgment, Marcus."

Battle laughed. "Maybe some," he said. "Not all."

Lola looked at the dirt. "Masochism isn't attractive," she said and took a step closer to Battle. She stood on her tiptoes, pulled him forward by his shoulders, and kissed his cheek. She blushed. "I'm taking that nap you suggested," she said and ducked into her tent without waiting for her dumbstruck mark to react.

Battle stood motionless for a moment. It had happened so quickly and he'd acquiesced without pulling away. What did that mean?

"It means you're human." Sylvia's voice was back. "It means you haven't entirely lost who you are."

Battle hastily unzipped his tent and crawled inside. Although the soft bluish hue of the interior was calming, he was agitated. He pulled off his boots and tossed them into the corner. They kicked up dust when they clanked against the taut blue nylon wall and the top of the metal spike affixed to the outside of the tent.

"You're not listening to me," Sylvia droned. "She's telling you how she feels. She wants to connect with you, Marcus. There's nothing wrong with that."

Marcus tried to ignore Sylvia and instead concentrated on what Paagal had said to him before she'd turned away in anger. She'd quoted Sun Tzu for a reason. She'd chosen those passages from his work for a reason. It wasn't arbitrary.

She wanted him to know what the plans were without appearing to have given in to his demands. She wanted to appear strong and resolute. Battle acknowledged to himself that was a smart thing to do. Baadal, and others, could only respect a strong leader who refused to negotiate.

If she'd outright told him her plans after he complained, it would get back to others that she'd caved against her better judgment. It would filter through the camps that Battle had bullied Paagal into divulging sensitive information.

She'd appear weak. He'd appear to be strong. The Dwellers could turn on her and follow him, defer to him, die for him.

Battle sat on the spongy cot that filled most of his tent and pulled his knees up to his chest. He crossed his ankles and wrapped his arms around his legs, holding them there with clasped hands. He rocked, thinking back to the conversation in Paagal's tent that morning.

He remembered the hypnotic sound of the rain slapping the tent, the ethereal red glow that filled the space, Paagal's calm temper. She'd as much as told him then how the war would begin on her terms.

"Ever since the truce," she'd said, "we've been dispatching cells. They've lived and worked amongst the Cartel in those cities you mention. They've painstakingly recruited allies. All of them are ready to pounce when we signal them. We can end the Cartel. You've come at the right time."

She'd signaled them. The viral cells she'd implanted within the Cartel were live. They were spreading. She was doing what the Cartel least expected, attacking them on their own turf without warning.

Paagal was smart. Battle stopped rocking, let loose of his hold around his legs and fell back onto the cot. It was only moderately more comfortable than the dirt, and it had the dank smell of mildew and sweat. It would do. He'd slept in worse places.

He turned onto his side and closed his eyes, trying to envision the chaos enveloping the Cartel's major cities. He smiled thinking about it.

Battle dozed off into a light sleep, contemplating the odds. They might have a chance to win, or at the very least degrade the Cartel enough that they could find passage beyond the wall.

***

Felipe Baadal sat across from Paagal in her tent. She was gritting her teeth, rapping her knuckles on the desk. She'd not said a word to him in the half hour since Battle had incited her, but Baadal was as curious about her plans as Battle had been.

"What's beyond the wall?" he asked. He was taking the circuitous route to the point.

Paagal stopped thumping her knuckles. "Why?"

"I'm curious," he said. "I'd never given it any thought. Now Battle wants to cross it. I'm wondering what he's going to find."

Paagal leaned on her elbows and sighed. "I don't know what he'll find," she said. "It depends on where exactly he crosses. It depends on what time of day it is. It depends on so many different things."

"You've crossed the wall?" asked Baadal, thinking he'd gotten the conversation started. "You've been to the other side, then?"

"Twice," she said. "That was enough."

Baadal's brow furrowed. "What do you mean?"

"So you've not crossed the wall?" asked Paagal. "I'd have thought as a sentry and a scout you might have been north of it."

Baadal lowered his eyes and shook his head.

"It's not what Battle thinks it is," she said, her gaze softening into the distance over Baadal's shoulder. "It's not..."

"Not what?"

Paagal's mind was elsewhere. Maybe it was beyond the wall, visiting things she'd as soon have never seen. Maybe she was thinking about the war at hand. Baadal waved his hand in front of her face. She blinked and snapped back into the present, into the confines of her command tent.

"Sorry," she said. "It's not easy to talk about." There was a quiver in her voice. Her eyes suddenly appeared glassy.

"I'm the one who should be sorry," Baadal said. "I didn't know."

"You wouldn't know," she said, wiping the corner of her eye with her finger. "Not unless you'd been there."

Baadal shrugged. "So why does anyone want passage to the other side?"

"People always want what they think they need," she said. "Rarely do they need what they have. It's the human condition. It's the idea that something out there can fulfill them, can make their lives better, fill the holes within their being."

Baadal leaned back in his chair, away from Paagal. "Isn't that called hope?"

"How so?"

"I mean to suggest…" Baadal searched for the words. "I have not lived a life of purity. I've sinned. I've been a perpetrator and a victim. But always in the back of my mind was this idea that I could be better. I thought things would get better. I wanted to believe that I would find a happier…" He used his hands to search for the words.

"Existence?" Paagal suggested.

Baadal nodded. "Yes," he said. "Perhaps that's the right word. Existence. A happier existence. That's not me being ungrateful for surviving the Scourge, having a roof over my head most nights, or food on most days. It's me being hopeful."

Paagal sat silently. She adjusted her elbows on the table but said nothing.

"Maybe that's all Battle wants," he said. "Maybe he's hoping for something better."

"He won't find it on the other side of the wall," she said.

Baadal leaned in. He pressed his hands flat against the table. "Why don't you tell him that?"

"He has to discover it for himself," she said.

"That's not—"

"Nice?"

Baadal shrugged.

"I told you, Felipe," she said. "I'm not a good person. A leader doesn't have to be good. She has to be strong. She has to do what's right for her survival."

Baadal nodded. He understood the strong pull of self-preservation at the expense of morality. He decided against asking about the plans already under way. He'd find out with the rest of them. Maybe not knowing was better.

CHAPTER NINE

OCTOBER 25, 2037, 5:35 PM
SCOURGE +5 YEARS
HOUSTON, TEXAS

Dead weight was a colloquialism Ana Montes had never fully understood until she helped carry one. General Harvey Logan was not a small man. Disposing of his body was not a minor task.

"A few more feet," said Sidney Reilly, grunting as he walked backwards and grappled with Logan's arms. "Just. A. Few. More. Feet."

"You keep saying that," Ana moaned. She kept losing her grip on Logan's heels as they maneuvered their way along the narrow hallway that separated the sitting area from the bedrooms.

They bounded along the hall, banging into the walls as they moved. They reached the end of it and struggled through the doorway into the master bedroom.

Ana crossed the threshold and dropped Logan's feet. "Hang on." She waved at Sidney and bent over at her waist. "I need to catch my breath for a second. He's so heavy. Remind me why we couldn't have left him in the sitting room? We're leaving here anyhow."

"It might be a couple of days," Sidney said, still holding Logan's wrists. The general's head was flopped backward, his Adam's apple exposed. "You don't want a dead body lying on the floor."

"Maybe," she said, wiping the bloom of sweat from the back of her neck.

"The tub is already filled with ice, right?" he asked.

"As filled as I could get it," she said.

"I thought you had a freezer full of ice in the garage," he said. "He's a general. Ice is a perk, isn't it?"

"We have ice in a freezer, sure," she clarified. "But it wasn't full. It was never full."

Sidney rolled his eyes, huffed, and dropped Logan's wrists. He turned to go to the bathroom and the dead man's head hit the floor with a thud. Even though he was dead, the sound was painful to Ana.

Sidney called from the bathroom. "This is enough," he said. "This will keep the body cold enough for a day or two." He reemerged and bent over to pick up Logan's arms. "Let's finish this, Ana."

She bent at her knees, grabbed Logan's ankles, and heaved upward. A few awkward steps and they'd navigated the rest of the distance. They rolled Logan's nude body into the tub and onto a bed of ice.

Ana stared at the body for a moment, recalling the wretched way in which the father of her child had died. It was hard to reconcile what she'd done, despite knowing it was for the greater good.

Sidney put his arm around her shoulder, leading her out of the bathroom. "You did a good job," he said. "This was the first step. It was the most important."

"I don't know," said Ana, stopping at her bed and dropping to sit on its edge. "I'm not any better than them."

Sidney knelt down in front of her as if he were proposing marriage. He took her hands in his. "What you did was self-defense. What we are all doing is self-defense. It will end the Cartel's hold over us. It will bring about a new time. Things will be better than they've been in years."

"I wish I could believe that," said Ana. "I wish I knew what we were doing was right."

Sidney squeezed her hands. "C'mon, let's go." He stood and pulled her from the bed and opened his arms wide, offering her a consoling hug.

She took his offer and buried her face in his chest. She closed her eyes and wrapped her arms around his back. She didn't see him pull the knife from his waist, but she opened her eyes in time to see the glint of the blade reflect in a wall-hung mirror.

She jerked away from his hold as he swung the knife around toward her back. Ana deflected the swipe with her forearm and instinctively drove her knee upward with as much force as she could muster.

The shot to his groin slugged into him the moment he drove his arm downward. The blade sliced the back of Ana's arm, and she repeated the upward movement of her knee, slamming him for a second time.

Sidney dropped the knife and grabbed himself as he crumpled to the floor, groaning. There was drool pooling on the floor beneath his mouth.

The pain of the wound numb from adrenaline, Ana scooted back onto the bed and away from Sidney. She rolled over and grabbed a large leaded-glass candlestick from the bedside table.

Sidney was struggling to find his feet. He looked up at Ana with the gaze of a drunk. His mouth was agape, his eyes clearly unable to find their focus. He mumbled something, drool leaking from the corners of his mouth.

Ana tightened her grip on the large candlestick and bounded toward Sidney. She reared back and swung the glass like a hammer onto the back of his head. The glass vibrated in her hand as it smacked his skull.

Sidney dropped flat to the floor, unconscious. A dark stain of blood spread across the back of his head.

Ana dropped the candlestick to the floor. Her heart was pounding against her chest, her pulse thumping against her neck. She had trouble taking deep breaths.

She willed herself to contain the panic threatening to overcome her. She pursed her lips and slowly drew in a breath and released it. In and out. In and out.

Ana took a step back from Sidney, grabbing the knife and squatting down at a safe distance. She couldn't tell if he was breathing or not.

Ana focused on the stream of blood trickling from the back of his head, down his shirt, and onto the floor. Between the double shot to his groin and the violent strike to his head, she imagined he'd be incapacitated for a while even if he were alive.

She would have liked to have asked Sidney why he would kill her. She'd done what he'd asked. She'd joined the resistance. She'd borne the child of a man she detested and then lived with him. She'd been a servant to the cause.

She wondered if Sidney had planned on killing her from the very beginning. Was it always part of the plan?

Ana had long expressed doubts of the strength and motive of the resistance. Sidney, Nancy Wake, and Nancy's husband, Wendell, had repeatedly allayed her fears until they bubbled again to the surface. Of all the conspirators, she was taking the biggest risk on a daily basis, she'd told them. She was living with the enemy.

They'd acknowledged her commitment and sacrifice. They'd promised her the effort would be worth it when the Cartel fell. Yet here she was, having escaped an assassination attempt in the hours after fulfilling her promise to them. She wondered if the exercise of moving Logan's body was an effort to fatigue her so she might be an easier target.

The sting in her arm was ballooning into a dull throb as the intensity of the moment waned. Ana looked at her wound. It wasn't deep and probably wouldn't require stitches. She'd been lucky. Still, it hurt.

Ana decided it didn't matter whether Sidney was dead or alive. She wasn't staying long enough to find out. She stood and kicked him in the back. He didn't move.

She folded the blade into the bolster and stuck it into her pocket. She might need it again.

Ana stepped over Sidney's body and flung open the closet. On the top shelf was a backpack she used to carry baby supplies. She yanked a couple of shirts from hangers and stuffed them in the empty pack. She moved quickly to the bathroom and emptied the medicine cabinet into the bag. Medicine of any kind was at a premium. She could use it. She could trade it. It was good to have.

Ana moved with purpose from her room to Penny's. She pulled a package of reusable diapers, a couple of outfits, and some Vaseline from the shelf above the changing table. She stuffed them into the now bulging pack. She unzipped the front compartment and was able to squeeze a single bottle inside of it.

Traveling the untamed wilderness of the Cartel's vast territory with a baby would be tough under normal circumstances. Ana was about to do it in the midst of a burgeoning war in which both sides were her enemy. She slung the backpack over her shoulders, unfolded the collapsible stroller in the corner of the nursery, and picked up her sleeping child.

Penny's eyes cracked open as her mother set her into the stroller's fabric and buckled the three-point harness holding her in place. Ana popped a pacifier in Penny's mouth and spun the stroller on two wheels. Penny sucked on the plastic until she fell asleep again, her head bobbing from side to side with the motion of the stroller. Ana was speed-walking north toward downtown. She let go of the stroller with one hand and felt for the sharp bulge in her right pocket. The keys were there. Three blocks to go and she'd be on her way out of Houston and toward somewhere else.

Ana was quickly reaching the conclusion, right or not, that the resistance wasn't about freedom. It wasn't about making life better. She believed trading one power for another wasn't always good. She'd experienced it in her personal life: taking power away from one bad man and giving it to another. Life didn't improve.

Instead, she'd come to understand that any alternative ruler when it took power often became an oppressor worse than the one it dethroned. So afraid were the newly empowered of losing the control they fought so hard to win, they morphed into the very thing they fought against.

Ana suddenly knew where she needed to go. She needed to reach the canyon and the leader called Paagal before it was too late. Paagal, she'd heard from the others, had access to the wall and a way across to the northern side. She would find Paagal, explain what she had done for the resistance, and then gain passage across the wall.

CHAPTER TEN

OCTOBER 25, 2037, 6:15 PM
SCOURGE +5 YEARS
LUBBOCK, TEXAS

The sun was dropping low in the sky. It would sink below the dusty horizon within forty-five minutes. General Roof wondered how many more sunsets he would see. Not a one was guaranteed. They never had been. He knew that. This one, however, he considered with more contemplation than usual. This one was as singular, he believed, as the one he'd enjoyed the night before he first shipped out to Syria some eighteen years earlier.

There was something simple about a sunset that evoked a complex combination of emotions. Maybe it was the joy of having survived another day mixed with the uncertainty of what the next sunrise might bring. Maybe it was the fear of the dark night ahead. Maybe it was both.

Roof didn't try to psychoanalyze himself. He didn't want to be that self-aware. Inward ignorance was bliss as far as he was concerned. Still, he reached into his shirt and pulled out his dog tags and rubbed them with his fingers, melancholy about the sun's shifting light.

Despite his mood, he relished the solitude. All of the grunts, bosses, and captains had finished their preparations for the coming departure. He stayed behind, tending to his work in the relative peace of the moment, though not before sending them off with a rousing speech.

Roof had praised the dozens of men for the expediency of their work. He'd told them they were ready for whatever challenges lay ahead. He'd assured them they would win and find their collective way back home, wherever home might be.

They'd cheered him. He'd tipped his hat to them and dismissed them, warning them not to be late the next morning. They'd left and gone to eat, sleep, and do whatever else rotten men do before heading off to war.

He was sitting in the bed of a HUMVEE, checking the weapons he'd chosen to bring. The Browning, a tactically stupid choice he'd always thought, was at his feet. Although he had never wanted the Cartel to fight with shotguns, he had been overruled. They had access to ridiculous numbers of the Brownings and what seemed to be a limitless supply of ammunition.

Given how many grunts were horrible shots, Generals Logan and Manuse had made the decision to make the Browning the standard-issue weapon.

Roof had relented to their demands, believing for so long that the sheer size of their infantry was more than enough to make up for the impotency of a shotgun. It was a mistake.

He knew that. He'd always known it. He was all the more certain of it as he checked the Trijicon optical sight of an FN SCAR 17 assault rifle. He pulled out and checked its twenty-round magazine and slammed it back into place. It was loaded with the heavy .308/7.62x51 military rounds. A voice from behind him interrupted his concentration.

"General?"

Roof swung the weapon with his shoulders as he turned to face whoever belonged to the voice. The young man stepped back, his eyes wide when Roof aimed the rifle at his head.

He raised his arms. "General? Sorry. I didn't mean to disturb you."

Roof kept the weapon trained. "What do you want?"

The man swallowed hard. "My name is Grat Dalton. I'm the one you and Captain Skinner sent to follow and observe."

Roof peeked over the sight. "I don't know what you're talking about."

"When you banished them folks from the Jones," Grat said, "you had Captain Skinner assign us to follow them. It was me, my brother Emmett, and Jack Vermillion."

Roof held his aim for a moment more and then lowered the SCAR 17. His eyes narrowed and he waved the man toward the side of the HUMVEE.

"I know who you are now," said Roof. "You lost your brother near Abernathy. Right?"

The grunt bowed his head. "Yes, sir."

"You lost my horses and weapons too," said Roof. "Right?"

"Well," Grat said, "I guess we—"

"You guess?"

"I just—"

"You just?"

Grat shrugged.

"What is it you want?"

"I want to make it up to you, General," he said. "I know you're heading north to fight. I'm not attached to any posses. I'd like to ride with you."

Roof put down the SCAR 17 and hopped over the side of the HUMVEE's bed. He stepped to Grat. "You want to make it up to me? Is that it? Or do you want revenge for your brother's murder? Which is it?"

Grat hesitated. He curled his lips inside his mouth and bit down.

"Answer me the right way and you can go," said Roof. "Answer wrong, you stay here with the women and children. Be honest. I'll know if you're lying."

Grat Dalton folded his arms across his chest. He looked Roof in the eyes and nodded. "I want revenge. I want that Mad Max dead. I want to kill his woman and that boy."

Roof stared into Grat's eyes after the man had stopped talking. He searched his face, judged his posture, the way he stood across from him.

"Good answer," said Roof. "We leave in the morning. Be here outside the Jones at sunup."

Grat exhaled, releasing the nervous anticipation, and thanked Roof. He offered his hand to the general.

Roof looked down at the offer and ignored it. "Your friend Vermillion isn't invited," he said and grabbed the side of the HUMVEE. He hopped back into the bed and picked up another rifle. He was a minute into the task when he sensed a figure still standing watch. He waved his hand to shoo the grunt away. "I'll see you tomorrow, Grat Dalton," he said without looking up.

"It's not Grat Dalton," said Porky. "It's me Porky. I need to talk to you about Skinner."

Roof cursed and let out an aggravated sigh. "Can't a man get any work done?" He looked up at Porky. "We got a war to fight."

Porky's fingers were tugging on his empty belt loops. "Yes, sir."

"Why can't Skinner come talk for himself?"

"He can't talk, General," said Porky. "I told you —"

"Right," Roof snapped. He rolled his eyes. "His tongue. I get it. Why are you here?"

"He wants to ride with you tomorrow," Porky said. "He sent me to ask if it was all right."

Roof rolled his tongue across his front teeth. "I guess," he said. "If he's up to it."

"Thank you, General," Porky said and scurried off toward the Jones.

Roof looked around. There were a dozen vehicles ready to roll out. He knew down the street there were horses primed to ride. The sun was sinking and cast a pinkish hue. He blinked and squinted as he looked into the setting sun, tipping his hat lower on his forehead. He soaked in the light and then closed his eyes, letting the afterimage burn into his mind.

This was a final day of peace. War was coming. It would be bloody. It would offer another kind of scourge to the land inside the wall.

CHAPTER ELEVEN

OCTOBER 25, 2037, 6:01 PM
SCOURGE +5 YEARS
PALO DURO CANYON, TEXAS

The burning impact of the twenty-two-caliber bullet drilling through Battle's shoulder spun him toward the direction of the shot. He peered into the distance, unable to see from where the projectile was fired. He was in an abyss, standing alone in a vast emptiness.

A second jarring slug penetrated his chest, and Battle grabbed at the wound as if his touch could do anything to ease the instantaneous, painful throb.

Battle reached for his waistband, searching for McDunnough. He couldn't find it. It wasn't there. The weapon he'd named for Nic Cage's character in the Coen Brothers' classic film *Raising Arizona* was missing.

He'd always identified with McDunnough: a man whose good intentions led him deeper down the rabbit hole with every step. The more he watched it on his computer in the aftermath of the Scourge, one of the two dozen films in his hard drive rotation, the closer he felt to the bumbling, oddly intelligent convict.

Battle searched his hip for the weapon. Nothing.

Another bullet zipped through the air and stung him in the thigh, dropping him to one knee. He cried out into the darkness.

"What do you want?" he asked.

There was a howl from the darkness. It was animalistic in tone, but was definitely human. The howl was echoed by a chorus echoing the ghostly call.

"I'm alone," Battle called. He narrowed his eyes, trying to adjust to the darkness. He couldn't see anything. A fog rolled toward him from the darkness. Hidden within the mist was a volley of shots. Each of them were true, stabbing Battle from too many directions to count and forcing his body to convulse and wrench with each connection. Battle felt his life spilling from inside him, draining into the blackness.

"You were always alone…" called a hollow voice. It echoed, repeating the last word again and again. "Alone. Alone. Alone."

***

Battle jolted awake and sat straight up, panicked by the dream and by not remembering where he was. It was dark. He had no concept of how late it was. He was drenched in sweat, which at first he worried was blood. He pressed his hands against his shoulders, his chest, and his legs until he was certain there were no leaking wounds.

He blinked back the sleep in his eyes until they adjusted. He was in his tent. He took in a deep breath and let it out slowly. His heart slowed.

Battle slid off the end of the cot and pulled on his boots. He climbed out of his tent and scrambled to his feet. He scanned the rows, looking for signs of life along the seemingly endless lines of pitches. He saw none.

"Lola," he called and stepped toward her tent.

No answer.

"Lola," he said, "I'm coming in." He unzipped the flap and poked his head through the opening. The space was empty save two cots and a pile of clothes in the corner.

Battle withdrew his head and scanned the tent city again. It was devoid of activity. The moon provided some visibility but not much as he peered as far as he could see. He planted his hands on his hips.

Where was everybody?

He was still groggy, his mind cluttered with the remnants of the violent dream. He started one way and then turned back toward the center of the encampment. Row after row, nobody was there. Then, in the distance, he could hear the low rumble of a conversation. Occasionally there was a roar of applause or a collective howl.

He walked toward the sound, and as he drew closer to it, he could see the amber glow of a fire flickering against the face of those gathered around it. A woman's voice was louder than the others.

"...of being the Cartel's minions..."

Battle picked up his pace, marching toward the gathering, his boots crunching the dirt floor of the canyon. He looked above and saw a thick cloud move across the moon. The ambient light disappeared with the moon, but he was close enough to the gathering for the fire to guide him.

"...guiding the course of our own destiny..."

He approached slowly, and the size of the group around the fire was larger than he'd thought. It appeared as though every Dweller was present.

"...securing a future better than our past..."

Standing close to the fire, speaking slowly and with purpose, was Juliana Paagal. She stopped when she saw Battle stop at the edge of the assembly. She looked at him and smiled. He could feel the eyes of the entire gathering staring at him.

"For someone so interested in our plans," she said, "you are remarkably late to learn what they are."

The meeting.

He'd overslept, and in his haste to square his surroundings, he'd completely forgotten about it. The sting of the bullets from his dream still tingled on spots across his body as if they lacked circulation.

"My apologies," he said and found an empty spot at the outer edge of the circle. He scanned the crowd for Lola and Sawyer but saw neither of them.

Baadal was seated nearest Paagal. He offered Battle an uncomfortable smile. Battle nodded.

"So—" Paagal sighed and turned her attention elsewhere "—as I was saying, we have already eliminated major threats in several of the larger cities. Our operatives have freed us of one general, six captains, and two dozen bosses. This leaves the Cartel grunts without critical guidance as they begin their assault on us."

There was a smattering of applause that grew into an ovation and then an uproarious cheer. Battle watched the joyous reaction of those around him. At first, he sat quietly observing the masses. They were a mixture of men and women, young and old. There were some children. There were some elderly.

"Our numbers are greater than they know," Paagal said. "We have been lying dormant. Now is the time."

The Dwellers were white, black, Hispanic, and Asian. They were representative of the oppressed, Battle thought. What they lacked in strength and cunning, they made up for with grit and will. They were fighting for a way of life, protecting their freedom and their future. And they were transfixed by the leader as she circled the fire, delivering what was part strategic briefing and part religious revival.

"This is our moment," she exalted. "This is our moment." Her words echoed off the canyon walls. The assembly howled their agreement. The more Paagal spoke, the more interested Battle became in what she said and how she delivered it.

He listened to her as if her words, her message, weren't directly meant for him. He spun himself into a fly on the wall, careful to observe the Dwellers without any judgment on his face. They were enraptured.

"We have cut off the snake at its head," she intoned in a guttural roar. "However, that does not mean its venom lacks poison. It does not mean the tail won't instinctively whip and flail in defense."

Battle was a disciple in church. He was listening to a sermon, acutely aware of his own failing faith. He'd not prayed in days. Worse was that he'd not missed the ritual. Without the graves of his wife and son to remind him of the need to ask and seek forgiveness, he was straying from that path. Battle half expected Sylvia's voice to fill his head at that moment. She was silent, as was Wesson. He looked around and saw the deep belief in the faces of gathered Dwellers.

The congregants were restless. They were ready to give their souls and believe. They were anxious to plunge their heads beneath the waters of salvation and emerge again clean and pure.

Paagal was the path to dominion. She was the conduit to what all of them sought.

She quieted the crowd with a finger to her lips, her face glowing in the firelight. "These small victories are valuable on the eve of what comes," she said. "But they do not, in and of themselves, guarantee victory."

Her voice was strong and clear. Battle sensed the cult of personality, her aura blanketing her followers. On this stage, she was electric in a way he'd not sensed up close.

"What will guarantee our victory will be your sacrifice," she said, her arms flexing, her eyes wide with enthusiasm. "What will guarantee our victory will be your cunning, your intellect, your measured patience."

Her voice was growing in decibel and intensity. Battle felt the rush. The rhythmic cadence of her oration was intoxicating.

"We will fight them where they live," she promised. "We will beat them where they live. We will fight them where we live. We will beat them where we live. And when we do…"

Battle leaned in, growing as anxious as anyone to hear what was next. His eyes were focusing on Paagal. Everyone's eyes were focused on Paagal.

She played the crowd, lowering her voice to above a whisper. "And when we do…" she repeated.

"And when we do!" a man in the crowd shouted.

"And when we do!" mimicked one young woman and then another. There was a chatter building in the crowd until Paagal raised her hands to silence it.

"And when we do," she said, throwing her fists up into the air and bellowing, "they will die where they live! They will die where we live! There is no other way. *There is no other way.*"

The hundreds, maybe thousands, gathered around the fire stood and cheered. They high-fived and fist-bumped and hugged each other. They howled.

Battle found himself joining in, unwittingly amped by the energy Paagal provided the assembled. He was ready to run through a wall.

Paagal rounded the fire, pumping her fists into the air. She was biting her lower lip and strutting like a heavyweight champion. She was in control. She paraded in a large circle, pointing to Dwellers in the crowd. For what may have been ten minutes she repeated her victory laps.

As the crowd's energy waned, Paagal flapped her arms to quiet them. "Shhh!"

The congregation grew silent. Those still talking were coaxed by their neighbors to stop.

"I leave you with this," she said, pointing to the sky. "You know your jobs. You know your task. Stick to your job. Complete your task. If you have questions, see your coordinator. We begin when the sun rises. Go sleep."

On cue, the Dwellers moved back toward the tent encampment en masse, pushing past Battle. He stood on his toes to see above the flood rushing by him, bumping into him. He tried to spot Paagal. She was still at the fire, shaking hands and offering hugs as Dwellers left the meeting.

Battle swam upstream, sliding in and out of men and women walking in the opposite direction. As he maneuvered his way to the fire, he searched for Lola and Sawyer. He didn't see either of them until the density of the crowd thinned and he neared the pulsing heat of the bonfire flames.

They were standing with Paagal. The leader had her hands on Lola's shoulders. Lola was nodding her head. Paagal's eyes moved to Sawyer and back as she spoke. It seemed none of them saw Battle until he was within a couple of feet. Virtually all of the Dwellers were gone. Though, for the first time, Battle noticed Paagal's security. A quartet of large armed men with prison physiques were stationed at four equidistant points about twenty yards from Paagal. The orange reflection of the fire danced on the barrels of their rifles.

"Battle," Lola said, "you made it."

"Yeah," he said. "Why didn't you wake me?"

"Sawyer said you were sleeping," she said. "I know you haven't slept well in days."

Battle was incredulous. "Really?"

"Well," she stumbled, "I—I—"

Paagal raised her hand to interrupt. "I told her to leave you," said Paagal. "I'd have filled you in on whatever you missed."

Battle folded his arms across his chest, hiding his fists. "Why?"

Paagal nodded at Lola. "She was right. You needed your sleep. There was nothing here tonight I couldn't tell you later."

Battle laughed, squeezing his fists tighter. "Later? We fight tomorrow," he said. "What later?"

"My plan," Paagal explained, "was to roust you before sunrise. I didn't say anything here tonight, other than reveal our successful infiltration into several Cartel strongholds, that you needed to know. This was a—"

"Pep rally?"

A smile spread across Paagal's face. "Yes," she said, "a pep rally."

"They believe in you," said Battle.

"They do," Paagal agreed. "But more than that," she said, stepping away from the fire and toward Battle, "they believe in themselves. They believe they can defeat a stronger enemy. Belief in one's own self is a powerful weapon."

"It's almost a little like a cult," said Battle. "You had me swept up in the moment there."

Lola whipped her attention to Battle and shot him a wide-eyed glare brimming with embarrassment. "Marcus!" she said. "That's not fair."

Paagal waved her off. "I understand that, Battle. I do," she said. "To the outsider, any collective faith may seem unhealthy. I assure you, that's not an issue here. Not only is every Dweller here of his or her own free will, it is free will for which they fight."

The more Battle listened, the more wary he became. Despite his momentary lapse of reason, he sensed something maniacal in Paagal. It wasn't as overt as he'd seen in some of the Cartel leadership. Nonetheless, it was there.

Everything in him told him that staying to fight was a bad idea. His gut told him they were better off taking their chances at the wall. He looked at Lola. Her eyes pleaded with him to relent, to stand down. So he did.

"I'm sorry," he said. "I shouldn't have said that. It wasn't fair. You've been very kind to us."

Paagal nodded. "Apology accepted. It's best we're on the same page when our fight begins. I'd hate to find us on opposite ideological sides."

Battle ignored the veiled threat. "We should talk tactics," he said. "Timing. Placement. Attack. Defense. Retreat."

Paagal laughed. "There will be no retreat, Battle," she said, clasping her hands behind her back. She began to walk toward camp. "I can promise you that." She glanced at one of her sentries, and the four of them moved with her, keeping the same distance.

Battle took the hint and followed Paagal away from the fire. Lola and Sawyer trailed a step behind. Battle motioned for them to walk beside him.

"Let's go to my tent," she said, marching toward the encampment. "We'll discuss the particulars there. Lola and Sawyer are welcome to join us. Since you're here, there's no need to wait until the morning."

CHAPTER TWELVE

OCTOBER 25, 2037, 6:40 PM
SCOURGE +5 YEARS
HOUSTON, TEXAS

Ana fumbled with the key and struggled to slide it into the slot in the side of the door. She'd tried the fob first, pressing the unlock button repeatedly without luck. The battery was dead or the mechanism was broken.

Either way, she was forced the work the key itself with shaky hands. She kept looking over her shoulders, finally unlocking the car door with a reassuring click. Ana pulled on the handle and swung open the door, the sound of its dry hinges echoing against the concrete of the parking garage.

It was dark except for a flickering streetlamp outside the garage. The bulb was even with the third-floor deck and gave Ana enough light with which to work.

The car, a 2028 Lexus, was a hybrid. It was plugged into one of three charging stations on the third level. Ana had no way of knowing whether the car's battery had any juice. Even though Houston had better power than most of the Cartel's two hundred and seventy thousand square miles, it was intermittent. Add the daily surges of power across the unreliable grid and the charging station might not work under the best conditions.

Ana sat in the driver's seat, put the key in the console to her right, and was about to press the start button to test the vehicle when she thought better of it. The sound of the engine starting, however low a hum, would alert anyone nearby. She'd need to be on the move once that happened.

She pulled herself from the car and walked to the passenger side. She tugged on the door. It didn't work. Ana slapped her forehead with the palm of her hand, huffed, and walked back around to the driver's side to press the unlock button in the door panel. She heard the stereo click of all four doors unlocking simultaneously and repeated her move to the passenger's side.

The door swung open and Ana left it there as she went to the rear of the car and pulled Penny from her stroller. The nine-month-old was still asleep, the pacifier bouncing in her mouth with a deliberate sucking sound.

Ana sat her child in the front passenger seat and tried the automatic adjustment lever at its side. It didn't work. She opened the rear passenger door, folded the stroller, and laid it across the backseat.

Gently she closed the rear passenger door, the front passenger door, unplugged the charging cable, and returned to the driver's seat. She looked back at the charging station and noticed a red flashing light atop the machine. It hadn't been flashing before. Ana disregarded it. Her finger hovered over the start button and she closed her eyes. Then she pressed it and the engine rumbled to life, settling into a low hum.

Ana pumped her fists. "Yes," she said between her teeth and leaned over to adjust Penny's seat. She lowered the back as far as it would recline and then pulled the seat belt across her sleeping child's torso. She yanked on it until the belt locked into place. It wasn't a car seat, but it would have to do.

She adjusted her own seat, setting it higher and closer to the steering wheel, before adjusting the side and rearview mirrors. Ana had only been in a car twice in five years, and she hadn't driven since the Scourge.

The Lexus, which had belonged to General Harvey Logan, was in surprisingly good condition for its age. It had a full tank of gas and a working electric motor, and Ana remembered Logan telling a captain the car could travel close to seven hundred miles.

Palo Duro Canyon was six hundred miles away. It would be close.

She ran through a mental checklist as if she were to pilot a plane. She checked the turn signals, the lights, the space between the gas pedal and the brake.

Ana shifted the car into reverse, pressed the accelerator with too much force, and was forced to slam on the brake. Her right arm instinctively flew outward to protect Penny.

The child stopped sucking for a moment and then resumed, still asleep. Ana shifted into drive and gently pushed on the accelerator. The high-intensity beams shifted as she turned the wheel and lit her path toward the exit.

She turned left, maneuvering around the two other hybrid cars plugged into their charging stations, and then turned the wheel right to enter the circular exit ramp. Ana sat forward in her seat, straining against the shoulder strap, her hands tightly gripping the leather steering wheel. Slowly she descended the ramp, her foot gently pumping the brake, letting the car's idle propel her forward.

Ana rolled to the second floor and then the first, to the traffic arm at the exit to the street. She rolled down her window to find something that might initiate lifting it, finding nothing. She turned back, determined to drive through the orange and white arm, when she saw a man standing in her way.

Ana jumped in surprise at the sight of him and let out a squeal before realizing it was Wendell Wake, Nancy's husband and a posse boss. He was on the other side of the arm, his hands in his pants pockets. He tipped his brown hat forward, leaving much of his face in shadow. He ran his hand across his throat, telling her to cut the engine. She didn't.

She rolled down her window, leaned out, and forced a smile, calling to him over the reverberation of the engine. "Wendell, I'm glad you're here. Can you please help me get the arm up?"

Wendell waved his hand across his throat again and then pointed to the headlights. "You set off an alarm," he said. "Where's Sidney?"

"I'm trying to help Sidney," she said. "We need the car. Could you please give me a hand?" She ducked back inside the car and looked across the hood at Wendell.

"Cut off the engine," he said. "I can't hear you."

Ana could hear him. She didn't comply.

"Ana," he said, taking a step forward, "if you want my help, you'll need to turn off the car. What did you do to Sidney?"

Do to Sidney? How would he know?

"He tried to kill me, Wendell," Ana said. "I defended myself."

"Defended yourself? I always doubted your resolve," Wendell said. "I wondered whether you could follow through. Sidney trusted you would, but agreed with us that you were too much of a liability going forward. The Dwellers told us to do what we saw fit, to do what was best for the whole."

Ana couldn't believe what she was hearing. They had planned on killing her. The resistance was no better than the Cartel. She gripped the steering wheel, waiting for Wendell to divulge more of their plans for her.

He didn't. Then he reached around to his back. When his hand emerged, he was holding something.

By the time Ana recognized Wendell was armed and aiming a gun at her, he'd already spent two rounds. The percussive blasts killed both headlights and startled Penny, who awoke and started crying. It was instantly dark. Ana pressed the button to roll up her window. She thumbed the shifter into what she thought was reverse and slammed her foot on the accelerator as Wendell shone a flashlight in her eyes. She was momentarily blinded and the engine roared, but the car stayed in place. Ana pressed the accelerator again. It responded, but the car didn't move.

Ana searched for the gear indicator. It read N for neutral. She pressed the brake and tried shifting into reverse. A piercing bright light followed by the stinging spray of shattered glass stopped her.

Wendell's powerful, rough hands grabbed at Ana, groping for the wheel. He tried opening the door and one hand caught her chin, forcefully turning her head toward the open window, and a finger grazed her lips. She opened her mouth and bit down as hard as she could, feeling the crunch between her teeth.

Wendell cried out in pain and cursed Ana, still managing to wrangle open the door. Ana shifted her weight and grabbed the handle with both of her hands. She pushed outward at first, giving Wendell enough space to move his arm inside the car and grip her shoulder. Then she pulled back, slamming the door on his arm at his elbow.

He cried out again and withdrew his arms, giving Ana enough time to find the gearshift and slip the car into reverse. The car shuddered at the sudden shift but propelled backwards until Ana slammed on the brake.

"Shhh," Ana said to Penny. Her hand found the child's forehead and she stroked it gently. Penny was on the verge of hyperventilating and was squirming against the seat belt restraint.

The flashlight Wendell had used to blind Ana and break the window was on the ground, its thin beam spreading outward on the ground near the posse boss.

Ana could hear him screaming at her, so she had a sense of his general location, but she couldn't see him clearly until he bounded in front of the car and was standing three feet in front of it with the handgun leveled at her.

She flipped the gearshift into drive and drove her foot down onto the accelerator and ducked, putting her body on top of Penny's. She heard a rapid trio of gunshots and felt another spray of glass across her back before the car shuddered and lurched. It bounced as if the tires had run over a speed bump. Ana's foot was still pressed to the floor and the car gathered speed, barreled through the exit gate arm, and exploded into the street. She moved her foot to the brake and sat up to retake the wheel.

The car screeched and spun, its tires burning off the top layer of rubber on the asphalt. Her hands again white knuckling the leather, Ana crinkled her nose at the acrid smoke filtering its way into the air around the Lexus.

Penny was still crying, her arms flailing. Ana leaned over and popped the latch. She pulled her daughter from her seat, cradling her flat against her body and stroking the back of her head. Penny's lungs filled with air and then stuttered as she breathed out.

"Shhh," Ana whispered. "It's okay, baby. It's okay. Shhh."

Penny pushed herself away from her mother to look at her. Even in the virtual darkness, Ana could see the shine of snot covering the lower half of her face. Her eyes were swollen with tears.

"Mamamama," Penny said. "Mamamama." Her tiny, wet hand touched Ana on the cheek. "Mamamama."

Ana smiled and thumbed away the tears from underneath her daughter's eyes. For a split second she forgot the urgency of the moment. It flooded back when she saw someone sprinting toward her car. It was a woman, maybe fifty yards from her, lit by the ambient light of a streetlamp in the distance.

"Hang on, baby," Ana said and rebuckled Penny into her seat. Penny protested, but didn't have a choice.

Ana checked the gear, flipped into drive, and slapped her foot onto the accelerator. The tires spun wildly against the street while she struggled to correct the wheel. The windshield was gone, and pieces of glass slid off the dash as the car increased its speed.

Ana aimed for the woman. Sitting forward in her seat, she drove straight at her. Not thinking about the lack of a windshield and the possibility the woman's body could fly into the car, she turned the wheel to make sure she made a direct hit.

At the last instant, she recognized the woman as Nancy Wake. She was armed with a shotgun or a rifle. Ana couldn't tell the difference in the dark.

Nancy screamed and tried to dive out of the way when it was apparent Ana wasn't trying to avoid her. It was too late. The car clipped her, spinning Nancy like a helicopter blade into the air before she landed face-first on the street.

Ana looked in her side-view mirror and saw the dark heap in the road, the long gun lying nearby. She slammed on the brakes while holding back Penny's forward momentum with her arm.

"Mommy will be right back," she said, holding up a finger to Penny. She leaned over and groped the floor until she found the pacifier. "Here," she said and popped it in her daughter's mouth like a cork. Penny blinked at her but seemed okay.

With the engine still running, Ana hopped out of the Lexus and marched back toward Nancy. In the span of less than a few hours, she'd killed three, maybe four people. The reality of it didn't set in until she stood over Nancy's dying body.

The woman's arms and legs looked like a broken puppet's. She was on her back, her eyes staring blankly into the sky. Ana moved closer and squatted down by Nancy's head. She could hear the ragged, wet air leaking from Nancy's lungs.

A knot thickened in Ana's throat as she surveyed her handiwork. She swallowed past it and gulped. "Why?" she whispered.

Nancy turned her head slightly and licked her bloody lower lip. Her eyes jerked toward Ana and narrowed.

"Why, Nancy?" Ana repeated louder. "I did what was asked of me."

Nancy sneered, closed her eyes, and said nothing. Her breathing slowed.

"Tell me, Nancy," she repeated. "You owe me an explanation."

Nancy laughed and then coughed. She winced from what Ana imagined was ridiculous pain. There were multiple compound fractures on each limb. Ana supposed the internal injuries were worse.

"I don't owe you anything, you whiny piece of—" Nancy coughed again and then wheezed when she tried to inhale.

A rush of anger coursed through Ana's body. She pushed herself to her feet and then stepped on Nancy's deformed left arm as if it were the accelerator in the Lexus. The pressure elicited a squeal that sounded like air leaking from a balloon. Nancy's eyes bulged.

"I killed your husband too," Ana said. She spat on Nancy's face and turned to find the gun. She picked it up with both hands and carried it back to the Lexus without turning around to see Nancy take her final breaths.

Ana stood at the car door and looked at the weapon. It was a nasty-looking machine. The stock was a varnished wood grain, as was the pistol grip. There was a round drum attached to the rifle underneath the barrel, which Ana believed was called the "magazine." It was angled forward toward the front of the weapon.

She pulled the weapon to her shoulder and looked through the iron sights. It was heavy in her arms. She imagined it was not an easy weapon to fire. She knew enough about guns to use them. Ana lowered the rifle, found the safety lever on the right side, pulled it up into the "safe" position, and set it on the floorboard of the rear passenger compartment.

Penny had fallen asleep again. The pacifier was still. Her chest was moving quickly up and down as she breathed.

Ana touched her leg and rubbed it with her thumb before strapping on her own seat belt. She looked at the electronic compass in the car's display panel. She was facing northwest.

"Perfect," she said to herself and put the car in drive. "Six hundred miles to go."

CHAPTER THIRTEEN

OCTOBER 25, 2037, 7:10 PM
SCOURGE +5 YEARS
PALO DURO CANYON, TEXAS

From a distance, the glow of the bonfire was a pulse of orange light. Felipe Baadal admired it from his perch on the southern rim of the canyon. He'd run to his spot after the meeting, stopping only once to drink water on his way. Paagal, his new lover, had entrusted him with what she believed might be the frontline of their defense.

Baadal turned from the canyon and into the wind that blew northward. It was a cold, steady breeze that added an unwelcome chill to the air. He slid his pack from his shoulders and pulled out a thin knit sweater. It was full of holes and thread pulls, but it was enough to keep his mind off the dropping temperature and focus on the task at hand.

He was standing guard with a half dozen other men. They were one of the many squads that made up the southern rim platoon. They were armed. They were ready.

He unclipped the radio from his overly cinched belt and pressed the transmit button. "This is Red squad one," he said with his mouth close to the microphone. "Please advise of your status. Over." He let go of the button and then held the radio to his ear.

There was static and then a voice. *"Red squad two. Status normal. Over."*

"Squad three, Red," buzzed another voice. *"Status normal. Over."*

Seven more squads responded. All ten were good. Baadal would check with them again in a half hour. As midnight approached, he would shorten the interval. Paagal had warned him the most likely time for an attack might be in the hours before dawn. That was when she had told him he must be the most diligent.

Even though she wasn't planning to deploy most of her resources until after sunrise, she told him to be prepared. They might have only minutes' worth of warning from those standing guard beyond the rim.

Baadal also knew that many of the embedded spies who'd been living amongst the Cartel would deploy the next day. They would squeeze the advancing Cartel forces, giving them nowhere to retreat. They'd be trapped.

Paagal had told him, in confidence, he would rule at her side when they won. She would entrust him with her protection and lead the forces that would forge a new age in the territory. Despite his lack of military experience and his deep desire for peace, he'd been flattered and had agreed to stand beside her as her protector and confidant. She'd chosen him, she had said, because he had survived the Jones. That was enough.

Baadal took in a deep breath, the cold air stinging his nostrils. He clipped the radio to his belt and turned to join the others.

"You know," one of the men said to Baadal, "this ain't the first war to happen in this canyon."

Baadal looked over at the man. He recognized him but didn't know him well. His name was Itihaas. People called him It for short.

He was older. His angular face bore a long scar from his left eye to the corner of his lip. It gave his eye a permanent droop, and his mouth was always pulled into a sly smile. He was missing a pinkie on his left hand and walked with an almost imperceptible limp. Baadal didn't know what had scarred him. A lot of people had scars in the post-Scourge world. Some of the wounds were visible. Some weren't. Looking at Itihaas, Baadal imagined his scars were deeper and wider than the ones he could see.

"It was more than one hundred sixty years ago," said It. "It was the United States against some Native American tribes."

"Which ones?" asked another man. The group was gathering around It to listen.

"Kiowa, Comanche, and Cheyenne. I think. It was part of the Red River War. Ended the war, really."

"The battle here?" asked Baadal, referencing the canyon behind him with bony fingers.

"Yep," said It. "It was the Battle of Palo Duro Canyon."

Baadal shrugged the pack on his shoulders. "What happened?"

It shifted his weight and folded his long arms across his narrow chest. He looked out into the darkness of the canyon and nodded toward it. "Palo Duro was a safe place for the natives," he said. "They could hide there, protect their women and their young, store supplies. They were like us."

One of the sentries, who looked to Baadal as if he were no more than fifteen years old, interrupted. "What do you mean?" he asked.

It rubbed the scruff on his chin. "They were hiding from the white man, who wanted them all corralled up on reservations, where they could control what the natives were doing. We're hiding from the Cartel, who essentially does the same to us."

The sentry lowered his hand and his head. "Oh," he said, apparently not liking the comparison.

"So the natives were stockpiling their supplies for the winter in the canyon," said It. "There were minding their own business. There was this colonel named Mackenzie who wasn't havin' it. He had permission to follow the natives wherever they went. So he did."

Baadal noticed the other men were nearly as spellbound as they'd been at the bonfire. Their eyes were wide and they leaned in as It wove his tale.

"Mackenzie had some native scouts," said It. "They found a fresh trail leading to Palo Duro. Mackenzie and his men got off their horses and walked down the narrow path single file. They surprised one of the native camps and destroyed it. A couple of other camps disbanded. They ran for the walls and opened fire from the rim."

The same young sentry interrupted again. "Did the natives win?"

It chuckled. "No," he said. "They didn't. They didn't even kill a single one of Mackenzie's troops. Maybe fifty or sixty natives died. The rest ran. They left their supplies, their horses, everything. By nightfall they were run off. Mackenzie controlled the canyon."

Baadal cleared his throat. "I don't believe that's an effective motivator," he said, "especially given your comparison between the natives and us."

"The point wasn't motivation," said It. "I was passing along some history. That's all."

Baadal nodded. He stepped back to the rim. The orange pulse was dimming. It wouldn't be long before the fire was out. He ran his hand across the top of his smooth head and sucked in another deep breath of cold air.

Standing on the rim, on the edge of the dark chasm below, Baadal thought about the countless nights he'd spent in the dark on behalf of the Dwellers. He'd been a lone sentry for so long, he'd almost forgotten what it was like to live amongst others. He'd missed it, even if he hadn't realized it at the time. Those endless nights tracking the Cartel's movements, cataloging their strengths and weaknesses, had become all consuming.

Now he was amongst people again. He had a woman about whom he'd instantly become passionate. They were on the verge of a great victory. An unconscious smile spread across Baadal's face as he envisioned a future filled with light.

They were Mackenzie's troops, he told himself, and the Cartel were the natives. It wasn't the other way around.

CHAPTER FOURTEEN

OCTOBER 25, 2037, 8:22 PM
SCOURGE +5 YEARS
LUBBOCK, TEXAS

Cyrus Skinner looked like he'd eaten a rattlesnake fangs first. His purple, swollen tongue poked out between his lips. Even with his eyes closed, he appeared to be in pain. His eyes were drawn together, his brow furrowed. He was slouched in a chair, holding his hat on his lap. His legs were crossed at the ankles and rested on the seat of a chair opposite him.

General Roof didn't know whether his captain was asleep or pretending to be. He didn't care. He walked into the room inside the first floor of the Jones, intent on talking to the man he'd savagely beaten a few hours earlier.

"How's your mouth?" he asked from across the room. Roof found a chair and dragged it across the floor.

Skinner's eyes opened slowly and stopped at a slit. He looked over at Roof and shrugged.

"Still can't speak?"

Skinner shrugged again and shook his head. Roof noticed one side of Skinner's face was a nasty palette of fresh scabs and bruises.

Roof spun the chair backwards and straddled it. He leaned on its back with his elbows. "I guess I should apologize," he said. "I really had no cause to whip you the way I did."

Skinner merely sat there, leering at Roof through the razor-thin space between his eyelids.

"Yeah," said Roof. "Guess you can't respond. That's my fault. Look—"

Skinner raised his hand, waving off Roof's apology. He closed his eyes and put his hat on his head, lowering the brim over his brow. His tongue still protruded from between his lips. He cleared his throat and clasped his hands at his belly.

"Whether you want to hear it or not," said Roof, "I'm gonna tell you what's what."

Skinner opened one eye and shifted in the seat. He flared his nostrils and tried adjusting the placement of his swollen tongue in his mouth.

"You're not going to the rim," said Roof.

Skinner opened his other eye, but didn't otherwise respond.

From behind Roof, Porky ambled into the room. "Oh," he said, "I'm sorry. I didn't mean to interrupt you, General."

Roof turned around and looked at the chubby grunt. He studied the man's cherubic face and wondered what had driven kind-looking Porky into the Cartel. "You're fine," he said. "What do you want?"

Porky held up a large glass bowl. "I found some ice," he said. "I thought Captain Skinner could use it."

Skinner waved him over and took the bowl. He set it on his lap and delicately fingered a jagged chunk of ice into his mouth. He squeezed his eyes closed and held his mouth open. His hands gripped the arms of the chair and his body tensed as he rolled the ice over his wounded tongue.

Porky stood beside the chair, his face contorting in a way that mimicked Skinner's pain. He swallowed hard and took a step back.

Roof was observing the grunt's sympathetic movements. "That's thoughtful of you," he said. "You seem like a good man..."

"Porky, sir," said the grunt. "Everybody calls me Porky."

"You seem like a good man, Porky. Why are you in the Cartel?"

Porky tilted his head and pursed his lips. "What do you mean?"

Roof pointed at Skinner and then himself. "You're not like us," he said and aimed his finger at Porky. "I can tell that. You have a kindness about you. There's a soft heart underneath all of that." He waved his hand over Porky's overhanging belly.

Porky sucked in his gut as much as he could and pulled up on his pants, using the empty belt loops. His face flushed.

"Seriously," said Roof. "I'm not joking. Why are you in the Cartel?"

Porky looked at Roof as if he didn't understand English. "I'm not sure what you mean, sir."

Roof looked at Skinner and then back at Porky and chuckled. "It's a simple question," he said. "Why. Are. You. In. The. Cartel?"

Porky tugged on his pants again and squeezed his eyebrows together. He pulled his shoulders up to his ears. "Because I had to, I guess."

Roof nodded. It was an honest answer. "Why did you have to join?"

"I didn't want to die," said Porky. "I was told if I worked for the Cartel, I'd have a job, a place to stay, food to eat. They said if I didn't, I could either leave town or die. I had nowhere to go. I wanted to stay alive. So…"

Roof knew that was how the Cartel grew exponentially in a short period of time. He and the three other generals had insisted their most trusted soldiers go about proselytizing the masses. It was their own version of the Crusades.

It was brilliant, really. Heavy handed and brutal, but brilliant. Posses went from town to town, ranch to ranch, house to house, and converted the nonbelievers at gunpoint or worse.

When there was resistance, Roof made certain his lieutenants knew to make examples of those who failed to comply. It was not hyperbole when a posse boss threatened to put someone's head on a stake or burn him alive. It led to a strong foothold in nearly every city and town within their territory.

For close to five years, ruling by fear had served the Cartel. Now, on the edge of war with those few who refused to succumb to their threats, who resisted with uncommon resolve, Roof thought better of it.

He looked at Porky — softhearted, roly-poly Porky — and saw the weakness in their numbers. How many other men about to fight for the Cartel were doing so because their only other options were exile or death? How many of them served out of fear as opposed to loyalty?

Porky, and the countless grunts like him, were conscripted soldiers. They were an entirely different proposition from the men and woman who would fight for the Dwellers because they chose to do so.

He knew from his days in Syria that a strongly held belief was more powerful than an HK. The fighters there, in their limitless number of factions, all fought for what they believed was right. They risked their lives and took those of their enemies based on the simple premise that they were doing so for a righteous cause.

It made them difficult to defeat, given that American soldiers, sailors, airmen, and Marines were fighting because it was their job to do so. They weren't in country because they were seeking a moral high ground. They weren't purging the world of infidels. They were getting paid to be there. The esoteric idea of patriotism and democracy didn't work the same way.

Skinner grunted and drew Porky's attention. The captain was holding the bowl of ice, shaking it loudly.

Porky reached out his hand slowly, as if he were afraid of losing it. "You're finished with it?"

Skinner nodded and shoved the bowl into Porky's hands. The grunt took it and lowered his head, leaving the room like a dismissed manservant. Both men watched him leave and then locked eyes.

"I need you here, Cyrus," Roof said. "I've got men staying here to hold down the fort, so to speak. Lubbock is critical to our trade with the Mexicans and with the users north of the wall. We can't leave it entirely unprotected while we march on the canyon."

Skinner's face was frozen with disgust. Roof started to further make his case when Skinner snapped his fingers and pointed over the general's shoulder, waving his finger at a desk on the far side of the room.

Roof turned around and saw a large notepad on the desk. He swung his leg over the chair and maneuvered his way to the desk. The pad was irregular and discolored from water stains, and most of the pages were already covered with illegible pre-Scourge notes.

Roof picked it up and showed it to Skinner. "You want this?"

Skinner nodded.

Roof walked around to the other side of the desk and fished through the unlocked drawers, looking for a pen. He found one, uncapped it, and scribbled on the paper until ink trailed onto it from the ballpoint.

He carried both back to Skinner and handed them over, standing over Skinner while he wrote on the crinkled paper and then ripped it free of the pad.

Roof took the note, held it close to his eyes and then pulled it back to focus. Skinner's handwriting was hard to read. It resembled the left-hand offering of a right-handed kindergartner.

"You need me at the canyon. I don't want to stay here with the losers and women."

Roof looked up, still holding the note in his hand, and sighed. "You can't put your tongue all the way in your mouth. You can't talk. Your face is swollen like you stuck it in a hornet's nest."

Skinner scribbled another message and ripped it from the pad. Roof would've laughed at the comedy of it if he hadn't been to blame.

"That's why you can't keep me here. I can't be in charge. I'll follow you to the canyon."

Roof considered the argument. Skinner was right. He was probably more effective as a grunt than a leader given his injuries. The captain handed him a third message.

"I'm in the Cartel 'cause I want to be. Not 'cause I had to be."

Roof nodded. "Fine, you're a frontline grunt. Hope you're happy."

Roof was happy. He needed as many Skinners as he could get. Skinner had a cause.

He *wanted* to fight. It wasn't about survival for him. It was about living.

CHAPTER FIFTEEN

OCTOBER 25, 2037, 9:07 PM
SCOURGE +5 YEARS
PALO DURO CANYON, TEXAS

Paagal took a long, slow drink from a tall metal thermos. She moaned softly as she drank, tilting the bottom of the thermos higher and higher until she'd emptied its contents.

"Coffee is such a treat," she said. "Are you certain I can't offer you any?"

Lola shook her head. Battle sighed.

"I suppose I'm boring you," said Paagal, one eyebrow arched higher than the other.

"You haven't told us anything," Battle said. "We've been here for I don't know how long, and I have no more sense of your tactical plan than I did when you were preaching to the choir."

Paagal eased into the chair across from her guests. They were sitting at the rough wooden table in her tent. She reached down and pulled a large map from beside her. It was rolled into a tube and she unwound it, placing it on the table.

Paagal spun the map around so the Texas Panhandle was on her side. There was a thick black line that circumnavigated the old state boundaries. Paagal ran her finger along the markings.

"This is the wall," she said. "That should give you a decent idea of the territory. We are in this location." She dragged her finger to the canyon, which was encircled in red.

Battle noticed there were numbers written by the names of most of the larger cities. Some of the numbers were crossed out and new numbers written beside them. He tapped the number 729 near Austin and 1050 at San Antonio.

"What are these?" he asked.

Paagal looked up from the map with a smile. "Those are the numbers of Dwellers we have in those locations."

Lola pointed to the number 2512 above Houston. "So you have twenty-five hundred people in Houston who are sympathetic to your cause?"

"Twenty-five hundred and twelve," said Paagal. "And they're not sympathizers, Lola. They're revolutionaries."

Lola's eyes darted from marking to marking on the map. "How?"

"We didn't start with these numbers," said Paagal. "We began two years ago with maybe five or ten in each city. Each of those people recruited those who they thought might fit our way of thinking. They in turn recruited more people. It organically grew exponentially from there."

Battle waved his hand over the map. "And all of these revolutionaries are doing what right now?"

"For starters," she said, "they've attacked the leadership in each location."

"You said that at the bonfire," said Lola.

"Yes," Paagal said. "I did. But I didn't say what comes next."

Lola leaned in. "Which is…?"

"Half of the revolution takes place in the cities," she said. "The element of surprise is a powerful force. Once we've degraded the Cartel enough that neutral actors see we can win, they'll join our side."

"What about the other half?" asked Battle.

"They advance," said Paagal. She held her hands in front of her face and interlocked her fingers. "They squeeze the Cartel. If we hold them at bay long enough here at the canyon, we win. They'll have nowhere to go. Retreat becomes an impossibility."

"Not impossible."

Paagal leaned back, her eyes widened and brow arched. "Oh?"

Battle ran his fingers along the map, indicating stress points for the Dwellers. He showed Paagal areas from which the Cartel could make them vulnerable. He traced escape routes for both the Dwellers and the Cartel.

Battle had lost so much of what he'd learned at West Point and on the battlefields of Afghanistan and Syria. The space in his memory reserved for military gamesmanship was fragmented. He'd made so many stupid mistakes since the Scourge, it was as if he'd never been a soldier. His survival to this point was as ridiculous as it was miraculous. It was the stuff of dime-store novels.

As he worked the map bathed in the red glow of Paagal's tent, those disparate memories flooded back. It was as if he'd awoken from a long sleep and was lucid for the first time in a long time.

"Let's assume they'll be attacking from all points." Battle ran his finger along the map, tracing the multitude of routes available to the advancing troops. "They'll have men moving from these roads here and here."

"It doesn't matter," Paagal said, running her finger along the map next to Battle's. "They can't access the floor from any of these points. They'll have the high ground to provide cover fire and to occupy our people, but they'll have to funnel their advance into these spots here. They're the only ways down to the floor."

Battle nodded. "So where do you want me?"

Lola nudged him with her shoulder. "You mean us. Where does she want us?"

Battle acquiesced. "Us."

Paagal tapped a point on the map near the southern rim. "I think you'd be best utilized at the entrance here. That's one of the funnel points. You're good with a weapon. I'll need you picking off combatants as they emerge from their descent."

"Got it."

Battle and Lola left Paagal in her tent, walking slowly back to their own shelters. Neither said anything at first until Battle broke the ice.

"Why didn't you wake me up?" he asked, his voice dripping with suspicion. "It seems kinda strange."

Lola looked up at Battle as they stepped in sync. "It was pretty chaotic," she said. "Everybody was rushing over there. Sawyer didn't want to be late. I checked in on you and you were asleep. I started to wake you, but Baadal tugged on my arm and told me to hurry up."

"So you left me?"

"I did try to wake you up, actually," she said. "I said your name loudly a couple of times. You rolled over. You were wheezing a little bit. I'm sorry, I should have gotten you up."

"You should have. I agree." Battle believed her. Still, he was skeptical of the Dwellers. "I don't trust them."

"You don't trust anyone."

"Not true," Battle said. "Maybe it's not that I don't trust them. I don't think their motives are as pure as they'd have us believe."

"Get over it." Lola laughed condescendingly. "Nobody's motives are pure in this world. Everybody's trying to survive by hook or by crook. For such a skeptic, it's like you still want to believe in Santa Claus."

Lola reached over and took Battle's hand. He allowed it, welcomed it really, and squeezed gently once their fingers were fully intertwined. A jolt of electricity sparked through his body. His chest tightened. He looked over at Lola and smiled. She smiled back and then looked away demurely, as if embarrassed by their connection.

Battle was content to walk quietly, hand in hand, back to their tents. He thought about what Lola had said about motive.

She was right, of course. There was no Santa Claus. He'd died from the Scourge.

CHAPTER SIXTEEN

OCTOBER 25, 2037, 9:42 PM
SCOURGE +5 YEARS
INTERSTATE 45, SOUTH OF BUFFALO, TEXAS

The headlights cut a narrow, bright path ahead along the cracked asphalt of the highway. Interstate 45, as it used to be known, was the direct north-south link between Houston and Dallas.

Ana planned to take the shortest path north before jogging west. She didn't have time to avoid the highway in search of more desolate, less traveled paths. This was her best option.

She squinted as she drove, pretending as if she were piloting a rocket ship; the reflective white dashes separating the lanes were like stars speeding past. She imagined she were hurtling through space towards some distant planet, one without violence or disease or guilt.

Penny was awake in the seat next to her, content to suck on the pacifier. Ana knew it wouldn't be long before the child would be hungry and she would have to stop to feed her.

Ana didn't want to stop. She wanted to be at the canyon.

It was ice cold in the car. Without a windshield, the wake of air displaced by the car rushed through the cabin. Ana had found a blanket in the trunk that she'd wrapped around Penny, but she herself was cold. Her hands were especially uncomfortable.

She looked down at the speedometer and saw she was pushing the Lexus at forty miles per hour. Though there wasn't much about cars she could recall, she did remember hearing once that the faster the car moved, the more fuel it consumed. She hoped that by driving fast enough to outpace anyone on horseback, she might save some fuel and arrive at the canyon without problem. It also reduced the wind swirling through the open cabin.

Driving through the darkness, she occasionally caught a gray glimpse of a building or abandoned vehicle along the side of the highway. She was thankful the journey to this point had been in the dark. Ana didn't need the distraction of what the Scourge had wrought and what it had done to the world as she tried to free herself from what it had done to her and what she had done as a result.

It wasn't as though Ana had lived a life of leisure before the pneumonia killed her mother, her grandfather, her sister, and the man to whom she was engaged. Every last one of them was a drunk or an addict who couldn't find their way past the eighth step.

None of them had ever made amends. Even on their respective deathbeds, as the consumption took their breath and their lives, they refused to take responsibility for their actions or their interaction.

The Lexus cut through the dark and Ana was focused on that eighth step. She tried to recall all of the people she had wronged. She couldn't get past the four people she'd killed that day: her child's father, a resistance recruiter, and two foul people who she did not like but whom she'd rather not have murdered.

Ana leaned forward in her seat and rubbed her palms on the leather steering wheel, trying to generate some friction and heat for her hands. She looked up above the horizon, the wind whipping through her hair and drying her eyes as she peered into the dark, searching for a star or the moon. She couldn't find either.

"Mamamama," Penny babbled. "Mamamama."

Anna pulled her hand from the wheel, popped the pacifier back into Penny's eager mouth, and placed her hand gently on Penny's leg. She squeezed it and rubbed it with her thumb.

"Mama is right here, baby," she said.

Ana looked over at Penny and reassured her daughter they would stop soon to eat. She wondered, as she soaked in the beauty of her child, what the fractured world might hold for her. Ana couldn't imagine it would be good. Her smile melted and she looked back at the road.

It was already too late.

Directly in front of the car, dead center in the pale yellow fan of the headlights, was a large coyote. Its eyes reflected the light as it stood frozen in the center of the highway. It had a dead animal in its mouth.

Ana pressed firmly on the brake. The tires screeched in protest against the highway. Her right arm snapped outward to protect Penny, who was already sliding forward in her seat, her little body straining against her seat belt. Ana tried swerving to the right to miss the animal. She failed. She hit it as if she were aiming for it.

The impact brought with it a sickening crunch as the front of the Lexus pulverized the scavenger. Its mangy carcass was tossed onto the hood of the car, and for a split second Ana was sure it was headed directly through the open windshield. Instead, the limp rag doll bounced over the windshield, hit the roof, and slid off the trunk.

Penny was crying as the car came to a shuddering stop. Ana immediately noticed wisps of smoke coming from underneath the hood of the car. A rush of adrenaline flooded her body and she began trembling. Her pulse quickened and her chest felt heavy. She tried taking a deep breath and found herself unable to inhale.

She unbuckled Penny and pulled the baby to her chest. Ana rocked, whispering into her daughter's ear and calming her. Once Penny was quiet, all Ana could hear was the low hum of the engine. The smoke from under the hood had dissipated, but there was a large dent in the hood from the coyote.

She held Penny with one arm and used the other to open her door. She climbed out of the Lexus and walked around to the front of the car.

The signature Lexus emblem was missing and the front grille was a mess, barely resembling the mean, sleek black grate that had decorated the front of the sedan. It was decorated with pieces of the animal, tufts of grayish hair stuck in clumps in the plastic.

The hood was concave at the point of impact. The car looked like it belonged in a junkyard. Ana held Penny and shielded the child's eyes as she moved into the headlights. Looking at them, they were brighter than they'd seemed to be as she drove. The engine still humming softly, she walked around the passenger side of the car and to the rear. She wanted to see the animal.

Ana stepped deliberately toward the coyote. It was only twenty-five yards or so behind the car. As she got closer, she could hear its high-pitched whimper. Somehow it had survived the collision, if only for a few minutes.

She circled the animal at some distance, afraid to get too close. Its eyes were open, its body mangled. Its torso, or what was left of it, rose and fell with difficulty. The dead rabbit it had been carrying was lying beside its mouth.

The coyote's whimper drew Penny's attention, and Ana spun to keep the child's eyes from the dying beast and walked back toward the car. Short of putting a bullet in the animal, there was nothing she could do to ease its suffering. It was merely another living being cut down while trying to survive in a post-Scourge world, a scavenger looking for scraps where it could find them.

Ana reached the Lexus, opened the rear driver's side door, and leaned into the backseat. She placed Penny upright on the passenger's side, thinking it would be warmer, and likely safer, if her child were in the backseat of the car.

The child was buckled in and Ana was closing the door when she heard a rustling noise and the sound of soft voices spoken above a whisper. She shut the door with her backside and saw a man and a woman standing on the edge of the road.

The man had a long gun perched on his shoulder. The woman was aiming hers at Ana. She whispered something into his ear, keeping her gun leveled. The man snickered. Ana couldn't hear them above the purr of the car.

It was dark enough that Ana couldn't make out their features or their clothing, but she could see enough to know they wore desperation. The man's jaw moved up and down as if he was chewing on something.

Ana inched along the side of the car. She kept her eyes on the couple and started to open the front door.

"Ah, ah, ah," said the woman. "I wouldn't do that."

Ana left her hand on the door handle. "What do you want?"

"We want your car," said the woman, "and whatever you got inside."

"You can't have it," Ana said defiantly. "You'd leave me stranded here."

The woman stepped forward. "We're not asking your permission," she snarled. "We're telling you that we're taking your car."

"And whatever you got inside," added the man.

When the woman got closer and stood on the edge of the glow from the car's headlights, Ana could see she was missing an eye. There was no patch. There was a scarred hole where the eye used to be. Her lips were worm thin and most of her front teeth were missing.

She was wearing a soiled, ribbed white tank top and baggy cargo shorts. Her legs were a canvas of wounds and bruises. Her feet were bare.

"The car's not going anywhere," Ana said. "It got damaged when I hit the coyote. I don't think it'll drive."

The woman cackled, sending a chill along the back of Ana's neck. "You think we're stupid? You just said us taking your car would leave you stranded. Now you're saying you're already stranded."

Ana struggled to say something that might dissuade the carjackers. She came up with nothing.

"You're gonna need to step away from that car," said the man. He kept his position on the edge of the road, but he'd lowered the long gun and was aiming it at Ana from his waist.

"Step away," said the woman. She stepped closer. Ana could see the grit under the woman's long fingernails. They were as black as the land beyond the highway.

Ana took a deep breath and raised her hands. "Fine," she said. "Let me get my baby out of the backseat."

"You got a baby?" the woman asked. "A real live baby?"

Ana hesitated. "Yes."

"She got a baby," the woman called back to the man out of the corner of her mouth without taking her eye from Ana.

"I heard that," said the man. "A real live baby."

"We had a baby," said the woman. "A little girl."

The woman's shoulders curled forward and she lowered her aim. Her gaze drifted for a moment.

"She caught the Scourge," said the man. "Died fast."

"I'm sorry," said Ana. "I—"

"You're not sorry," snapped the woman. Her shoulders squared and the aim returned to Ana's head. "You got no reason to be sorry. You don't know us."

"I'm only—"

"Shut up and get the baby," the woman said, moving the barrel as she talked. "I wanna see the baby."

"Is it a girl?" the man asked.

Ana nodded.

"Get the girl," said the woman. She took another step forward. "I wanna see her."

"What's her name?" asked the man, stopping Ana as she reached for the rear door handle.

Ana pulled on the door handle and cracked open the door, triggering the interior light. "Penny."

"Oh," cooed the woman. She craned her neck to see inside the car. "I think I see her. I think I see that beautiful girl."

"We may have to take the girl too," said the man. "The car and the girl. I think that's how it's gonna have to be."

"We did say everything inside the car," said the woman, the joy evaporating from her face as she looked back at Ana. "Hurry up."

Ana turned her back on the couple and reached into the car. She whispered to Penny, "Mama will be right back," and she grabbed the automatic rifle. She slapped the safety lever down and spun around with her finger on the trigger.

She shoved the rifle to her shoulder as she depressed the trigger, holding it in place, spraying its contents at the couple. Ana didn't expect the recoil and was knocked back into the car. She kept firing, the fully automatic shots sounding like keys on an electric typewriter as they zipped through the air.

The first volley arced into the air. As Ana fell backward from the recoil, the weapon aimed upward. The first several bullets from the seventy-five-round barrel magazine were close to true and hit the woman twice in the gut. She dropped her long gun and grabbed her midsection, crying out in pain and cursing Ana.

The man reacted quickly. He fired off a pair of shots aimed at Ana's head. She fell back into the side of the car from the recoil, the twin rounds missing her head by inches and slugging the Lexus.

Ana regained her balance and pushed her right hand against the wooden club stock to tighten the rifle against her shoulder and applied steady pressure to the trigger. This time she unleashed a sustained volley of rounds. The first dozen drilled the woman to the road face-first. Her body twitched on the highway as if she were trying to break-dance.

Convinced the woman was no longer a threat, Ana swung the weapon to her left and found the man as he approached. A sting in her left arm near her shoulder altered the first couple of shots, but the trail of gunfire found its mark and cut a swath across the man's chest. His arms flung outward and his long gun rattled to the ground. His body shuddered and convulsed before he stumbled forward and slid onto the asphalt.

Ana held the trigger for a moment longer, the stock thumping against her right shoulder as she struggled to hold the heavy weapon in place. As the last of the shots echoed into the expanse on either side of the highway, Penny's whimper became audible. The child wasn't inconsolable, but Ana could tell she was upset. How couldn't she be? The sound of screaming and gunfire would bring virtually anyone to tears. Ana took a deep breath and exhaled, trying to slow her racing pulse. She stretched her mouth wide, trying to ease the thick ringing in her ears.

It wasn't until after she'd lowered her weapon that she realized she'd been shot. She was bleeding. When the adrenaline of the moment left her body, the wound began to throb.

Ana winced and carried the weapon with her right arm, walking over to the would-be carjackers. She checked the woman first. She was dead on her side, her neck turned awkwardly. The bottoms of her feet were black. The rest of her was coated in grime and blood.

The man was flat on his stomach. Ana couldn't see his face. Blood leached onto the highway from underneath his body. She turned back to the car, reset the safety, and gently laid it where she'd retrieved it.

She consoled Penny for a moment and then turned back to grab the other weapons from the couple, who wouldn't need them any longer. The woman's weapon was a shotgun of some kind. It had two barrels. Ana took the weapon back to the car and then searched the woman's grisly remains for any ammunition. The pain of the bullet wound was spreading down her arm. Her hand felt stiff.

She found a handful of red and brass colored shells in one of the wide pockets in the woman's cargo shorts. Rather than try to carry them, she used her right hand to remove the woman's shorts. She struggled to yank them over the hips, but once she'd managed that, the task was easy. Ana balled up the shorts and tossed them into the foot well of the driver's side rear seat next to her rifle and the woman's shotgun.

She trudged back to the man's rifle. It was smaller than hers and lighter. She flipped its safety and carried it back to the car to place it with the others. Unlike the woman, the man had an ammo pouch on his hip.

It was looped into his belt, a thin braided leather, and she couldn't pull hard enough with one hand to remove it.

Ana cursed and sat down on the road next to the man's body, careful to avoid the pool of his blood. She used her heels to flip him over onto his back so she could unlatch the belt buckle and free the ammo bag. He turned over like a drunk man, his tongue hanging from his mouth and his eyes wide open.

He stared toward the sky. It was a blank, distant stare Ana thought looked peaceful. As if the man had seen the stars or the moon for which she'd been searching and was imagining a better life far from the planet on which he was stuck.

Ana leaned over, trying not to look at his eyes, and undid the buckle. She plucked the brass prong from the braid and then tugged on the buckle's frame. It slid easily from the belt loops in his pants and the ammo bag dropped to the road. She took the ammo bag without looking in it and tossed it into the back of the car.

She felt light-headed and leaned against the open door, her forehead resting across her right forearm. She knew she was losing blood and she touched her right hand to the back of her shoulder. There was no exit wound. The pain was intensifying.

Ana knew she'd need to take care of the wound. Otherwise, she'd be a one-armed unconscious single mother stranded in the dark on a lonely post-apocalyptic highway.

CHAPTER SEVENTEEN

OCTOBER 25, 2037, 10:21 PM
SCOURGE +5 YEARS
PALO DURO CANYON, TEXAS

Baadal was on first watch. As the leader of his squad, he took the first two hours of the rotation. Twenty minutes in, several of the men were already asleep. A couple of them snored loudly enough that Baadal wondered if he'd be able to fall asleep when his turn came.

He had nine minutes until the next radio check. This would be a long night.

Baadal walked along the rim, his feet dragging in the dirt. When he stepped farther from the snoring, he could hear a whistle.

At first he thought it might be the wind, but the closer he moved to its source, the more apparent to him it was a tune, a melody of some kind. Baadal didn't recognize it, but it was catchy.

His pace quickened, and he raised his rifle, closing the twenty-yard gap between the whistling and his spot along the rim. He was within a few feet when he recognized the whistler.

Baadal stopped and lowered his weapon. "It?"

The whistling stopped and the man turned around. "Baadal? That you?"

"Yes," Baadal said. "What're you doing?"

Itihaas turned to fully face Baadal. He drove his hands into his pockets. His rifle was slung across his back. "Just whistling," he said. "Can't sleep."

"What're you whistling?"

"It's an old song," Itihaas said. "It's called 'New World in the Morning'. It's by a fellow named Roger Whitaker. My father used to whistle it. I picked it up."

"Got my attention," said Baadal. He looked out over the rim again, straining his eyes to see anything beyond the darkness.

"I don't know," said It. "I thought it was appropriate. Tomorrow brings a new world, right?"

Baadal shrugged. "I suppose." He turned back to It. "May I ask you a question?"

Itihaas nodded. "Shoot."

Baadal traced his finger down his face. "How'd you…"

"Get the scar?"

Baadal nodded.

"It was on the other side of the wall."

"You've been over the wall?"

It nodded.

"What was it like?"

"That's a tough question to answer," said Baadal. "How do you describe chaos disguised as order? It was deceptively dangerous. No better than here, really. On this side of the wall you can see the danger coming. Up there, on the other side, it's too late by the time you sense it."

Baadal took another step closer to It. "How so?"

"There's a government," he said. "There's a military. There's power, most of the time, and there's food."

"That's all good," Baadal said.

"It's all window dressing," It said. "It's corrupt. It's smoke and mirrors. There's no such thing as an honest living there. I mean, don't get me wrong, if you're willing to go along to get along, it's better up there than it is down here. But if you want to make a go of it, if you want a piece for yourself, you gotta fight bigger, nastier dogs for it. Problem is, you never see their teeth until they're ripping into your throat. By then it's too late."

"Is that why you came back?"

"I didn't come back by choice," It said. He ran his finger along his scar. "After I was attacked, I was tossed back here. Exiled."

"How'd you end up in the canyon?"

"Scavengers along the wall stripped me of everything. They left me for dead," he said. "Some sentries found me, patched me up, and brought me here. That was more than a year ago. I was thankful enough that once I healed, I became a sentry."

Baadal checked his watch. It was time for a check. "Hang on a second," he said, raising a finger to Itihaas. "I gotta get on the radio."

Itihaas nodded. "You do what you gotta do."

"This is Red squad one," said Baadal. "Please advise of your status. Over." He let go of the key and then held the radio to his ear.

There was static and then a voice. *"Red squad two. Status normal. Over."*

"Squad three, Red," buzzed another voice. *"Status normal. Over."*

Six more signaled their situation was normal. The last one, southern rim squad ten, did not.

Baadal looked over at Itihaas and then pulled the radio close to his mouth. "This is southern rim squad one," he said calmly. "Please advise of your status, squad ten. Over."

Nothing.

"Squad ten." Baadal's voice carried more urgency. He shook the radio as he spoke into it. "This is Red squad one. Please advise of your status, squad ten. Over."

Static. Then nothing.

Itihaas moved next to Baadal. The two of them glared at the radio, as if somehow looking at it might produce a response Baadal knew wasn't coming.

"Who's the closest squad to ten?" asked It. "I know we're in the middle of things."

"Eight," said Baadal. He pressed the radio. "Squad eight," he said, the urgency having morphed into desperation. "Please advise of your status, Red squad eight. Over."

The response was immediate. *"Red squad eight. Status normal. Over."*

"Red squad eight," said Baadal, "shift half position east to squad ten location. Advance with caution. Squad ten is not responding. Over."

"You're moving squad eight?" It asked.

"Half of them," said Baadal. "We can't leave a gap." He spun a knob on the top of the radio. "Blue squad one. Please advise of your status. This is Red squad one. Over."

The radio crackled and beeped. *"This is Blue squad one. Status normal. Over."*

Baadal pressed the radio key. "Blue squad one, please provide assistance to Red. Red squad ten not responding. Squad eight moving now with half response. Over."

"Copy that." The radio was overmodulated but intelligible. *"Shifting half position Blue squad nine to assist. Will advise. Over."*

"This isn't good," Baadal said. He switched his frequency again so he could communicate with Paagal. She wouldn't be happy.

"So much for the new world starting tomorrow," said It. "It's happening now."

***

The leader of General Roof's reconnaissance posse couldn't believe his good fortune. The team of six men, all of them smart and wily posse bosses, had moved quickly north to the edge of the canyon's easternmost southern rim three hours ahead of schedule.

Roof had told them to expect sentries to interrupt their progress or misdirect their path. Neither had happened and they'd easily found themselves in an enviable position. They'd stationed themselves behind a clump of large rocks about seventy-five yards from the rim and what appeared to be an unprepared patrol squadron.

The squadron included a larger number of armed combatants than the quick-footed recon posse, but they were inexperienced. They didn't carry themselves with swag. They were too relaxed.

Rather than the Browning shotgun that most of the Cartel carried as standard issue, the recon posse was armed with SCAR-17s similar to General Roof's. There were bipods connected to the barrels, twenty round magazines, and stock was designed to make it easier to secure the weighty weapon against the shooter's shoulder.

In the years before the Scourge, Russian crime lords had provided caseloads of SCAR-17s to those engaged in the Afghani heroin trade. Those same weapons found their way to South and Central America and the nasty drug gangs that populated that early part of the twenty-first century.

Other than the Brownings, which were the most plentiful weapon post-Scourge, the SCAR-17 was the Cartel leadership's weapon of convenience. Six seasoned malevolents armed with the semiautomatic rifle capable of quickly emptying the magazine were likely to defeat most similar-sized opposition.

The leader signaled for two of the men to take positions on either side of the rocks. Both of the men had the added benefit of AAC Cyclone silencers on their weapons. The suppressors lessened the volume of the rifles when fired, making the shots sound more like pneumatic nail gun shots than full-blown semiautomatic rifle fire.

Each man took his position, prone, and set their respective bipods in the dirt. On the leader's signal, they took aim.

One by one, like a shooting gallery at a carnival, the men smacked their targets. Some of the targets were already on the ground. In the dark, the shooters could only see the jerk of their bodies as the .308-inch rounds drilled into the opposition two or three at a time. The others, who were standing, dropped instantly from the staccato rhythm of those brass slugs peppering the life out of them.

Within fifteen seconds, the entire Dweller patrol was done. The recon posse hadn't broken a sweat, and they moved quickly to search their marks. They took what weapons and rations they could use and stuffed them into the light rucksacks on their backs.

The leader opened a satellite phone and awaited the signal before he dialed General Roof. The ring warbled twice before the general answered.

"What?"

"We've made our first contact," said the leader. "Easy pickings. Probably a dozen of their sentries are down."

"No resistance?" asked Roof.

"They never saw what hit 'em," said the recon posse leader. "We've got maps, a radio, some weapons, light rations."

"Good job," said Roof. "Keep me posted. Move along the rim, disabling whatever defenses they have working the edge. The more damage you do, the easier it'll be tomorrow."

The leader hung up, closed the satellite phone, and slipped it into his rucksack. It was dark, but the clouds were clearing, and the moon was providing enough light for the tasks at hand.

He was turning to the group to relay their instructions to the other five bosses when the radio crackled to life. A series of squads checked in with their base. He listened to the number of sentry squads placed along the southern rim: six, seven, eight, nine…

Nobody answered at number ten. The commander called out for number ten again. No response.

"I'm guessing that's us, boys," said the leader. The men chuckled in agreement.

The radio squawked again. *"Red squad eight,"* said the anxious voice sending the orders. *"Shift half position east to squad ten location. Advance with caution. Squad ten is not responding. Over."*

The leader turned to his left and pointed into the darkness. "We're gonna get company," said the leader. "It's gonna be coming from the west. We need to look for it."

The radio chirped. The voice ordered another squad to move.

"We're gonna get it from the north too," one of the men added. "What do you want us to do?"

"We head back to those rocks," said the leader. "They're far enough back with a little elevation. We'll have three positioned facing west and three perched on the other side facing north. We'll hit both of them as they get near."

The men retreated to the rocks. They each set up their attack position and waited for the approaching Dwellers.

CHAPTER EIGHTEEN

OCTOBER 25, 2037, 10:40 PM
SCOURGE +5 YEARS
LUBBOCK, TEXAS

General Roof set down the sat phone. "That was a recon posse," he said to Skinner. The captain was struggling to stay awake. His head kept bobbing up and down as he worked to keep his eyes open. Roof had told him repeatedly he could go to sleep. He'd promised not to leave him behind in the morning. Skinner apparently hadn't believed it.

"They're at the southern rim already," he added. "They're gathering some good intel and they've already taken out some Dwellers. It's off to a good start."

Skinner scribbled on the notepad still on his lap. He ripped free a piece of paper and handed it to Roof.

Roof read it aloud. "What is a recon posse?"

Skinner shrugged and held out his hands expectantly.

"This recon posse is out of Wichita Falls," said Roof. "It's six bosses. All of them are meant to observe and report. That's all. If they have to kill in the process, so be it."

Skinner nodded. He dropped the pad and pen onto his lap.

"Get some sleep," Roof said. "I'll be down the hall."

The general left the captain in his bed and moved into the long hallway that ran the interior of the Jones. He rubbed his eyes. He needed sleep.

He thought about the recon posse's efficiency and wondered to himself how different the last couple of weeks might have been had he made one available to Skinner. Maybe the posse, with its speed and ruthlessness, would have captured and killed the woman and her boy before she ever found Battle's ranch.

Battle would be holed up in his private world, fending off the occasional incursion. He wouldn't have done so much damage to the Cartel. Roof wouldn't have found himself in the difficult position of having to keep Battle alive out of a debt of gratitude.

Still, Battle's involvement and survival had ultimately given them the opportunity to infiltrate the Dwellers inside the canyon. That was a benefit.

Skinner, though, had gotten to Roof. He'd found the festering wound and picked at the sore. That was why Roof had attacked Skinner so mercilessly. It was a mistake. Roof acknowledged that to himself.

He hoped he was wrong about Battle coming back to haunt him. He hoped Skinner was wrong. He reached the door to his room and shouldered his way into the cool darkness of it, an uneasy feeling swirling in his gut.

Despite an early victory and an overwhelming force heading toward the canyon, something told him the worst was yet to come. He fell into his bed and closed his eyes.

No sooner had he begun to drift into that comfortable space between consciousness and sleep when through his lids he could see the bluish-white flicker of the monitors on the wall.

"Roof?" It was Parrott Manuse. "Roof? You there?"

Roof pushed himself to his elbows and called across the room. "Yeah. I'm here." He rolled out of his bed and walked over to the screens, flipping the light switch on the way.

Parrott's face was white, his eyes bloodshot. "Have you heard?"

"Heard what?"

"Harvey Logan is dead."

Roof looked into Manuse's eyes. They were swollen. "What?"

"He's dead," said Manuse. "Somebody killed him. He's dead in the bathtub of his house. His woman and kid are missing."

"Did she do it?"

"I dunno," said Manuse. He hadn't blinked since he'd started talking. His eyes were watering. "When he didn't answer your call, I tried him again later. He never answered. Given what we got going on tomorrow, I thought it was hinky. About a half hour ago I sent a team by his house."

Roof rubbed his face with his hands. He couldn't believe what he was hearing.

"They found a man dead in the bedroom," Manuse explained. "It looked like there was a struggle or fight. They went into the bathroom and found Logan's body on ice in the bathtub."

"Dwellers?"

"Probably," said Manuse, blinking for the first time. "It gets worse."

Roof wasn't sure he wanted to know, but he bit. "What?"

"We have a dead posse boss too. Run over by a stolen car. His wife is dead as well."

"Let me guess," said Roof, "the car was part of the Cartel fleet that belonged to Logan."

"Yep."

Roof clasped his hands behind his neck. "Do we have problems in other places?"

"I dunno."

"Are you safe?" asked Roof. "If they can get to Logan, they can get to you."

"Or you."

"I'm fine," said Roof. "I'm in the Jones."

"I'm good. I've got my security team here at the house." He looked over his shoulder at the team lead, a black- and red-booted boss named Hoodoo Brown. "Why do you think they took the wife and kid?"

Roof shrugged. "Leverage maybe?"

"What do you want to do?"

"We need to move now," said Roof. "We need all posses advancing ASAP. Can you handle your end of things?"

"Yes," said Manuse. "The teams from Houston are already moving. I'll get the ones here in Dallas heading toward the canyon."

"Good," said Roof. After Manuse turned off the screen, Roof began pacing. He had no doubt the Dwellers had killed Logan. Somehow they'd infiltrated the inner workings of their organization.

The inner workings.

It was the wife. She was the infiltrator. Roof's instinct told him she was to blame. If he was right, it meant the Dwellers were more organized than they'd anticipated. They had a greater reach and larger numbers than they'd estimated.

The wife.

Roof felt a rush of anger course through his body. His teeth clenched. His eyes narrowed. He balled his hands into fists and punched the air as he roared his displeasure.

He thought about the various ways he'd like to make the wife pay for what she'd done to Logan. He'd make it slow and painful. He'd give her hope before he took it away. She'd be begging him to end her life.

Roof reared back and drilled his fist through the wall, leaving a wide tear and a mess of dust and insulation on the floor as he slowly withdrew his arm.

He took a deep breath and shook his head clear of the anger. The wife was the least of his worries. Things were accelerating. The pieces were moving now. The war was at hand.

CHAPTER NINETEEN

OCTOBER 25, 2037, 10:45 PM
SCOURGE +5 YEARS
INTERSTATE 45, SOUTH OF BUFFALO, TEXAS

Ana's back stuck uncomfortably to the leather driver's seat. She sat forward and tried to pluck the shirt fabric from her skin, blinking past the sting of sweat in her eyes. The car's air-conditioning, on full blast, did little to help cool her off.

She'd spent the last half hour tending to her wound. When she shifted the Lexus into gear and spun the wheel to correct the car's path northward on the interstate, she swore she could feel the bullet grinding against a nerve in her arm. She knew it was psychosomatic, though that didn't lessen the discomfort and throbbing pain.

Ana wasn't a doctor and had virtually no medical training, but she knew better than to try to remove the bullet. Not only would it have taken too much time, she might have done more damage to her already wounded upper arm. The key was stopping the bleeding.

She'd grabbed her baby bag and withdrew a couple of cloth diapers and some baby powder. She'd laid one of them open on the hood of the car. In the glove box, she'd found a fifth of whisky. From the trunk, she'd taken a large emergency kit that apparently came with the car. She placed both on the diaper and unzipped the kit.

Inside she'd found a pair of road flares, a screwdriver with multiple heads, some zip ties, a tire pressure gauge, and some electrical tape. She'd taken the tape, a flare, and the screwdriver.

With one hand, Ana had popped the top on the whisky. She taken a swig and recapped it. One swig wouldn't affect her breast milk or her driving, but the slug might help with what she was about to do.

She'd used both hands, enduring the pain emanating across every nerve in her left arm, to crack one of the flares, lighting it. She'd held the flare in one hand and used the other to handle the screwdriver. She'd held the widest flathead attachment in the flare to heat the metal until it glowed. Then she'd tossed the flare toward the woman's dead body, took the extra diaper, and stuffed it into her mouth, lodging the cloth between her teeth. She'd bitten down, closed her eyes, and pressed the glowing bit onto the bullet hole. She'd pressed her eyes closed against the pain and had clenched her jaw until she'd thought she might break a tooth. A radiating burn had exploded through her flesh, traveling the length of her arm and into her chest. Her scream, from the depth of her gut, had been muted by the cloth. She'd nearly gagged on the diaper but managed to control the reflex.

Ana had flipped the still searingly hot bit onto its other side and pressed again to be certain she'd burned the entirety of the wound's circular entrance. Her chest had been heaving as she'd struggled to control her breathing.

She'd dropped the screwdriver to the asphalt and pulled the diaper from her mouth. Her mouth had filled with saliva and she'd bent over at her waist to let the drool drip to the ground. Once the burning sensation had localized around the wound, she sprinkled baby powder on top of it, hoping to aid the cauterization.

Overheated from the self-inflicted surgery and still weakened from the blood loss, she pressed the gas until the speedometer hit forty miles per hour. She found the cruise button and depressed it to set the speed and took her foot off the pedal.

Ana angled her rearview mirror so she could see her daughter in the backseat. Penny was restless. She kept popping her pacifier in and out of her mouth. She was babbling and tugging at the seat belt. In the chaos of the carjackers, the resulting gunfire, and the impromptu wound repair, Ana had forgotten to feed her.

Ana looked at the dark road ahead. It was endless. It was dangerous. She didn't want to stop again. She knew she'd have to, though. Better now than later.

After struggling to remember how to slow the car while in cruise control, she reluctantly tapped her foot on the brake to disengage the accelerator. She pressed firmly on the brake, slowing the car more rapidly, and steered to the highway's shoulder.

There was a cluster of trees lining the median between the north and southbound lanes. The eastern edge of the highway, adjacent to the northbound shoulder, was wide open and empty. There were no trees, no buildings, and no vehicles.

She made sure the car doors were locked and climbed over the front seats into the back of the cabin. Ana sat next to Penny, her feet resting on her collection of long guns, and unbuckled her daughter from the belt.

Ana raised her shirt, lowered her bra, and brought Penny to her chest. The child eagerly removed the pacifier and replaced it with her mother's breast.

Ana leaned her head back and closed her eyes. Her arm was throbbing, as was her head now, and having her child pressed against her didn't do anything to keep her body cool.

Penny hungrily sucked her nourishment. Ana wondered, without any food for herself, if she'd eventually have to partake of her own bounty. The thought of it was nauseating, but so much of what she'd done in the last few hours had been no less vomit inducing.

Ana slid her hands underneath Penny's armpits and maneuvered her to the other breast. Penny looked up at her mother as she fed. Ana smiled at her daughter and gently tickled the child's forehead with her fingers.

Once finished, Ana elicited a couple of good burps from her satiated daughter, changed her diaper, and was back on the road. Within a couple of miles, Penny was asleep.

Ana figured she had four or five hours of uninterrupted driving ahead of her. She could be well past Dallas by that point. The cruise was set at forty-five miles per hour, trying to make up for some of the lost time. She figured another five miles per hour wouldn't waste much more gasoline.

She held the wheel with her right arm and cruised along in the dark, resting her left arm against the driver's side door. The throbbing from the cauterized wound was constant and strong enough to make her mind stray from whatever thoughts she conjured to try to distract her from it.

Ana narrowed her eyes against the wind and flicked on the high beams, watching the lane markers zip past her. Her hair whipped around her face as the car powered forward. She was trying to recreate her trip through space.

A loud ping interrupted the game. Ana looked at the dashboard. An icon that looked like a thermometer dipped in water was lit, as was the check-engine light. Ana looked at the temperature gauge. She didn't know much about cars, but she knew the Lexus was on the verge of overheating.

She thought back to the coyote and the damage it had done to the front of the car. She remembered the smoke billowing from underneath the hood. There was no way the car would make it to Amarillo, let alone Dallas.

Suddenly, the pain in Ana's arm numbed. It was gone, replaced with an overwhelming sense of fear. Her body tensed. Her heart thumped harder and faster against her chest.

Ana knew that any moment the car would die. She and Penny would be stranded.

CHAPTER TWENTY

OCTOBER 25, 2037, 10:52 PM
SCOURGE +5 YEARS
PALO DURO CANYON, TEXAS

Paagal forced her way into Battle's tent without warning or permission. "I need your help," she said. "I need it now."

If her intrusion wasn't enough of a signal, the exasperation in her voice told Battle something was wrong. He popped up and was sliding on his boots before Paagal could tell him why she needed his help.

"One of our squads on the southern rim is unaccounted for," she said. "We have other squads moving in to determine what happened. I need you up there."

Battle rubbed his eyes, trying to adjust to the dark. "On the rim?"

"Yes," said Paagal. She backed out of the tent and Battle followed. "Baadal has dispatched parts of two other squads. They're on the move. Still, I don't like the sound of it. I want an additional team to respond. If this is the beginning of something, we need to quash it quickly."

Battle slid a pack over one shoulder and scratched his head. "I'll need a weapon. My nine millimeter isn't going to be enough." He checked the bag for extra rounds for the handgun.

Paagal waved forward one of her guards. He brought with him an HK416. It was the same rifle Battle had used in Syria. The guard handed it to Battle by the front hand guard and told him it was loaded.

"The buttstock telescopes," said the guard. "It has a thirty-round magazine."

Battle was already extending the buttstock. "Got it." He pulled the weapon to his shoulder and aimed it at the ground to check the sights. "Thanks." The weapon felt good in his hands. It was familiar and immediately became an extension of his body.

"I'm going with you," said the guard, tossing Battle three extra magazines. "I know the shortest route to the southeastern rim."

"We're going too." A pair of masculine Dwellers, whose appearances reminded Battle of off-the-books operators in Syria, stepped forward. Both were armed with broad chests, thick wiry beards, and the similar M4 pattern rifles as Battle.

"We have sentries posted along all of the typical inbound routes," said Paagal. "None reported seeing anything unusual. If the Cartel is employing some sort of team that slipped by our scouts undetected, we need to respond in kind. That's why I want you up there."

"You don't know anything has happened," Battle said. "It could be a bad radio."

"It could be," Paagal said. "It could also be the beginning of the war."

Battle tucked his nine millimeter into the waistband of his pants and dropped the extra STANAG magazine into his bag. He looked at Lola's tent, thinking about the brief moment they'd shared before going their separate ways. He sighed and then stepped to the guard. "Let's go."

"Thank you, Battle," said Paagal. "Thank you."

"Don't thank me yet," he said and followed the three others through the maze of tents toward the southern rim.

***

The recon posse couldn't have been in a better position than behind the cluster of large rocks at the southeastern corner of the rim. It couldn't have been worse for the first squadron of Dwellers tasked with responding to that spot.

The squad approached from the west. They traveled due east, hugging the rim as they moved deliberately forward.

The two recon posse bosses couldn't see the Dwellers until they got close enough for the moonlight to project their shadows or outlines of their bodies and weapons. When they did, their suppressed rifles unleashed a torrent of deadly projectiles, riddling every last one of the men. None of them knew what had hit them, and their bodies dropped no more than fifteen yards from the dead squad whose status they'd come to investigate. Not a one returned fire.

The team moving south along the eastern rim was more fortunate, initially. There were four men and a woman working their way toward the position at which they believed they'd find southern rim squad ten.

The older man leading them was named Praacheen. He stepped deliberately, as if avoiding land mines, and urged the others to proceed as cautiously as he. They ignored his warning until the first echoes of semiautomatic gunfire caught the group's collective attention.

"That's suppressed," said Praacheen. He stopped moving and closed his eyes to listen. "You can tell by the hollow, metallic click. I'd suppose there are two shooters."

"How do you know that?" whispered one of the followers. "It sounds like one gun to me."

Praacheen shook his head. "No," he said. "It's two or more. I'm sure of it. We're not far from them."

The lone woman leaned toward the leader. "Should we radio the other approaching squad?"

"No. There's a fair to middling chance the Cartel has our radios," Praacheen said. "If they've taken out two teams, we're better off not revealing our position."

As if on cue, the radio crackled against Praacheen's hip.

"Red squad eight. Blue squad nine," said Baadal, his voice digitized and overmodulated. *"Please advise status. Over."*

The woman looked at Praacheen and then at the radio on his hip. She bit her lower lip.

Praacheen raised his finger to his lips. "Wait," he whispered.

There was no response to Baadal's query. The radio was silent until the southern rim leader called again. *"Red squad eight. Blue squad nine. Please advise status. Over."*

"They're going to think we're dead," whispered the woman. "They might endanger more squads if they think we're dead."

Praacheen pinched the volume dial on the top of the radio, spun it to the left, and turned it off. "He also let the Cartel know we're on the way."

"What do we do?" asked one of the squad, a portly middle-aged man with a mangy beard. "We're walking into a trap. Now that they know we're coming, they'll blow us up like target practice. Especially with those assault rifles they're using."

"We wait here," said Praacheen. "I'd say fifteen minutes. Then we advance to the corner. It's only two hundred yards from here."

"Why?" asked the portly Dweller.

Praacheen nodded at the woman. "She's right," he said. "They'll send another team, if they haven't already. Two teams are better than one."

The portly Dweller scratched his chin. "Aren't you going to want the radio on? That way we know who's coming. Damn sure the Cartel's going to be listening."

"My guess is," said Praacheen, "whoever they're sending won't be exposed on the radio. They have to know they've already done enough damage by talking."

"I hope you're right," said the portly Dweller.

"Fifteen minutes," said Praacheen, "and we'll know."

***

The hip pack bounced against Battle's side as he jogged quickly upward. He was following the guard and the two operators toward the southern end of the canyon.

The moon, which had escaped the earlier cloud cover of the night, provided the only illumination for the men.

Battle was winded, still recovering from the smoke damage to his lungs he'd suffered weeks earlier. He moved forward as fast as he could, his boots crunching against the dirt and his legs burning from the ascent. It was as if he were back "in country", performing an extraction or manning a patrol.

As the men gained altitude toward the rim, it grew warmer, lacking the breezy chill of the canyon's floor. When they reached the rim, the guard held up his hand in a fist to stop the foursome.

"We're taking the long way around," he said. "If they're attacking the southeastern corner, we need to come at them from behind. They'll be less likely to expect an attack from the west or the north."

The guard waved the team forward and they marched quickly. They accelerated and were at a full run as they passed one of the cabins perched on the rim's jagged edge. Before the Scourge, it had served as a rental house for canyon park visitors.

Battle imagined the view from the cabin would've been spectacular. The vision evaporated as quickly as it formed, and the four of them pushed ahead. He found the going much easier on level ground. Still, his thighs were thick with fatigue from the upward hike.

Starting their turn west some two hundred yards south of the rim, in the distance Battle heard the rat-tat-tat of semiautomatic gunfire. The men exchanged glances but said nothing to each other when another volley of snaps punctured the quiet air surrounding the southern edge of the canyon.

To Battle it sounded like a typical night in the midst of a war. His mind drifted as he ran. He recalled the night he spent wondering how close that gunfire would come to his position. He thought about Syria and being trapped with an injured man whose life depended on him. His eyes drifted to the horizon, expecting to see the flash and glow of tracer fire.

Rat-tat-tat. Rat-tat-tat.

It was obvious to Battle someone was engaging the Dwellers stationed to protect the edge of the canyon walls. He slowed, following the lead of the guard and the two operators.

"We should head north from here," said the guard. "Follow my lead."

The foursome stepped as quietly as possible, covering the distance between their position and the rim with caution. Battle adjusted his grip on the HK and shifted it to a low carry position that would allow him to quickly shoulder the weapon and fire.

The moonlight helped with the detail's vision, but also exposed them should the Cartel team get the drop on them as they approached. Battle didn't like it.

Rat-tat-tat.

The quick burst came from closer than Battle would have thought. He was looking for its source on the near horizon when a second burst dropped one of the operators.

Rat-tat-tat.

Battle dove to the ground. He grabbed the injured operator's ankle, crawled a few feet to his left while dragging the man, and found relative protection with his back against a tree trunk. The operator was alive, but the blood from his wound was profuse. The moonlight reflected in its sheen as it leaked from a wound at the man's neck underneath his beard.

Rat-tat-tat.

Battle laid down his weapon and pulled the man's upper body into his lap. The operator's eyes were wide and dancing with fear. His breathing was ragged and his body shuddered. Battle placed a hand on the operator's cold, sweaty forehead.

"I'm here," Battle said softly, trying to keep the man's attention focused on his voice. "I'm with you." He found the operator's hand and held it with his. "Squeeze my hand," he said.

The man was trying to talk. He was stuck on the first word and couldn't get it out. His grip was weak.

Rat-tat-tat.

Thump. Thump. Thump.

The guard was returning fire.

Thump. Thump. Thump.

"Do you pray?" he asked the man, surprised the question had popped into his head, let alone come out of his mouth.

The operator was losing focus. His eyelids were flickering. Losing consciousness, he managed a slight nod.

Battle squeezed the operator's hand tightly. "Our Father, who art in heaven, hallowed be thy name…" He recited the rest of the Lord's prayer. By the time he was finished, the operator's breathing had stopped. His eyes were frozen half open, his body limp.

Battle closed the man's eyes and then his own. "As far as the east is from the west," he whispered, "so far has He removed our transgressions from us."

For an instant, Battle felt whole. His faith, somehow, was still there. It was buried deep within him. It was becoming increasingly difficult to find, as was his humanity. In that moment he found both.

Battle shook himself from the introspection and gently pushed the operator from his lap. He rolled over onto his stomach as if he were getting ready to do a push-up and picked up the HK.

He adjusted the rifle so it was in line with his body, spread his legs, and pointed his toes outward. He kept his ankles as flat as he could, but his knees resisted. A foot or so from the rifle was a medium-sized rock. The rock was wide and relatively flat. He slid it over underneath the barrel of the rifle to act as a stabilizer. Although a bipod would have been better, Battle had no choice.

He pulled the stock into his right shoulder, raised his body and then lowered it. He relaxed his frame into the ground, keeping the barrel on the rock. Battle knew his aim wouldn't be perfect without the stabilized bipod. There'd be recoil he couldn't mitigate.

He settled in and checked the sights, pivoting to search the darkness. He couldn't see anything at first. The moon only provided so much light.

Battle looked to his right and saw his two surviving partners. The other operator was crouched behind a berm. He was kneeling and kept peeking for opportunities to fire.

The guard was ahead of them by twenty feet or so. He was lying flat on the ground, in similar position to Battle. He had a large boulder protecting him and was unloading his rifle into the dark.

Battle looked back through his sights. Still nothing.

Rat-tat-tat.

There it was. A muzzle flash. It gave Battle a target. He took in a deep breath and released it, applying pressure to the HK's trigger.

***

"I think that's our signal." Praacheen waved his team forward. It was only a ten-minute wait. "Move carefully. We're stepping into a gunfight."

He led his team south toward the cacophony of gunfire. Ahead of them, he could see the intermittent fire and light of the assault rifles. They looked like fireflies dancing in the distance.

They were within fifty yards when Praacheen stopped his team. They were behind the Cartel, which was turned to face whoever had engaged them from the south.

He counted three shooters from the spacing of the flashes, but it was too dark to know the number for certain. Praacheen signaled for his team to stop and provide cover for him as he moved slyly forward.

The closer he got, the easier it was for him to make out the outline of a large outcropping of boulders. The muzzle flashes were partially obscured by the rocks. There was no way for him to know exactly how many enemies he was facing.

Beyond the rocks, maybe another fifty yards or so, were flashes from two or three additional weapons. The echoes of those rifles sounded different from the ones closer to him. They were likely friendlies, Praacheen surmised. If that was the case, they had the Cartel pinned in their positions. Better yet, with their attention turned south, they might not see his team approach from the north.

Praacheen turned back to the men and woman of eastern rim squadron nine, anxious to tell them of their fortune. He took a couple of quick steps north when he felt a sharp, deliberate punch to his lower back. The impact was followed by an intense heat that radiated outward until he felt nothing.

He lost his footing and fell forward. Praacheen caught himself with his hands before he planted his face into the dirt. His rifle flew forward and slid a few feet from him.

Still unsure of what had socked him in the back, Praacheen tried pushing himself to his feet. He needed his weapon. His feet, his legs, and his hips wouldn't cooperate.

They were dead weight.

Praacheen rolled over onto his back, propping himself up on his elbows, to look at his legs. They were there, outstretched and seemingly unscathed, but he couldn't feel them.

They became blurry. He squeezed his eyes shut and reopened them to regain focus. He was dizzy. His mouth was cotton thick.

He looked into the distance, toward the rock and its muzzle flashes. A shot zipped past him, close enough for him to hear it displacing the air next to his head.

Trying to stay conscious while maintaining his wits, he dragged himself backward on his elbows. He glanced over his shoulder. He couldn't see his teammates yet.

Quickly, he worked his arms to pull himself away from the threat. His left elbow dug into the jagged edge of a rock and he bent his arm in pain. At that moment a round slugged the dirt next his right leg. A third punched into his thigh at a shallow angle and bored its way up toward his hip.

Praacheen looked at the wound but couldn't feel it. Then he noticed the thick dark smear trailing behind him in the dirt. He was bleeding from his back.

He kept inching backward on his elbows, sweat stinging his eyes. He wanted to call for help, but knew that would draw a perfect shot that might end him.

He caught another flash before he felt the burn of a shot through his right arm. He fell over onto his right, his arm collapsing underneath him. Praacheen grunted and rolled to his left, his arm flapping wildly, and tried dragging himself with his one good limb.

His fingers clawed at the dirt, digging for a grip. His mouth was so dry.

"Praacheen," called the woman. "Oh my —"

"Grab him," said one of his men. "Under his arms. Don't worry about the wounds."

In the haze of shock, he couldn't tell whose voice it was. He felt the strong pull of two people dragging him farther from the flashes, farther from the Cartel.

He swallowed hard against the fiberglass lining his throat. A gravelly, weak voice he didn't recognize gave his team the warning. "There are three or more men behind the rocks," he said. He sucked in as deep a breath as he could muster. "We have a team to the south."

The woman knelt beside him. "I'll stay with you," she said. "The rest of you, go get them. Take them out. Find the team to the south."

Praacheen closed his eyes. A rush of comforting warmth enveloped his damaged body. Muffled against the sensation of calm, he could hear the voices of his team members. They were arguing. They were debating. Praacheen did not care. Suddenly, none of it mattered. He let the warmth take his breath from him.

Praacheen was dead.

***

"We've got 'em on both sides," said the recon posse's leader. "Hold your positions. We've got nowhere to go."

He'd instructed the men to his left to target any approaching Dwellers from the north. The men to his right were engaged with an unknown number of assailants approaching from the south. He moved between the groups.

His most recent shot in the dark had found its target, slugging a wounded Dweller trying to inch his way toward safety.

Without night vision, they would have been fighting blind. With a near full moon beginning to wane, they had some sight. They were in good shape, behind the rocks, from any northern approach. The southern attackers were a different matter.

They were aggressive. They had untold numbers. So far, two positions had opened fire. They might be a distraction; they might be cover. The recon leader couldn't be certain of anything.

"Why don't we have scopes?" asked one of the bosses. "Woulda been nice."

"We're running light," snapped the leader. "With a full moon, we didn't see the need. The scopes are extra weight."

Thump, thump, thump.

An incoming volley from the south smacked against the boulders.

"Another stupid move," said another boss. "If I were running this—"

The elder growled. "You're not. Focus on your job. Complain later."

"There ain't gonna be a later if we get killed," one of the men said. "We're trapped here without an escape. There's not enough light to effectively pick them off. There's too much light to sneak away and retreat."

"You knew the job," said the leader. "Now do it!"

The other bosses stopped their tantrum for the moment and returned to the steel sights of the weapons. They were silent except for the sound their rifles emitted as they unloaded rounds in both directions.

The one who'd called the move stupid was on one knee, aiming south, when a barrage of bullets from that direction tore through his chest. His body rattled against the rock and he collapsed in a heap, falling onto the man next to him.

Thump, thump, thump, thump, thump.

Another volley peppered that boss across his midsection above his waist. He convulsed and dropped onto the dead man next to him.

The leader moved to take their position, and he steadied his weapon toward the direction of the shots that killed a third of his posse. He crouched low behind their bodies, feeling them jerk and shake as another assault sprayed their corpses. Without sight, he returned fire.

Rat-tat-tat. Rat-tat-tat.

"We're down two!" he called to his men over the gunfire. "I need the focus south. One stay north. The other two join me this way."

"I got it," called the one who'd complained about the lack of scopes. "I'll take the north. Watch my —"

A trio of slugs found his back. The impact thrust him forward, twisting against the boulder, and he slid to the ground. The recon posse was shrinking.

The leader shifted his position again. "I'll take the north," he said. He climbed over the third dead boss and pressed himself against the boulder. The leader peeked around the edge of the rock and saw an advancing team of Dwellers. There were three or four of them. They were grouped tightly together, likely to mask their numbers.

They were stuck. This was not going to end well.

***

Battle's aim was instinctual. Even with the slim bluish light of the moon, he was able to make out enough of the silhouette attached to the muzzle flash that he was confident when he squeezed the trigger.

He couldn't be sure he'd hit his mark, so he adjusted his aim infinitesimally to the left and squeezed again. The kick against the flat rock he used as a steadying pod was inefficient at best. The barrel moved with the recoil.

Battle believed he'd hit his mark when the muzzle flashes from that spot stopped popping. He'd hit his target. He waited for the next mark.

To his right, both the guard and the surviving operator were returning fire. With a closer vantage point, the guard might have a better shot, but he was too exposed.

Rat-tat-tat.

A grunt followed by a pubescent-sounding scream told Battle the guard was hit. His screaming alternated with heavy guttural moans. Battle resisted the urge to tell him to be quiet so as not to give up his own location.

Rat-tat-tat.

The guard was silent.

Battle was watching the guard and didn't spot the location of the flash. He had no distinct idea of where to aim. He didn't want to indiscriminately fire either. That would be as bad as had he called out to the guard to tell him to shut up.

He considered his options, looking at the moon slip behind a bank of clouds moving slowly across the Amarillo sky. He could move or advance. Both of those possibilities exposed him to return fire.

He could stay in place. There was no threat in any direction but from the rocks to his north. That was the best bet.

***

The portly Dweller was side by side with the woman marching south. The two of them moved cautiously, taking advantage of the cloud cover to advance more quickly than they might have otherwise, especially given they were inching forward on their bellies.

The muzzle flashes had momentarily stopped. A breeze swirled, whistling through the dry foliage clinging to the trees dotting the area near the rim.

She'd sent a pair of Dwellers southwest and two more southeast to provide cover on either side. If the friendlies attacking the Cartel from the south were still alive, something of which she could not be sure, they'd have the enemies outflanked.

The woman Dweller had taken the lead because nobody else seemed willing to do it. They'd listened to her and were taking her direction. Even the portly Dweller followed orders.

The woman, who'd come to the Dwellers as the lone Scourge survivor among her husband and four children, had never asked for much. She'd given greatly, always eager to volunteer for whatever task Juliana Paagal assigned her.

That included raising her hand to take a shift on the rim. She had nothing to lose and was willing to sacrifice herself to warn or protect those in the canyon below.

She'd taken the Dweller name Ma-an. None of the men in her squad had asked her name, however, so she'd not shared it with them.

As Ma-an and the portly Dweller drew closer to the rocks, she could sense his fear. His breathing was short and loud, and the rifle rattled in his hands.

"What is your name?" she whispered.

He glanced at her wide-eyed. "Galaphulla."

"I'm Ma-an."

Galaphulla nodded. He inched ahead of Ma-an and stopped, pointing to their right.

One of the Dwellers sent to the southwest was standing. He had his rifle pulled tight to his shoulder. His large silhouette was intimidating in the moonlight escaping the patch of clouds.

Ma-an readied her rifle. She motioned for Galaphulla to do the same. The standing Dweller took a pair of shots at the rocks directly ahead of them.

***

The shots came from the left, unexpectedly. They shattered the relative silence of the moment and took the life of the boss crouched next to the recon leader. The leader was jolted and spun to face the new threat.

He was looking west now and saw a gunman standing in the moonlight. His rifle was aimed straight at the leader. There was no time to take proper aim in defense. The leader closed his eyes, resigned to his fate, when a loud percussive echo exploded behind him.

Rat-tat-tat.

The only other surviving boss had sighted the standing gunman and opened fire. His quick trigger downed the standing gunman.

Rat-tat-tat.

Another quick trio of shots found another Dweller crouched in the same spot. Two down in a matter of seconds.

The recon leader spun to thank the boss for saving his life in time to see a muzzle flash from the corner of his eye. It was from the southwest.

Thump, thump, thump. Thump, thump, thump.

The boss's head snapped backward and he dropped. His eyes were fixed to the leader as the shots drilled through his brain. The leader blinked away the spray of blood that splattered across his face and neck. He was alone. The last survivor.

The leader, as mean a cuss as anyone could find, was like most sad men when faced with the prospect of pending death. He raised his hands and begged for his life.

He tossed his rifle to the ground. "I surrender!" he said as loud as his shaky voice would carry. "I surrender."

His head swiveled, searching the dark for approaching Dwellers. His body tense, he raised his hands higher above his head, anticipating a rifle shot to the gut at any second.

"I surrender," he repeated, his words falling flat in the air. "I'm the last one. I give up. Don't shoot."

***

Battle jumped to his feet and pressed the HK's stock into his shoulder, advancing slowly. He'd heard the man announce his surrender. He caught the operator's eyes, and the two of them moved in tandem toward the rocks.

From behind the rocks, a woman's voice said, "Move toward me. Slowly. Hands above your head."

Battle pressed forward, and the man began to move. He was wearing a dark cowboy hat. Battle guessed the man was a posse boss. His hands raised high, he shuffled away from the rock and to the west.

"We're right behind him," a man's voice announced from the east. A pair of Dwellers, rifles at the ready, emerged from the darkness, following the boss.

One of them noticed Battle and the operator. "Who are you?" He switched his aim, pointing his rifle directly at the operator.

"We're Dwellers," said Battle. "Paagal sent us to help. She told us one of the squads was hit."

"Just two of you?"

"No," said the operator. "We lost two others."

Battle motioned his rifle toward the recon boss. "Let's all row in the same direction. Keep our weapons aimed at the boss here. Move slowly. We can figure it out on the other side of the rocks."

The Dweller nodded. "We've got two more coming with us," he called out to the woman. "We're all armed."

"Got it," said the woman. "Move slowly."

The five men, including the posse boss, rounded the rocks. The woman and a short, chubby Dweller awaited them.

The woman had her eyes and weapon trained on the boss. "Is he it? Is he the only one left?"

"It looks like it," said Battle.

The woman looked Battle up and down. "And who are you?"

"My name is Battle," he said. "I'm...helping out."

"I know you," said the portly Dweller. "I saw you at the bonfire. You're not a Dweller."

"No. I'm also not the issue right now." Battle nodded at the posse boss. "He is."

"Agreed," the woman said. "We need to get him to Paagal and find out what he knows."

"We can take him," said the operator.

"Good," said the woman. "We'll take care of this and radio the other squads."

"I'd keep the radio talk to a minimum," said Battle. "We don't know yet if this is the only team, and this guy has one of your radios."

The woman stepped forward and grabbed the radio from the boss. She glared at the prisoner then turned to Battle. "Go ahead," she said. "Take him to Paagal. We'll get back to work here."

CHAPTER TWENTY-ONE

OCTOBER 25, 2037, 11:40 PM
SCOURGE +5 YEARS
INTERSTATE 27, NEW DEAL, TEXAS

Roof sat in the passenger's seat of the Humvee. The low rumble of the engine, the smell of diesel, and the threadbare interior of the vehicle stimulated his memory.

He ran his fingers through his beard and stared out the window at the moonscape along Interstate 27. His mind drifted from the northbound convoy to the moments before his life changed in Syria nearly eighteen years earlier.

The patrol was routine. He and the five others were alone in an area not far from the university. They'd completed countless similar missions in Aleppo with no casualties. They were armed, they were doing their job, but Roof, known then as Sergeant First Class Rufus Buck, had the sense they weren't as vigilant as they should have been.

Despite warnings from their superior officer, Captain Marcus Battle, they'd been talking about their upcoming leave. The men were looking forward to their R&R. Or as Roof had called it, I&I. Instead of rest and relaxation, he'd joked, it was more about intoxication and intercourse.

That sort of irreverence was a tricky proposition in the Muslim nations that jailed people for virtually any public displays of affection. Roof was schooling the younger men on ways to subvert authority and where they could find forbidden fruit when Battle chastised them for their lack of focus.

Roof was walking behind Battle with the other men. They were six or seven steps behind him. Roof silently mocked him with a lazy salute. The other men laughed. When Battle turned around, one of them poked his rifle at a moldy stuffed Elmo doll lying in their path.

The doll was filled with carpenter screws, ball bearings, and a pipe containing explosive material. Elmo exploded as the soldier stood above it.

He and the two men closest to him died instantly. Roof, Battle, and another soldier were thrown clear of the immediate blast.

No sooner they got their wits about them when the man next to Roof was gunned down. They'd stepped into an ambush. The combatants who'd detonated the doll were showering them with lead.

Roof was hit and dropped. His leg below his knee was mangled. He was trapped and unable to move.

The man he'd mocked moments earlier was his only salvation. From behind a concrete barrier, the fearless captain found the source of the gunfire and neutralized it.

He then returned and, at the risk of his own life, helped Roof to safety. It was the longest night of his life before the Scourge took hold. It was the night he learned what heroism was. He also learned he wasn't capable of it.

When they crossed a bridge and checkpoint the following morning, they underwent a thorough debriefing. Every aspect of the previous afternoon and night was discussed repeatedly.

Battle was insistent he receive no medal for his actions. He'd told his superiors that if he'd done his job, if he'd kept his men focused, they never would have come under fire.

Roof, more jealous of his comrade's selflessness than thankful for it, agreed that Battle had not commanded his patrol with authority. While he was grateful for the captain's efforts to save his life, he didn't promote the idea of any commendation. His ego wouldn't allow it.

Both men were sent home from the tour. Roof never saw him again, except in nightmares when he relived the pain and embarrassment of relying on someone else to keep him alive.

And then karma played its hand. Battle, of all people, was the thorn in the Cartel's side. On the eve of the war that would give them dominion of their lands, the fight that would put an end to the only organized opposition, Marcus Battle reappeared.

Roof was certain that when he confronted Battle before the Jones, the good captain would recognize him. For some reason, he hadn't. Battle had no idea who Roof really was. The general was so shocked by it that he had to let the man live. He had to give him the same gift he'd received. So he did. He thought it would ease him of his guilt, the inadequacy that guided his life.

It didn't.

Instead, it only reopened the festering wound, left it gaping and subject to infection. Letting Battle live was a mistake, just as Battle's having let him live so many years ago was a mistake. Had Battle let him die, the Cartel never would have risen to power.

Now they were back where they began. Together in war. This time, though, they were on opposite sides. They were enemies. One or both of them would have to die. Karma, Roof believed, demanded it.

A knock on the thin window behind Roof's head shook him from his trance. It was Skinner. He was riding in the back of the Humvee with the ambitious grunt Grat Dalton.

Roof looked over his shoulder. Skinner was pointing across the highway. Roof nodded and leaned forward to look through the front windshield. There was lightning off in the distance. The forks and flashes illuminated the storm clouds gathering in the dark. They spread wide across the direction in which they were heading.

It was impossible to tell how far north the storm might be. He hoped it would dissipate or move on before they drove into its path.

Roof turned around and acknowledged Skinner. He shrugged. There wasn't anything he could do about it.

CHAPTER TWENTY-TWO

OCTOBER 26, 2037, 12:00 AM
SCOURGE +5 YEARS
INTERSTATE 45, RICHLAND, TEXAS

The Lexus rattled to a stop. Steam poured from underneath the cratered hood. The car was overheated. There was nothing Ana could do about it. What she'd hoped would be a straight trip to the canyon without interruption was stalled for the third time.

Ana pounded her fists against the top of the steering wheel. It was midnight in the middle of nowhere. She unbuckled her belt, slung it off her waist, and huffed.

She knew from the rusting green road sign on the side of the highway that she was outside Richland, Texas. That meant nothing to her except that it wasn't Palo Duro Canyon. Ana would have to start walking.

Penny was asleep in the backseat. Ana looked at her and pursed her lips. Waking a sleeping baby was never a good idea.

The car wasn't running, but its headlights still worked. She flipped on the high beams to give herself more vision ahead. They didn't do much. They did, however, reveal an exit to the right and what looked like a building in the distance.

Ana elbowed herself out of the Lexus and stood in the road. It was quiet aside from the chirp of insects and frogs. The air was still and edging on crisp.

She pulled out the stroller and popped it open. She stuffed the car emergency kit into the pouch hanging off the back of the stroller near its handles. She took the stuffed backpack from the trunk and noticed the rubber nipple poking out from between the teeth of the open zipper.

She'd forgotten she packed a bottle. It could have saved her some time had she remembered, and might have allowed her to get farther than Richland. It didn't matter now. She was glad to have the bottle. She opened the pack's main compartment to remind herself of what else she'd packed in the fog of a post-homicidal escape. There were some reusable cloth diapers, some clothes for Penny, and a half-empty jar of Vaseline. Ana rolled her eyes at her own lack of creativity and closed the pack to sling it on her back.

She grabbed each of the weapons she'd stored in the back of the car and laid them on the road next to each other. She could only carry one. She folded her arms and strummed her fingers on her elbow. She picked up the pair of weapons from the would-be carjackers and tossed them into the trunk of the car.

The weapon left in the road was the assault rifle she'd taken from Nancy Wake. She grasped its varnished wood stock and held it tight in her hand. It had the round drum of ammunition underneath the barrel. Ana knew it had to hold more ammunition than the smaller, lighter weapons the carjackers had unknowingly gifted her.

Having killed two people with it, the rifle already felt familiar in her hand. She made sure the safety lever was in the "safe" position and leaned it against the side of the Lexus.

Penny was awake. Her eyes fluttered and her brow furrowed as she stretched her nine-month-old body against the backseat. Penny's sighed with relief. She wouldn't have to wake her and face "angry baby wrath".

Ana reached into the car to unbelt her child. "Hi, baby," she cooed in the sweetest voice she could muster. Babies were like dogs, Ana had discovered in her short time as a mother. Tone and pitch mattered a lot more than words.

Penny smiled and patted her mother on her nose. "Mamamama," she babbled.

Ana hooked her hands underneath Penny's armpits and gently pulled her from the Lexus. Free of the car, she spun around in circles. "Wheeee!" she said, giggling and looking her daughter in the eyes as she twirled. "Wheeee!"

Penny giggled and cupped her hands together. Her dangling baby feet fluttered until Ana plopped her into the stroller and latched the nylon belt across her lap and between her chubby legs.

Ana placed the long gun over the stroller's handles and wrapped one hand around the wooden pistol grip. She shrugged the pack up more comfortably onto her shoulders and started pushing the stroller. The first twenty yards or so, she stayed in the center of the road, using the headlights to guide her path. When she walked past the edge of the dimming light, she moved to the edge of the highway, closer to the exit. The closer she got to the building, the more its form took shape.

By the time she'd exited, she could make out the high, steep ridge of the roofline. Another twenty yards and she saw a large welcome sign to the right of the road. It was fronted by dirt and a W-shaped wall made of jagged limestone rocks. The signage was a dark color, maybe rust, and was decorated with bold white lettering, some of which was missing.

It read "TE AS DEP RT ENT O TRAN PORTA ION" across the top and "N VARRO C U TY SAFETY RE T A EA". Ana stopped to make out the words. She chuckled to herself that the only word not missing any letters was safety.

She shoved the stroller past the sign, the wheels crunching along the pitted asphalt leading to the building. The rest area was larger than she'd anticipated from its moonlit silhouette.

It, like the signage, was built behind a limestone wall. A large area in front of the main building was a mixture of dirt, weeds, and tall unkempt grass. The building itself had a large covered porch and looked like a mix between ranch and shake architecture. It was constructed, best she could tell, of stone and wood siding. The siding was rotting so much in some spots it was evident in the dark. The large glass windows that framed the front of the first floor were dark. A couple of them were broken. Ana thought it had been some time since anyone had been here.

She inched her way up the path between the patches of weeds and grass and onto the porch. She rolled straight into a thick spiderweb that caught her across the forehead. Ana instinctively drew her hands to her face and head to swipe away the silky, sticky strings trailing across her eyes and mouth.

The gun fell and rattled against the concrete floor and reverberated against the walls and ceiling of the porch, making a noise loud enough to awaken anyone sleeping within a hundred yards.

It did.

CHAPTER TWENTY-THREE

OCTOBER 26, 2037, 12:30 AM
SCOURGE +5 YEARS
PALO DURO CANYON, TEXAS

The thunder snapped and rumbled an instant after a bolt of lightning targeted a lonely mesquite tree on the canyon floor. The tree caught fire, the flames crackling as they devoured the wood.

The sweet, rich smell burned in the cold air. It reminded Battle of the many fall evenings he would barbecue on the back porch with Sylvia and Wesson. He didn't grill, even though he had one with a direct line to natural gas. He didn't like the taste. Instead, he'd take mesquite chips and burn them over charcoal in a tin pot. Then he'd pour it into a big stainless basin, put a grate on top of it, and cover the grate with red meat.

Smell was the most powerful memory trigger. Battle inhaled deeply, enjoyed the scent for an instant, and then powered his fist into the recon posse boss's stomach.

All of the air left the boss's lungs. "Oooooof," he spat and then gagged, trying to catch his breath.

"Aren't you glad you didn't kill this one?" asked Paagal, standing watch over the interrogation. The operator asked the questions and Battle provided the muscle. They were a quarter mile from the main camp, near a thin trail of water that ran along the floor. In the rainy season it could swell to a river. For now it was not much more than a trickling creek bed.

The boss was tied to a tree, his hands knotted around the back of the trunk, his ankles bound and immobile. He stood there against the young, dying cottonwood. His head hung with his chin against his chest. Drool trailed from his lips.

"You came to us," said the operator. He was standing next to the boss, whispering in his left ear. "You surrendered. If you want to live, you need to give us more than your name." He turned to Battle. "What was his name?"

Battle rubbed his right fist with his left hand. "Frank Canton."

"Frank Canton," whispered the operator. "Frank Canton. Huh. Well, Frank, now is your chance. You need to tell us what you know. Specifically, how many more teams are on their way here?"

Battle flexed his hands, took a deep breath, and stepped back.

The boss licked the spit from his lips, breathing through his mouth. He sounded like a child gulping a glass of juice. He lifted his head to speak.

"They sent us for recon," he said. Each word sounded as if he'd carefully selected its use. "That's it. They want to know your positions and numbers."

"What else?" snapped the operator. "Give me more."

"We were the first team," said the boss. "I don't know how many more are coming."

The operator scratched his beard before running his hands through his hair. He leaned against the tree, standing behind the boss. "Good. What else?"

"I don't have anything else."

"Nothing?"

Drool flapped from Frank Canton's lips as he shook his head. "Nothing." His voice dripped with resignation.

"I don't believe you." The operator backed away from the boss. His eyes found Battle's.

Battle pursed his lips and looked over to Paagal. She nodded. Battle walked over to the tree and the man attached to it. He reached into his pocket and pulled out a pair of pliers. They were rusted at the joint and difficult to separate. Battle made a show of it. He held the instrument in one hand and then walked around the man to the back of the tree, watching Canton follow him with wide eyes.

Before he reached for Canton's hand, the prisoner began struggling against the ties. He squeezed his hands into tight fists, hiding his fingers in his palms.

Battle stood there, behind the tree and out of the man's sight. He did nothing. He knew the thought of torture, the anticipation of pain, was greater than the pain itself.

"Wait. Wait. Wait. Wait." The boss suddenly found a burst of energy deep within the part of his brain that triggered fear. "Don't. Don't. Don't. Don't."

Battle grabbed at the man's flailing hands and secured one of them. He pulled the man's thumb, the easiest of the digits to separate, and pulled it free of the fist.

The boss's voice rocketed a pitch higher. "Please. Please, please. Stop. Stop. Stop."

Battle drew the open jaws of the pliers to the man's thumb and touched the lower teeth to the spot where the edge of his nail met the skin.

The man cried out and whimpered. "Noooo!" he said through tears. "I'll tell you what I know."

"It better be good, Frank," said the operator. He folded his arms across his chest. "Talk."

Battle held onto the man's thumb. He removed the pliers.

A strong gust of wind howled through the canyon. It brought with it a drop in the temperature.

The boss shivered. He was on the verge of hyperventilating. His chest was heaving as he spoke. "I reported directly to General Roof."

The operator held up a satellite phone he'd retrieved from the boss. He shook it in front of the boss's face. "With this?'

Lightning flashed in the distance. Another crash of thunder rolled against the canyon walls. It was followed by an angry fork of light and a louder crack that ripped across the sky. The ground rumbled from the percussion.

The boss nodded. "I told him our position. I told him we'd taken out some guards. I told — "

The operator popped the boss on the forehead with the satellite phone. "Frank, what did he tell you? That's what I want to know."

The boss's eyes searched for the words. He swallowed and coughed on the phlegm in his throat. His eyes were glassy, and tears streaked through the dirt on his cheeks.

Battle squeezed Canton's thumb, and the boss tensed against his touch. His body straightened and he started wailing in protest.

"Fray-yank," said the operator, "c'mon now. We don't have time to baby you. We know there's an army heading this way. We need details. What did the general tell you?"

Frank Canton whimpered. "You'll kill me once I tell you," he said. "You'll kill me if I don't."

The operator laughed. "That's where you're wrong, Frank," he said. "You tell us what we want to know and you have a chance at living."

Canton's body relaxed against the tree. He sniffed and cleared his throat.

The operator lowered his voice and spoke slowly. "But if you don't tell us what we want to know, we're going to make you wish you were dead. And then we're going to send you back to your general. What do you think he'll do?"

A toothy grin snaked its way across the operator's face. A strobe of light flickered above them. The thunder crashed. He stared at Canton without blinking until the boss hung his head. Battle flexed the boss's thumb and quickly pressed the open pliers against the nail.

Another gust of swirling wind accelerated through the valley, and thick, cold drops of rain began to fall.

Canton cried out in anticipation of the pain that didn't come. His body shuddered against the tree. "Fine," he said throughout the slobber that coated his lips and chin. "I'll tell you everything I know. Everything."

CHAPTER TWENTY-FOUR

OCTOBER 26, 2037, 12:38 AM
SCOURGE +5 YEARS
INTERSTATE 45, RICHLAND, TEXAS

Ana was spitting the spiderweb from her lips when she saw it. It flashed out of the corner of her eye, and at first she didn't think anything of it.

When she bent over and picked up the rifle and checked to make sure she hadn't damaged it, she saw it again. The light swept across her face and then panned back. It was coming from inside the building. It shone directly in her face. Ana tried shielding her face with her hand despite holding the long gun. She was squinting, trying to see beyond the light. She couldn't.

A stern voice called from inside the building. "Drop the weapon."

Ana glanced down at Penny and then back at the light. "I can't do that," she said.

"Drop it," said the voice. "Or I drop you."

Ana couldn't tell if the voice belonged to a man or a woman. She bit her lower lip and raised the weapon, but kept the business end pointed away from the light. "You're gonna have to drop me, then. I'm not giving up my weapon."

The light danced across Ana's body, shifted to the stroller, and moved back to blind her again. In the moment it panned away from her face, Ana could see the large frame of the person holding the light. Her eyes couldn't adjust quickly enough to make out more than that.

"Who are you?" asked the voice. "Why are you here?"

"Who are you?" asked Ana. "Can you get that light out of my eyes? I can't see anything."

"That's the point. Give me your name."

"Ana."

"Why are you here?"

Ana sighed. "My car died."

There was a pause before the voice responded. "You have a car?" The question was laced with confusion.

"I did," said Ana. "It's overheated."

"Why do you have a gun like that?"

"Protection," Ana said incredulously. "Why do you have yours?"

The light went dark and Ana blinked past the afterimage until she could see a tall, broad-shouldered woman standing feet from her. She was inside the building at one of the broken windows. There was the hint of a sweetly accented sour odor coming from the building's interior.

The woman's hair was short and matted to her head. Her voice resonated with depth when she spoke. "I'm Michelle," she said. "I live here."

The woman, who must have stood six feet tall, was wearing a filthy tight-fitting Longhorns T-shirt and sweatpants torn at the knees. She was barefoot and was holding a hand-crank flashlight. Ana slowly lowered the weapon and nodded at the building. "This is your home?"

Michelle glanced at the rifle and then at Penny. "For a few weeks," she said. "Who are you running from?"

Ana looked over her shoulder. "Could I come inside, please? I don't like being out here."

Michelle took a step back from the window. "Leave the gun at the door and you can come inside."

Ana rolled Penny in through the front door. She laid the gun and her backpack at the entry, unloaded her pack, and gave Penny the lone bottle she'd brought. Michelle stood watch from a distance.

Ana looked around the space. She couldn't see much in the dark, but the foul odor was stronger. It smelled like spoiled meat. She walked toward Michelle, trying not to wrinkle her nose in disgust. "You're alone?"

Michelle nodded. "For a while now."

"I'm running from everyone," she said. "The Cartel mainly."

"Where are you headed?"

"The Wall."

Michelle's eyes widened. Even in the dark, Ana could see the surprise on her face. "Why?"

Ana looked down at her feet. "I need a fresh start," she said. "Long story."

Her eyes having adjusted to the darkness, she could see hints of Michelle's lifestyle. The place looked like the homeless encampments Ana used to see under highway overpasses or along the banks of Buffalo Bayou in downtown Houston. There were scraps of food, animal carcasses, and piles of clothing cluttering the floor.

Michelle frowned. "It's dangerous along the Wall," she said. "You shouldn't go there alone."

"I'm not."

The woman licked her lips. "Your baby doesn't count."

"I'm going to the canyon," Ana clarified. "The Dwellers will help me."

Michelle laughed. "Dwellers?" she said. "They don't exist anymore. The Cartel killed them off."

Ana planted her hands on her hips. "Who told you that?"

"Everybody. It's a fact. Dwellers are a myth."

"No," Ana said softly. "They're not. They live in the canyon. They have passage to the wall. They're about to overthrow the Cartel."

Michelle took another step back. She was shaking her head. "I don't believe you. That can't be."

"Michelle," Ana said, stepping forward, "it is true. I know because the Dwellers recruited me to help them."

Michelle backed up again. She vigorously cranked the flashlight before turning it on and shining it in Ana's eyes. "Who are you really? What do you want from me?"

Ana stopped her approach and tried shielding her eyes with her hands. "I don't want anything from you. I was looking—"

"I've been here by myself for months. I haven't seen a soul. Then you show up with your rifle and your lies. It doesn't make sense. Something's up. You need to leave."

Ana waved her hands. "I promise you, I am who I say I am. Wait...how long have you been here?"

"You need to leave," said Michelle. "I don't need a liar in my home. I've had liars here before. There was one the other day. I had to stop his lies."

"I thought you said nobody had been here for—"

Michelle flashed the light toward the door. Her voice was forceful and sharp. "You need to leave before something happens."

Ana looked over her shoulder, following the beam of light. In the corner, behind the door where she'd entered, was a dead, half-eaten animal. Ana squinted and focused on the remains, trying to identify what kind of animal it was. The bones looked familiar. The light moved away from the corner and back toward her. She turned to Michelle.

"What would happen?" she asked. "It's you and me and my baby. I don't want anything from you."

The woman was pacing. She started muttering to herself in a high-pitched, whiny voice. "I told you not to let them in," she rambled. "You insisted. This is your fault."

Ana took a step back toward Penny, keeping her eyes on the woman. "Michelle?"

Michelle kept muttering, the voice deeper this time. "Don't blame me for this. I'm not the one who let the last one inside. I'm not the one who believes the lying liars." She was shaking her finger at the air as she marched.

Ana looked toward the door. Her rifle was there. It was a few steps away, but she calculated she could get to it, release the safety, and take aim before Michelle closed the distance. She glanced back at Michelle, who was still in her trance, and made her move.

She bolted to her right and dove at the rifle, grabbing it with one hand and sliding the safety lever down with the other. She slid on the floor, her back hitting the frame at the door as she turned around to level the heavy assault rifle at Michelle. She wasn't fast enough.

Michelle was already on her by the time Ana turned halfway. She grabbed Ana with her thick, muscular hands and pulled her from the floor. Ana dropped the weapon, which slid across the floor. Michelle withdrew one hand and wrapped her arm tightly around Ana's neck. She squeezed and pulled back to lift Ana's feet from the floor.

"You can't be trusted," Michelle grunted through her clenched teeth. "You have to go."

Ana grabbed at Michelle's mighty forearm and failed to pull it from her throat. She tried kicking her feet backward, hoping to catch Michelle in the knee or groin. That didn't work either.

When Michelle turned her body, wrenching Ana from side to side, Ana caught her feet on the wall next to the door. Michelle leaned forward for an instant, and Ana, on the verge of losing consciousness, planted both of her feet and shoved backward as hard as she could. She timed it perfectly.

Michelle was stepping back at the moment Ana kicked. The momentum threw Michelle off balance and she stumbled backward. She tripped, lost her grip on Ana, and landed hard on her back, smacking her head against the floor.

Ana rolled to the floor on her side, close to where the rifle stopped its bounce. She grabbed it without turning to find Michelle and rolled onto her back. Sitting up and pulling the rifle to her shoulder, she scanned the room for the giant.

Michelle was five feet from her, lying on the floor, dazed, her legs splayed such that the black bottoms of her feet faced Ana.

Recognizing that she had the momentary advantage, Ana pushed herself to her feet. She backed away from Michelle and stepped to her daughter.

Penny was surprisingly content, still sucking on her near empty bottle. She'd need a diaper change.

Ana smiled at her daughter and tilted her head. Her neck throbbed. Her shoulder was sore. Swallowing was tinged with discomfort.

She stepped to Michelle, the rifle pointed squarely at the Amazonian's chest, making certain she was out of the woman's long reach. She stood watch as Michelle's haze evaporated.

"This isn't fair," moaned the woman. Her eyes were squeezed shut. "You're a liar. You should be gone."

Ana tightened her grip on the rifle and lowered her eye to the sight. She rested her finger on the trigger.

Michelle turned her head toward Ana and opened her eyes. She started to speak.

Ana tapped the trigger long enough to silence Michelle. She twitched reflexively, stiffened, and relaxed as if her body would sink into the floor.

Penny started crying and dropped her bottle. It bounced on the floor and rolled to a stop at Michelle's foot.

Ana heard the baby crying but didn't listen. She stood over her latest victim. When she'd awoken that morning, she'd never taken a life. Now she'd taken six, maybe seven, lives and killing Michelle had been way too easy. She'd not hesitated.

Ana stood in the dark, watching the blood drain from Michelle's body, her blood appearing black on the floor. Then it hit her; the animal in the corner. She knew what it was.

She scoured the floor for the flashlight. Michelle had dropped it or thrown it when she moved to attack her. Ana found it on the floor and thumbed on the bright white LED beam.

She panned the light around the room, stopping at the piles of clothes, the small mounds of bones and decaying flesh she now saw were swarming with flies. The bile rising in her aching throat, she walked toward the animal carcass by the door.

Her hand trembled and she aimed the beam at the half-eaten animal. Except, what she found partially clothed in the corner wasn't an animal. It was human.

Ana bent over at her waist and retched until her stomach pulsed. She now recognized the sweetly sour odor that overpowered Michelle's home.

It was death.

Ana shook off the nausea, wiped her face clean with her shirt, and lifted Penny into her arms. She pulled her sobbing child to her chest and swayed, moving her hips gently from one side to the other. She rubbed her hand along the back of Penny's head and whispered sweetly into her daughter's ear through the tears streaming from her eyes.

***

With a freshly diapered Penny sucking on her pacifier in her stroller, Ana refocused on the path forward. She needed a way north to Dallas.

The rest area was a sprawling piece of property. Ana would have been surprised by the lack of humanity there had it not been for the lack of humanity she'd witnessed firsthand in Michelle.

Rolling Penny in front of her, the pack slung over her shoulders, Ana somehow maneuvered the stroller while holding the rifle and the flashlight. She moved north along the grounds, looking for anything that might help her get closer to Dallas, the canyon, the wall, and a new life on the northern side.

Adjacent to the main rest building was a second one. It was smaller and looked to be where the public restrooms were. Ana stopped at its entrance and cranked the flashlight. There was a shattered Dr. Pepper vending machine chained to a metal eyehook cemented into the concrete. On either side of the machine were doorless entries to the restrooms. Ana had no interest in exploring them.

She was cursing her luck as she reached the edge of a second large building, when she heard noises coming from its far end. They didn't sound human, so she didn't reach for her gun.

She slowed her roll, though, and inched to the building's corner, where it met with more dirt and weeds, holding the light in front of her, illuminating her path like a headlight.

As the noise grew louder, it became more familiar. In front of Ana, its nose buried in the weeds, was a horse. Behind it were two more. All of them were tacked up. None of them seemed spooked by her presence or the light or Penny pointing at them and babbling.

Ana wasn't an equestrian. She hadn't even been on a horse since the Scourge, but if she was going anywhere anytime soon, it would be aboard one of the sweet animals she found in front of her. She closed her eyes and tilted back her head.

"Thank you," she said, apologizing for having cursed her luck moments earlier. She was thoroughly convinced the horses were a Godsend.

CHAPTER TWENTY-FIVE

OCTOBER 26, 2037, 1:30 AM
SCOURGE +5 YEARS
INTERSTATE 27, TULIA, TEXAS

Skinner pulled his collar up around his neck and lowered his hat over his face. Not that it did any good. The wind-driven rain was pounding him as the Humvee plowed through Tulia, Texas.

They were halfway to Amarillo, and were it not for the storm, they'd reach the canyon before sunrise as planned. Instead, they were crawling along the interstate at a snail's pace, making the deluge even worse for Skinner and Grat Dalton. Both of them were in the back of Roof's Humvee.

The water was pooling at the bottom of Skinner's boots, squishing between his toes. He looked over his shoulder at Roof, riding in the dry cabin, and yanked on his collar again.

"This ain't what we bargained for, is it?" said Dalton, trying to make light of the untenable weather. "I mean war is one thing. Getting rain soaked, though…" Dalton chuckled.

Skinner wasn't interested in small talk. Partly because he couldn't say anything and partly because he wanted to be left alone.

He'd never been outgoing. He never had a lot of friends. Even before the Scourge, his human interaction consisted of torturing prisoners he was in charge of guarding and dealing with those with whom he employed in his drug trade.

The Scourge had provided an exponentially more solitary existence save interactions with by-the-hour women and posse bosses he controlled. It wasn't all that different from working in a prison culture.

His encounter with Roof had served to reinforce his desire for solitude and self-preservation. It had also deprived him of the ability to enjoy a cigarette. His swollen tongue made it nearly impossible for him to smoke. He was more ornery than usual and his hands were trembling.

"I was kidding," Dalton said loudly over the beating rain. "Sheesh."

Skinner faced the grunt. He tipped back his hat, the rain pouring across his face, and caught Dalton's beady little green eyes. He held them there with his angry gaze, telling the boy to shut up and leave him alone.

Cyrus Skinner didn't need to talk to speak. Dalton got it and lowered his head like a scolded dog, wiped rain from underneath his eyes, and pouted.

Skinner looked over his shoulder, past the driver's door and into the storm. The cold pellets of rain peppered his face, stinging when they hit him. He opened his mouth and stuck out his tongue, catching the drops.

He closed his eyes and relished the water washing over the wound. Although it hurt, it soothed the throbbing ache at the same time.

Light flashed against his closed lids and he opened his eyes in time to see a fork of lightning reach the horizon. The sky flickered with a purple afterglow before the thunder rumbled in the distance.

Skinner was struck by the beauty of something so deadly. A bolt of lightning, as hot as 53,540 degrees Fahrenheit, could fry a man where he stood. That same bolt, from miles away, was a marvel.

The Scourge was the same, he reckoned. It was a scientifically beautiful connection of nucleic acid and proteins. He'd seen a model of it on television before it killed virtually everyone he knew. It looked like a dandelion. A dandelion that could kill a man where he stood.

Another bright flicker lit the thick layer of clouds that had built on their way north. The thunder was a soft vibration.

Skinner closed his mouth and turned back to face where they'd been instead of where they were headed. Both looked good from afar, especially in the dark. He chuckled, thinking how both were far deadlier up close. A sense of dread washed away the smile. For the first time in his life, Skinner felt mortal. He feared death. He wondered if that was because it too was drawing closer. The captain tilted his hat forward, leaned his back against the Humvee's cab, and closed his eyes. He needed rest. It might be the last he ever got.

Skinner didn't want to die as a man in need of a nap.

CHAPTER TWENTY-SIX

OCTOBER 26, 2037, 1:45 AM
SCOURGE +5 YEARS
DALLAS, TEXAS

General Parrott Manuse saw the intruder before he heard him. He was in his office, sitting behind his desk. He couldn't sleep.

He was reading a dog-eared printout of a thirty-three-year-old Army Manual titled "FM -3-07.22 Counter Insurgency Operations".

The manual was a nice refresher for a man who hadn't waged war since the last Dweller skirmish two years earlier. He was reading about convoy operations when he caught movement in the peripheral vision above his outdated reading glasses.

The office had a single entrance that fed to a long hallway. The hallway split at a four-way intersection, which provided access to various parts of Manuse's sprawling home. Unlike the other generals, who'd chosen comfortable but modest accommodations, Manuse squatted in a six-thousand-square-foot monster.

He put down the manual and reached for the handgun strapped under the desktop, a nine millimeter Glock. Its magazine was fully loaded. He pulled it out onto the desk and rested it there, his hand gripping it tightly.

"Hoodoo?" he said loudly, his voice echoing down the hallway. "That you?"

Hoodoo Brown was the head of the general's private security team. There were four of them. Brown was the best. He was ruthless in his protection of the general.

"Hoodoo?" The general's call went unanswered. Manuse searched his memory for the last time he'd heard from any of his security team. They typically checked with him every half hour during a heightened alert.

Manuse sat at the desk for a moment, Glock in his hand, watching the doorway through which he'd caught the movement. He took off his glasses and rubbed his eyes, wondering if he'd seen anything at all. His gut, and the hairs on the back of his neck, told him something wasn't right.

He reached over and turned off the dim desk lamp to his left. It was the only light in the room. With it off, he was in the dark. He pushed himself from the desk, crouched low, and moved around to its side, his dry, aging knee joints cracking. He squeezed into the space between the corner of the desk and a large floor-to-ceiling bookshelf.

Manuse was not a young man. He shifted his body in the space, trying to alleviate the discomfort in his lower back. He couldn't stay hidden there for long.

The only sound in the room was the ticking of an old grandfather clock on the opposite wall. Its deliberate brass pendulum clicked back and forth, sweeping the minute hand across the sun and moon design of the old timepiece. It chimed once to mark the quarter hour and startled Manuse. He cursed the clock under his breath and adjusted his position to take the pressure off his back.

For several minutes, there was no sign of an intruder. Manuse wondered if Hoodoo had told him he'd be going somewhere. His memory was clouded in the untrustworthy fog of an old mind.

Manuse had nearly convinced himself of his own paranoia when he heard the intruder outside the office. It was a whisper or a murmur.

The general peeked around the corner in time to see two dark figures entering the room from the hallway. He steadied himself and raised the Glock.

Before he could pull the trigger, the room exploded in gunfire. The intruders sprayed the desk with the lead from their assault rifles, muzzle flashes strobing. Glass shattered. Splinters of wood shot through the air. It was a deafening attack that left Manuse cringing in his tight space. Nonetheless, he took aim from his uncomfortable spot on the floor and repeatedly pulled the trigger. One of the intruders jerked awkwardly and fell to the floor. The other turned his aim on Manuse. A volley of bullets riddled the bookshelf to his right, shredding the old volumes that populated the shelf.

Avoiding the barrage, the general slid backward and crawled on his knees to the other side of the desk. A sudden, sharp pain struck his ankle above his foot.

He bit down on his lip to stop himself from crying out in pain and leaned around the desk on its opposite side. He was met with the barrel of a rifle inches from his face.

"Drop it, old man," said the intruder. "It's over."

Manuse dropped the Glock and slid it to the intruder. He dropped onto his stomach and spread his arms. "I'm injured," he said, laying his face on the cold, wooden floor. "My leg. I think you shot my leg."

The intruder reached over to the desk lamp and pulled its chain. Manuse could see the man's boots in front of him. The red overlay in the boot shaft was familiar. He recognized it, but couldn't place it.

The intruder crouched down and tilted his head so that Manuse could look into his eyes. There was a wide smile stretched across the intruder's face.

"Got any final words, General?" asked Hoodoo Brown. "Anything you want to say?"

Manuse felt the pressure of his own weapon against the side of his head. He pressed his eyes closed, forgetting about the burning ache in his ankle.

"Why?" he asked Hoodoo. "Why are you doing this?"

Hoodoo nodded. "I'm a Dweller," he said. "That's why."

Manuse swallowed hard, his Adam's apple dancing in his throat. He could taste his lunch. The general narrowed his eyes and spat the bile onto the black toe of Hoodoo's boot.

"A Dweller?" said Manuse. "You fu—"

Hoodoo interrupted him with the Glock. Twice.

The guard stood up and plucked a satellite phone from his back pocket. After inputting the correct connection information, he drew the phone to his ear.

"Paagal?" he said. "Manuse is dead. The Metroplex rebellion has begun." He listened to Paagal's instructions and hung up, tucked the phone into his pocket, and walked over to the coconspirator who lay dead on the floor. Hoodoo bent down and picked up the man's rifle. Carrying one in each hand, he marched from the office into the hallway.

Hoodoo had work to do. Killing the general was the first step of many. Chaos was building in the streets. Hoodoo had promised Paagal he'd contribute to it.

CHAPTER TWENTY-SEVEN

OCTOBER 26, 2037, 2:15 AM
SCOURGE +5 YEARS
DALLAS, TEXAS

The storm had subsided. The rain shower was intense but brief. It, and the accompanying electrical storm, drifted south. There were still flashes of light in the distance and long delayed booms of thunder. A steady, cold wind had settled in behind the storm. It was a damp wind that cut through Battle's soaked clothing and chilled his body. He rubbed his thumbs across the tips of his wrinkled fingers. He was drenched to the bone.

He looked at the others. They too wore frowns on their faces. Their brows were furrowed, their shoulders hunched.

Canton was the worst of them. Still tied to the tree, he'd braved the storm and the operator's relentless questioning.

As far as Battle could tell, recon posse boss Frank Canton had told them everything he knew about the Cartel's battle plan. They'd learned Canton had been in many of the key meetings where Roof and the other generals had discussed strategy. He was an intelligence gold mine. It only took Battle and the operator a little digging to find the choice nuggets.

They knew from Paagal that Logan was dead. So was Manuse. That left Roof as the only general alive.

He'd be dead too if he hadn't left his home for Lubbock. The Dwellers had no sway in Lubbock. As the hub of the Cartel's illicit trade, their infiltration efforts had repeatedly failed. The grunts and bosses working there were loyal beyond reason.

The operator told Paagal they'd extracted everything they could get from Canton, but she'd wanted more. She'd insisted they had time before the attack, which Canton placed at intervals after sunrise.

He'd advised them that they'd face attacks on all fronts. There would be wave after wave of offense. Paagal listened intently, making tactical adjustments in her mind.

"What can you tell us about Roof?" asked the operator. "What was he before the Scourge?"

Canton was obviously spent. He couldn't lift his head. His words were virtually inaudible. The operator had to stick his ear close to the boss's mouth to understand what he was saying.

"He was a soldier," said Canton.

"A soldier?" asked the operator. "As in the Army?"

Canton licked his dry lips and nodded. "Army." He coughed. "Syria."

Battle's interest was piqued. "He served in Syria?" He stepped around to the front of the tree and stood next to the operator.

Canton nodded again. "Then drug dealer. Built Cartel." His body sank against the tree and he winced against the pull of the binds on his bruised, raw wrists.

"He was a soldier and drug dealer?" asked the operator.

Canton tried lifting his head but failed. He whispered something.

"What?" asked the operator. "I can't understand you."

Canton's chin dropped to his chest and his head rolled to the side. He was unconscious.

The operator looked at Battle. "Wake him up."

Battle sighed and stepped to the boss. He took the man's face in one hand and slapped him with the other.

Canton gasped. His head jerked back against the tree. His eyes fluttered open. "Drugs," he spat. "He sold drugs."

Battle moved next to the prisoner and spoke softly into his ear. "How do you know he served in Syria?"

"Rumor," Canton said. "He wore dog tags."

Battle pressed. "What about Syria?"

"People say he almost died in Syria. They say Elmo almost killed him."

Battle stepped away from the boss and walked past the operator, past Paagal, consciously ignoring their stares. The wind was whipping through the canyon, the tail edge of a storm that brushed by them.

He stopped at a spot where the creek widened. He looked at the split reflection of the moon in the trickling water, trying to organize his thoughts.

It couldn't be. Could it?

There were tens of thousands of soldiers who'd served in Syria. Maybe it was more than a hundred thousand who'd done lengthy tours. That information didn't narrow the field.

Many of them might have turned to the high-profit world of drug trafficking or other illegal work. There had been limited opportunities for legitimate employment coming back to a weakened economy. Only men with spotless records were getting the consulting jobs Battle had landed. Roof's employment didn't necessarily make him exceptional.

There were countless deaths and near deaths during the Syrian War. That wouldn't distinguish Roof either.

But Elmo, that squeaky red Muppet with the big nose. That was the clincher. That was the one thing Battle couldn't shove aside into the evidence pile marked coincidence.

Standing on the edge of the water, Battle's balance wavered. The rain had swollen the creek. He lost himself in its run through the canyon floor, finding its way across the inhospitable terrain.

"You should have let him die," said Sylvia's voice. "Then maybe you'd still be home. You'd be with us."

Battle ran his hands through his sopping hair. He gritted his teeth. "You told me to leave," he said to Sylvia. "You wanted me to move forward."

"Because that's what the circumstances demanded, Marcus," she said. "If you'd let Rufus Buck die in Syria, there wouldn't be a Cartel. You wouldn't have needed to leave our home."

Battle tried to follow that reasoning. "But if I'd let him die," he argued, "I never would have met Nizar. I wouldn't have understood the need to prepare for the end of the world. I—"

"None of that mattered, did it?" asked Sylvia. "Your preparations, your stockpile, your rules. None of it mattered."

Battle crouched in front of the creek. It was deep enough that he could see the moon over his shoulder. His own filthy reflection stared back at him. "So what are you saying?" he asked. Sylvia's image appeared in the water, displacing his own. She was as beautiful as he remembered. She was as she looked in the photograph he carried in his pocket, the photograph he'd risked his life to save from the fire that consumed their house two weeks earlier.

"I'm not saying anything, Marcus," she told him. "I'm not here. My voice is your voice. You know that. You know I'm only telling you the things you don't want to admit to yourself."

Battle dipped his fingers into the cold running water. Expanding outward, the ripples distorted Sylvia's face. By the time they'd dissipated, a different face was smiling back at him. Sylvia was gone. The visage reflected in the water was Lola's.

Battle squeezed his eyes shut and wiggled his fingers in the water, trying to erase her. He couldn't. She was there.

"You're not crazy, Marcus," she whispered, her voice blending with the rushing water. "But if you don't forgive yourself for things you've done, or didn't do, you'll drive yourself insane with regret."

Battle drew his cold, shivering hands to his face and quietly sobbed into them. His tears mixed with the creek water and the remnants of rain that dripped from his hair. His chest shuddered as he cried.

He wept for his mistakes, for his miscalculations, for his arrogance. He mourned the Syrian named Nizar who'd sacrificed his own life to lead him and Rufus Buck to safety, the churchgoing woman who'd infected his son and wife with the Scourge, and his inability to protect any of them. He shed tears for Sylvia and Sawyer, for Lola's husband, and for Pico. He cried for himself, for his own lack of humanity and loss of faith.

The sudden knowledge that Rufus Buck was General Roof was a gut punch Marcus Battle greatly needed. It clarified his purpose. He would stop looking back.

He would miss his wife and son for the entirety of his life. If he ever returned to his home, he would visit their graves. But he resolved at the edge of the rising creek to put the man he had been behind him.

If he was going to live in this new world and survive, he had to get out of his own head. He had to trust again. He'd have to find joy where it existed, and forge happiness where it did not. He had to love again.

And above all else, he had to kill the man responsible for the Cartel.

CHAPTER TWENTY-EIGHT

OCTOBER 26, 2037, 3:55 AM
SCOURGE +5 YEARS
DALLAS, TEXAS

Ana tore at the jerky with her teeth. It was dry and leathery, but she was hungry. It was her fourth piece, the last in the saddlebag aboard her horse. There were a couple of canteens, a blanket roll, and a Smith & Wesson .357 double action revolver with a cinched pouch full of ammunition.

She'd ridden up the interstate more than sixty miles, somehow maneuvering the well-trained paint at a steady trot. She'd almost fallen off a couple of times, managing to keep her balance.

Penny was on her chest The rhythmic bounce of the horse had put the baby back to sleep. After all her misfortune in the last day, Penny's exhaustion was a blessing.

The child was stuffed into the backpack Ana had used to carry baby supplies. Ana had stuffed the Vaseline and extra diapers into the saddlebag. She'd used a folding jackknife she'd found on another horse and sawed two leg holes into the bottom of the pack.

She drew the straps tight and wore the pack against her chest, the baby sitting inside and facing forward, her legs dangling from the holes.

Ana saw Dallas from miles away. There was power in the city. She could see the lights flickering on and off. She wondered whether it was a mirage or whether the electricity was as spotty as it had been in Houston.

The horse kept a steady pace, its shoes clopping on the highway toward the city. Ana wondered if she was better off avoiding the city, but it was the fastest route to where she needed to be. On horseback, she figured she'd need to ride another fifteen hours. If she stayed on the highway, she and Penny would be fine.

On her approach, the city gleamed to the left. It wasn't as impressive as Houston's skyline, even in their varying degrees of disrepair. Ana rubbed the top of Penny's bouncing head with her hand, feeling the fine soft strands of hair. She kept her eyes forward and used her tongue to suck the remnant pieces of jerky from her teeth.

The highway was elevated twenty feet above the ground below. Above her was what was left of a highway directional sign. It was bent and sheared at the bottom.

Ana cranked the flashlight and aimed it at the reflective green face of the sign. She'd been using the light to make sure she was headed in the right direction.

The sign read BRYAN STREET. That didn't mean anything to Ana. She wasn't from Dallas and hadn't ever spent any time there, except when Logan had taken her to look at motorcycles.

There were Cartel outfits who used high-efficiency cycles to deliver messages and other things of importance. They were like a Pony Express, Logan had explained.

The Dwellers had always told her the motorcycle gangs were ruthless criminals. They were delivery boys and girls, but also high-RPM killers who could maneuver the wilderness of north and far west Texas faster than horses and more nimbly than Humvees or trucks. They typically hung close to the wall and traveled in packs.

Ana bounced in the saddle with the horse's trot. She wasn't a good enough rider to employ a full gallop. If she could find a motorcycle, though, she might be able to make it to Palo Duro before it was too late. It was a long shot. She had little recollection of where they'd been.

Ana kicked her heels into the horse's sides and it picked up its pace after snorting its disagreement. She read the overhead signs as they bounced along underneath them. Nothing looked familiar.

She took a deep breath and took the next exit ramp down into the city. Maybe from the surface streets, she would recognize where they'd seen the motorcycles.

No sooner she'd made the descent into the city than she regretted it. Gunfire popped in the near distance. Men and women screamed, children were crying. The sounds echoed and bounced off the high buildings that lined the streets.

Ana smelled smoke and burning rubber. She pulled her shirt up over her nose and draped a cloth diaper over her sleeping baby's head. Her eyes stung from the acrid smoke. She tugged on the reins to slow the horse and rubbed its neck.

At an intersection two blocks up, a man on fire ran into the street. He collapsed to his knees, howling, and rolled on the ground in a vain attempt to put out the skin-searing flames. A trio following him put him out of his misery with a barrage of gunfire.

Ana didn't know who was who. Was the Cartel winning? Were the Dwellers taking control of the city?

It didn't matter. Both were her enemies.

One of the men in the intersection pointed at Ana, and the other two looked her way. She couldn't see their faces from such a distance. Even the dim lights that gave the street a yellow glow from their perch atop curbside poles didn't reveal who they were.

Ana stopped the horse and tried to get it to turn around. The men were shouting. Two of them were running toward her.

Ana tugged on the reins. She jerked the horse's head to the left. It resisted. Penny lifted her head and yanked the diaper from her face. She sucked in a deep breath and started crying.

The men were getting closer. The horse stepped back and snorted, shaking its head. Ana tried yanking the reins to the right. She slammed her heels inward. Nothing.

Penny's cry grew louder as if she'd spun a dial and turned up the volume. Ana reared back and tugged again.

One of the men shouted, "Who are you? Hey! Stop!"

They kept coming. They were less than a block from her.

"She has a baby!" one of them yelled.

"Don't shoot her," another said. It was too late.

One of the other two fired a pair of shots. Neither of them hit Ana, Penny, or the horse, but it spooked all three of them.

The horse reared back onto its hind legs. Ana grabbed at the saddle's horn as she slid backward. Penny's weight drew Ana to one side and they barely stayed aboard the animal.

It returned to all four hooves and began a gallop straight toward the three men. They gave the horse a wide berth.

She raced past them without any of the three firing another shot while Ana struggled to stay squarely in the saddle. Penny's cries reverberated with the bounce as they put more space between themselves and the trio, riding deeper into the chaos.

The horse slowed to turn left, picking up speed as it raced out of the turn. Ana clung to the horse, fighting the inertia as the animal sprinted along the street. They galloped past the grotesque vignettes playing out on corners and spilling out of doorways onto the streets, the violence an indiscriminate blur.

Ana tugged on the reins to slow the horse, to try to gain some sort of control over its speed and direction. It kept chugging forward, huffing through flared nostrils, until it grew tired and slowed to a walk without any coaxing from Ana.

Penny was still crying, her wails interrupted by deep, ragged breaths. Ana pulled her closer to her chest, her hand wrapped around the backpack, and whispered into her daughter's ear.

"It's okay, baby," she cooed. "Shhhh. Shhhhh. It's okay. We're okay."

Penny flung her hand at Ana's face and a finger caught her mother in the eye. Ana reflexively pulled back and pressed her hand to the sting.

Blinking away the welling tears, Ana noticed a white building with a bright red awning to her right. Above the awning was a building-length panel that bore the name of the shop: DUCATI AMS DALLAS.

It was a motorcycle retailer. Ana rubbed her eye and smiled. She looked over both shoulders. She seemed to have distanced herself from the battle being waged downtown.

She guided the horse to a wooden utility pole at the right edge of the darkened showroom and carefully hopped off the horse, tying its reins to the pole. Ana took a canteen and a bowl from one side of the saddlebag. She poured water into the bowl and put it on the ground in front of the horse.

She took a swig of the water herself before stuffing it back into the saddlebag. Ana had the .357 tucked in her waistband. The assault rifle was strapped inside a makeshift scabbard underneath the saddle. She looked at it and considered bringing it, but didn't. She had six shots with the .357. It was either enough or it wasn't.

Penny was whimpering, though her cries had subsided. Ana cranked the flashlight and aimed it at the glass windows that covered most of the one-story façade. The tint on the window reflected the LED beam. She couldn't see anything inside the windows. She'd have to find a way in and hope there was a faster, less irritable form of transportation awaiting her.

CHAPTER TWENTY-NINE

OCTOBER 26, 2037, 4:35 AM
SCOURGE +5 YEARS
FM 1541, 12 MILES WEST OF PALO DURO CANYON,
TEXAS

The rifle shots struck the front window of the Humvee. Two of them found Porky's chest. He looked at Roof, his eyes large and drawn together with confusion, his mouth agape. His hands dropped from the wheel and his right foot dropped heavier onto the gas pedal as he slumped in his seat.

Roof ducked at the sound of glass shattering and grabbed his SCAR 17 from the floorboard. He was stuck between the hard dash and his seat as the Humvee lurched and accelerated forward.

The gunfire shifted from twelve o'clock to the vehicle's nine o'clock until Roof was slammed violently against the dash. He looked up in time to see Porky's body flip awkwardly and launch through the windshield. The grunt's feet caught on the steering wheel and kept his body attached to the vehicle.

Roof looked behind him, trying to unwedge himself from the floor, and saw Skinner standing in the bed, returning fire. Dalton had his back to Skinner's and was unloading his weapon in the opposite direction.

Roof struggled free and, staying low, pushed on the passenger's side door, but it met with resistance. It wouldn't fully open. Still, Roof squeezed himself through the narrow gap between the door and the Humvee's frame and pulled his SCAR 17 behind him.

The Humvee was smashed against a cluster of tall red cedar trees between the farm-to-market road and two lanes of asphalt that ran parallel to the highway before taking a sharp dogleg to the right toward the canyon. One of the low-hanging branches was lodged between the door and another tree. Roof snaked himself across the branch, scratching his face.

The rapid fire of the attackers was deafening. They were close and they were heavily armed. There was no space along the passenger side of the vehicle.

Roof ducked his head, losing his hat, and crawled toward the back of the Humvee before scooting underneath the bed, dragging the rifle with him in the mud. He positioned himself between the driver's side tires, held the rifle tight at his chest, and rolled out into the fray.

On his stomach and perpendicular to the Humvee, he propped himself onto his elbows and searched for a source of incoming fire. Straight ahead of him he caught a muzzle flash ten feet off the ground. It was coming from atop a building or shed. Roof leveled the rifle, angling it upward, and fired. A single pulse of the .308 projectiles ended the threat.

A collection of flashes lit what Roof could now tell was a group of buildings on the other side of the farm-to-market road. He guessed there were five more targets, but he couldn't place their exact locations. The light from one obscured the burst from another. He couldn't afford to waste what was left of the twenty rounds he had left in the rifle. A volley of shots missed him a few feet to his left.

Roof glanced over his left shoulder. Skinner and Dalton were holding their positions in the Humvee's bed, both of them using its sidewall as the front edge of a bunker. They'd dropped from their exposed standing position and had taken cover.

From the corner of his eye, he spotted the location of a single flash. It was roughly ground level. Roof couldn't tell if the target was fully or partially exposed.

He waited for another flash from the same spot, his finger resting on the SCAR 17's two-stage trigger. He applied enough pressure to take up the slack and narrowed his focus.

The target's muzzle lit perfectly within the frame of Roof's sights. He finished the pull and the .308 exploded from the rifle at faster than twenty-six hundred feet per second. Roof unleashed a second round and waited.

He couldn't see if he'd hit the target, but in the next thirty seconds he didn't see another flash. The dissonance of the gun battle was lessening in volume. Clearly they were killing the Dwellers one at a time.

Another torrent of bullets came close to Roof but missed. He checked over his shoulder again. Dalton was hunkered down in the Humvee's bed. He looked like Kilroy with the top of his head and his eyes poking over the edge of the side rail.

Skinner wasn't there. Roof scanned his surroundings and checked over his other shoulder but didn't see him.

Then, as he tried to refocus on the remaining threat, he saw a figure running toward the buildings from his left.

Roof scrambled to his feet, gripped the rifle in a two-handed "ready" position, and bolted toward Skinner. The bursts of gunfire zipped past Roof as he ran circuitously, trying to make targeting him more difficult.

Skinner stopped his advance behind a shed at the edge of the highway. He positioned his back against the rotting corrugated metal frame and waved Roof toward him.

Roof put his head down and came as close to a sprint as he could muster with his bad leg and motored his way to the shed. He parked himself on Skinner's right.

He looked back to the Humvee and saw intermittent sparks of light from Dalton's position. The kid wasn't giving up. He was probably wasting a lot of precious ammunition, but he had the right spirit.

Roof nudged Skinner. "There are maybe three left," he said. "Hard to tell."

Skinner crouched low and peeked around the corner toward the larger buildings. Without looking back at Roof, he held up two fingers. He then pointed up with his index finger before pointing down.

Roof understood there were two Dwellers left. One was up high, atop a building maybe. The other was on the ground.

He squatted next to Skinner. "I'll take the one up high. You get the one on the ground."

Skinner turned around. The tip of his tongue protruded from between his lips. He nodded and stood up. Roof was about to make a suggestion when the captain darted from the safety of the shed and disappeared from the general's view.

Roof edged closer to the corner and peered around it. He scanned the various elevations of the rooftops and saw nothing. He lowered his chin and swept the property at eye level. A series of flashes and a quick spate of gunfire caught his attention. Skinner had engaged his man.

The general lifted his eyes at the sight of some shadowed movement at the near end of the closest building. He narrowed his eyes, squinting into the gray night, and saw his man.

The Dweller was repositioning himself to take aim at Dalton. Roof lowered himself onto one knee, pulled the rifle tight to his shoulder, and took aim.

Three quick shots later and the Dweller was tumbling off the pitched roof, bouncing awkwardly. He hit the ground with a muddy splat.

Roof kept the rifle at his shoulder and moved forward cautiously, sweeping left and right, surveying the buildings for surviving threats. He stepped toward the spot where he'd seen the gunfight erupt between Skinner and the ground-level Dweller.

When he got closer, he saw two men on the ground in close proximity to one another. Neither was moving.

Roof spun at the sound of mud-sucked footsteps. "Sir." Grat Dalton was jogging toward him. "We've got help. A group of men on horseback is only a few hundred yards back."

The general looked past Dalton and saw a lone boss on horseback perched behind the Humvee. "Good," he said. "Go see if they have extra rides for us."

"Three?" asked Dalton. "I think Porky's dead."

Roof glanced over at the bodies and stepped toward them. "I don't know yet," Roof said. "Go ahead and ask for three, though."

Dalton glanced at the bodies, licked his lips, nodded, and jogged back to the boss.

Roof stood over the first body. It belonged to a Dweller. Death had frozen his eyes open. His corpse was bloodied and bullet-riddled. Roof kicked the Dweller's legs out of habit, receiving no response.

He took a dozen steps to the other body. It was Skinner. He was on his stomach. His head was turned to the side, blood leaking from his mouth.

Roof knelt down and placed his hand on Skinner's back. He felt the faint rise and fall of his lungs. Skinner was alive.

Roof laid down his rifle and rolled Skinner onto his back, revealing the twin wounds in his gut. Skinner's eyes were open. His hot, fetid breath came in heavy waves from his open, bleeding mouth.

"You killed him," said Roof. "You got the Dweller. You hit him four or five times. That's more than he got you." Roof tried smiling.

Skinner blinked. He reached for the bleeding holes at his midsection and found them, pulling his hand back to his face. He looked at his bloodied fingers, and then his eyes locked onto Roof's.

"It ain't good," Roof said.

Skinner turned his head to the side and spat. A spray of blood flew from his mouth. He closed his eyes and coughed. His eyes squeezed tight from what Roof imagined was ridiculous pain.

"He gonna die?" Dalton was back. There was a boss and a couple of grunts standing behind him. He motioned at Skinner lying flat on his back in the mud. "The captain? He gonna die?"

Still squatting beside the dying man, Roof looked at Dalton and nodded. He shifted his weight and placed his hand on Skinner's chest. "What can I do? I owe you for your loyalty."

Tears welled in Cyrus Skinner's eyes, spilling down his muddy cheeks. He looked up toward the sky and back at Roof. He dug his fingers into the mud and then waved for Dalton Grat to come closer before his hand plopped back to the ground.

Dalton slowly approached. He stood beside Skinner until the captain motioned for him to come closer. Dalton obliged and knelt down in the mud.

Skinner raised his left hand and, using his index finger, drew a letter on Dalton's stained white shirt. He dipped his finger in the mud and painted another letter. And another. And another.

When he was finished, Skinner pointed at the shirt. Dalton stood and tugged at the bottom of the shirt, stretching it to make the mud letters more legible.

KILL ME

Roof read the instructions and then grabbed Skinner by the jaw. He turned his face toward him so as to look him in the eyes. "You want me to kill you?"

Skinner coughed again and nodded. His complexion was gray. His breathing was irregular and shallow. He sounded as if he was panting.

Roof licked the front of his teeth and nodded. He looked over at Dalton and the others. "You all can go back to the rest of them. You have two horses?"

Dalton nodded. "Yeah."

"Then go," said Roof. "I'll be there in a minute."

The men retreated back to the posse. Roof could make out the rough shapes of the gathered men and horses waiting for him at the Humvee. He took a deep breath and exhaled.

Roof started to reach for his SCAR 17, then tried counting in his head how many 308s he'd used, but couldn't arrive at an answer, so he scooted to Skinner's side and lowered his head closer to the captain.

"This will only take a minute," he said. He placed both hands over Skinner's face, covered the captain's nose and mouth, and pressed down. Skinner's eyes bulged wide with surprise and fear.

"Shhhhh," said Roof. "Shhhh. Don't fight it."

Skinner struggled against the pressure, grasping at Roof's wrists. Roof responded by leaning on Skinner's chest with his elbows. He pushed his weight into the dying man, expelling his stored air and his will.

Cyrus Skinner's grip weakened until his hands slipped to the ground. His kicking feet slowed, twitched, and then stopped. The look of fear melted into one of resignation and acceptance. Like that, one of the most feared men in the western Cartel territory was dead.

Roof ran his fingers across Skinner's open eyes, sliding the lids shut. "I always figured it'd be the cigarettes that killed you," he said and used Skinner's body to push himself to his feet.

He turned back to the men gathered at the Humvee. "Men," he called with his hands cupped around his mouth, "come get the weapons from these Dwellers."

A group of grunts led by Dalton marched forward. While the others spread out in search of long guns, Grat Dalton stopped at Skinner's body. "I didn't hear a gunshot," he said. "How'd you do it?"

Roof wiped his hands on his thighs and reached over to grab his rifle. "I didn't want to waste the ammunition," he said. "We need every bullet we've got." He shot Dalton a look and stared at the grunt expressionlessly for a moment before walking past him toward the Humvee. "Sometimes you need to be careful what you wish for."

CHAPTER THIRTY

OCTOBER 26, 2037, 5:01 AM
SCOURGE +5 YEARS
PALO DURO CANYON, TEXAS

"It's time to go," Battle was saying before he stuck his head into Lola's tent. "Paagal wants us at the narrow entry point."

Lola was sitting cross-legged on the ground, eating a slice of cucumber. Sawyer was trying to squeeze his feet into his shoes.

Battle pointed at the boy but looked at Lola. "Where's he going?"

"With us."

Battle shook his head and stepped fully inside the tent. "Yeah," he said. "I don't think that's —"

"He's going," said Lola.

"We're going to be at the entry to the canyon," Battle said. "He's a kid. It's going to be way too dangerous."

Sawyer stood and wiggled his foot into the shoe. "I can handle it," he said.

"He can handle it," said Lola, pushing herself to her feet. "He's grown up surrounded by danger. Besides, I'm not leaving him here."

Battle shrugged. "I was just —"

"You were trying to tell me what to do with my son," she said. "I'm not letting him leave my side. I lost him once. That's not happening again."

Battle raised his hands in surrender. "Okay, okay," he relented. "He's coming with us."

Lola stepped to Battle and kissed him on the cheek. "Thank you," she said, patting his chest and sliding past him out of the tent.

"Ew," said Sawyer. The boy rolled his eyes before they hardened into a glare. "I'm not a kid, Mr. Battle. Not anymore."

Battle smirked and followed the boy from the tent into the predawn morning. They had three hours until sunrise. According to recon posse boss Frank Canton, the Cartel's onslaught would begin at some point in the next one hundred and eighty minutes.

The tent city on the canyon's floor was abuzz with activity. Men and women prepared themselves for the defense of the homes. Most of them were armed with long guns. Some carried crossbows and wore bolt-filled quivers across their backs. Others had knives or swords.

Battle surveyed the surreality of the scene playing out before him. It was as if he were caught in a medieval film. He half expected a knight in black armor to ride past him en route to a jousting tournament.

Battle told Lola and Sawyer to wait for a moment and ducked into his tent. He emerged with two rifles, both of them roughly identical to the HK he'd taken with him to the rim. The Dwellers to whom they'd previously belonged were dead.

He held one in each hand and extended his arms to the mother and son duo. "Take these," he said, his warm breath visible in the cold morning air. "You'll need them."

A smile spread across Sawyer's face. He took the weapon by its fore stock with a strong grip and tested its weight in his hand.

Lola took her weapon with less gusto. "Thanks," she said. "Got a name for this one?"

Battle pursed his lips to one side of his mouth. "Aldo."

Lola shifted the weapon to her other hand. "Aldo?"

"Main character in an old Quentin Tarantino flick."

"Who?" asked Sawyer.

Battle motioned for them to start walking. "He was a movie director," he said. "All of his movies were comically violent."

"Not sure I like the name, then," said Lola, sniffing at the cold.

Battle shook his head, thinking about the film in which actor Brad Pitt played the fictional World War II Army lieutenant. "Aldo was a bad dude," said Battle, "and I mean bad in a good way. He was one of the heroes."

Sawyer squeezed his way between his mom and Battle as they moved. "I wanna see it," he said. "I've never seen a movie. I've seen a couple of old television shows, but never a movie."

"When we make it to the other side of the wall," said Battle, "we'll find a copy. I'm sure it exists somewhere. Somebody will be able to find us a download."

Sawyer skipped ahead and walked backward, carefully maneuvering his way along an aisle of tents. "What should I name my rifle?"

Battle looked at Lola, who gave him a warning shot with her eyes. He sighed. "Let me think on that."

"Something good," said Sawyer, his mind distracted for the moment from the brutal reality of what lay in front of them. "Make it something good."

Battle led Lola and Sawyer through the maze of Dwellers. They reached the far edge of the encampment, clearing their way past the last of the tents. All three of them were outfitted with light packs that contained extra ammunition, folding knives, rations, and rudimentary first aid supplies. They also carried canteens.

They walked quietly amongst the flow of other well-armed Dwellers on their respective paths to war. Sawyer uncapped his canteen and pulled a long swig, losing some of the precious liquid from the corners of his mouth.

Battle pressed his finger against the wet spot spreading across the collar of Sawyer's shirt. "You're going to want to save that. Sip it. Don't guzzle. Just enough to wet your whistle. It's going to be a long day."

"Or days," added a Dweller slogging in the same direction. "Who knows how long we'll have to fight to keep them at bay?"

He was middle-aged, like Battle, but he was thinner and taller. His eyes were sunken with disappointment. His mouth appeared stuck in a permanent frown. The rifle he carried against his shoulder was as big around as the arm holding it.

"Days?" asked Sawyer, sounding more like an impatient child than the wizened teen who'd survived on his wit and guile. "Seriously?"

Battle put his hand on Sawyer's head. "Don't worry about it," he said. "We worry about what we can control. Nothing else. Got it?"

Sawyer offered Battle a smile and nodded. He tucked his thumbs under his pack straps and tugged. Battle caught Lola smiling too from the corner of his eye.

The thin man sped up his gait to keep up with Battle. "Where are you headed?" he asked. "What's your responsibility?"

"The narrow passage that descends into the canyon," said Battle.

The thin man's eyebrows arched and he motioned toward Sawyer with his head. "With the kid?"

Sawyer arched his back and set his jaw. "I'm not a —"

Battle put his hand on Sawyer's head, palming it like a basketball, and gently squeezed. "Yes," he said, "including this young man. He'll be an asset." Battle didn't fully believe what he was saying, but given there was no turning back, he deemed it better to praise Sawyer. The higher the boy's spirits, the greater his confidence, the better chance they all had of surviving the Cartel's advance.

The man's frown deepened, accentuated by his cold-reddened nose and cheeks. "Huh," he said. "All right then. I'm headed in the same direction. Have the same job. I'm not crazy about a child getting in the way."

Despite the frosty morning, the man's forehead was glistening with sweat. He kept rubbing his thumb across the buttstock of his rifle.

"We'll be fine," said Battle. "This kid here isn't a kid. He's seen and survived more than most. We're lucky to have him with us."

The man wiped his brow and grunted something unintelligible. He slowed his pace, allowing Battle, Lola, and Sawyer to march ahead of him.

Battle looked over his shoulder and waved at the thin man. "We'll see you up there."

Lola sidestepped to move closer to Battle, cursing the thin man under her breath.

"He's nervous," said Battle. His words weren't as easy to come by as they began their slight ascent toward the elevated plateau at the mouth of the narrow passage. He sucked in a deep breath through his nose and blew it out. "I've got a name for your rifle," he said to Sawyer, trying to distract him.

Sawyer's eyes lit up. A smile returned to his face. "What is it? Did you make it good?"

Battle was conflicted by the boy's internal dichotomy. On one hand, Sawyer was a grizzled survivalist who'd lived more than his share of heartache and knew too well the faces of evil. Then there were flashes of adolescent exuberance.

His eyes lost focus for an instant, the corners of his lips pulled downward. The Scourge had killed two-thirds of the world's population. It also killed childhood.

Sawyer nudged Battle's arm. "Battle? What's the name?"

Battle's eyes blinked back to the moment. "Jed."

"Jed?"

"Main character in the movie *Red Dawn*," Battle explained. "It was a movie about a bunch of teenagers who fight back when their hometown gets invaded by foreign enemies."

"Who were the enemies?"

"In the original, which is maybe fifty years old now, it was the Russians," said Battle. "In the remake, which I saw as a kid, it was the Chinese."

"That's another one to watch," said Sawyer. He held up the rifle in front of him. "Jed. I like it."

"What about you, Marcus?" asked Lola.

"What about me?"

Lola glanced at Battle's hands. "What are you going to name your rifle?"

Battle looked at the HK and shrugged. "It doesn't need a name," he said. "I've got people now."

Lola held his gaze for moment until Battle felt a burning sensation in his chest. He smiled and she looked at the ground in front of her.

Battle couldn't be sure if the redness in her cheeks was from the cold or from what he'd said. Sawyer answered it for him.

"You two are disgusting."

CHAPTER THIRTY-ONE

OCTOBER 26, 2037, 5:16 AM
SCOURGE +5 YEARS
DALLAS, TEXAS

The cavernous, eleven-thousand-square-foot motorcycle showroom was empty. Ana shone the flashlight across the gray tile floor and the gray-paneled walls of the front area. The red triangular Ducati emblem on the wall behind the service counter was cracked. A large square sales poster was ripped in half. Others were evidently missing, only the hanging mechanisms intact against the wall.

Ana jumped when a large possum scurried past her, its long claws clicking across the floor. It stopped in the beam of light and hissed at her, baring its tiny, sharp teeth before dashing off into a dark corner of the large room.

Without the stroller, Ana kept Penny on her chest in the pack converted into a baby carrier. Penny was chewing on her fist. Her lower teeth had begun to come in. She was drooling and babbling as she gnawed on the meat of her hand.

Ana scoured the showroom, methodically working through the connected rooms. There was nothing. It was a bust.

Dejected, she found her way back to the main room and the service counter. She swiped off the thick layer of dust and grime with her hands, clapped them as clean as she could, and unloaded her baby-filled pack onto the counter's grimy surface. She turned Penny around so she was facing her and gave her a kiss on the forehead. She turned off the crank flashlight and slid it into her pocket.

Ana stepped back clear of the counter and stretched her arms above her head. She bent over at her waist and touched her toes. Her lower back and shoulders appreciated the relief. She turned her head from side to side, wincing at the cracking sound of air pockets popping in the joint fluid in her neck.

She stretched her shoulders and her ankles. The exercise was as much an energizing tension reliever as it was a stalling tactic. Ana had no idea what was next. Then she saw a folded piece of paper on the floor, half of it sticking out from underneath the service counter.

She reached for the piece of paper and slid it out from under the counter. She picked it up and unfolded it. It was a map. She spread it out on the counter next to Penny.

She pulled the flashlight from her pocket, cranked it, and turned it on. The map was of Texas before the Scourge. It was tattered and torn in spots at the worn folds. There were stains that obscured some of the markings and town names. It had highlighted scenic motorcycle routes throughout the state. Most of them were far west of her in what used to be known as the Hill Country.

Ana aimed the light at Palo Duro Canyon, east of Amarillo. With one hand she guided the light along the straightest viable route to Dallas while she traced it with a finger from the other hand.

Looking at the legend on the bottom right, she estimated she had as much as four hundred miles to go. Ana looked over her shoulder toward the parking lot. The horse could move at maybe twenty to thirty miles per hour on average, she guessed. It would take her another day, if she were lucky, to get to the canyon. She hadn't been lucky so far.

She slid her finger north along Interstate 35 and aimed the light at Gainesville, Texas. It was only a few miles south of the Red River, the natural border between Texas and Oklahoma. She didn't know exactly where the wall was built, but she could reasonably assume it was somewhere between Gainesville and the river. That was maybe an eighty-mile trip. She could make that in less than half a day, no problem.

She could even detour a few miles to the east and find fresh water at Lake Ray Roberts. That made more sense to her than trying to find help at the canyon.

Ana was sure she'd find someone near the wall to help her across. She hoped she would. She prayed she would.

She refolded the map, careful not to worsen the existing rips and tears. She unzipped the front pocket of the baby pack and tucked it inside. She spun Penny around and slugged the pack onto her shoulders.

She had a new plan. A good plan. "We're gonna be okay," she promised her daughter. She nuzzled her mouth against the top of Penny's head. "We're gonna be okay." She kissed Penny's head and pushed her way out of the showroom, a new bounce in her step. Ana was hours closer to the freedom she sought than she thought she'd been minutes earlier.

The door rattled closed behind her and she walked to her horse. It was chewing on some weeds that had grown through a series of webbed cracks in the ruptured asphalt parking lot.

Ana untied the animal from its mooring at the utility pole, grabbed the saddle horn with one hand, and heaved herself into her seat. She popped a pacifier into her daughter's mouth. Penny grunted at the sudden movement, but seemed unaffected by the jolt. She was a good baby. Even teething, she was a trouper.

209

Ana settled into the saddle and adjusted her feet in the stirrup irons. She checked the rifle tucked into the scabbard to her right. She drew a six-shooter from the saddlebag to her left, popping open the cylinder to check it. It was loaded. She closed the cylinder in time to hear a man's voice behind her.

"Can I help you?" The voice was gruff and dripping with a deep Texas drawl. The *L* in *help* was barely detectible. "You look like you need some help."

Ana jerked her head and looked over her shoulder, leveling the pistol at the stranger. "I don't need any help," she said.

The man was standing in the middle of the street. His shoulder-length hair hung over his eyes. His thick, wiry beard came to an irregular point at his chest. He raised his hands above his head, revealing his flat stomach and a handgun tucked into the front of his baggy, tightly cinched cargo pants.

He took a step forward. "Okay then," he said. "I figured 'cause of the baby and all…"

Using one hand, Ana turned the horse to face the stranger. "Keep your hands above your head. Don't move any closer."

He took another step toward her. "No need to get your dander up, little lady," he said. "I ain't the boogeyman."

"I said don't step any closer."

The stranger moved another step, his boot scraping against the asphalt. "You ain't gonna shoot me." He smiled, shaking the bangs from his eyes. "I ain't done nothing to you except offer to help."

Ana waved the barrel of the pistol at him. "If you're trying to help me," she said. "Stop moving. Do what I tell you to do."

His smile spread into a cheeky grin. He lowered his hands slowly, almost imperceptibly, as he slid his boot forward on the street. He kept his eyes on hers until they shifted over her right shoulder for a split second. Ana caught the glance and turned to her right, but it was too late. The stranger's partner was already at her side, a shotgun inches from Penny's head.

The stranger cleared his throat. "You're gonna need to do what I tell you from here on out. That understood?"

Ana ran through an index of options, trying to instantaneously play out the result of each move. None of them ended well. She shifted in her seat closer to the stranger. Her muscles tensed; her face reddened; her heart pulsed with such force she felt it thump in the side of her neck. The horse snorted.

"Get that gun away from my daughter's head," she snapped at the partner while keeping the pistol aimed at the stranger.

"We can't do that," said the stranger. "Least not until you do as we say. We're gonna need that horse, your weapons, and whatever you got in those saddlebags. We done killed younger than your baby, so it ain't a problem if you can't work with us. Understood?"

"You hear him?" said the partner. He extended the shotgun closer to her daughter. "You gonna do what we say?"

Ana kept the pistol across her body and aimed at the stranger's head, drawing it lower the closer he came to her left side. She pressed her right foot against the stirrup iron.

The horse snorted again and shook its head. It stepped back. Its restlessness was palpable.

"Whoa," said the stranger. "Hold up there, fella." His hands were out in front of him, coaxing the horse to calm. "It's gonna be all right. We need your momma to drop that pistol to the ground and hand my partner there your reins."

The partner inched closer. "Drop the pistol," he spat. "Do it."

Ana held the stranger's eyes with hers. "Not gonna happen."

The stranger stopped moving. His eyes widened, the whites visible beneath the greasy bangs. "Excuse me? Did I hear you right? You know we got a gun pointed right—"

Ana's eyes narrowed. "Yeah," she said. "I heard you. I'm not anxious to comply."

"Comply," said the partner. "She's trying to trick us with fancy words."

Ana chuckled. "I have to know first who you work for," she said. "Cartel or Dwellers."

"Dwellers?" asked the stranger. "Heck naw. We're Cartel through and thr —"

Ana pulled the trigger and put a bullet through the stranger's left shoulder. At that same moment she lay back in the saddle, bringing baby Penny with her. It was that movement that forced her aim leftward, failing to deliver a fatal shot. It was enough, however, to drop the stranger to his knees. Ana, flat on her back, kicked her stirruped right foot upward, driving her toe through the partner's arms and into his chin.

He lost the shotgun before he knew what had happened and stumbled backward on the verge of unconsciousness before the back of his head slammed hard into the utility pole. He slid down the pole and sank to the ground.

Ana took aim, pulled the trigger twice, and fired two shots into a tight pattern on the man's chest before she used the reins in her left hand to pull herself upright. She found the stranger on his knees, struggling to grab for the gun in his waistband.

"Hey," she called, drawing his attention from the gun to her face in time to deliver a lucky shot through his left eye. It jerked his head backward, his body went limp, and he collapsed to the asphalt.

Ana took a deep breath and held it. Only when she exhaled through puckered lips did she hear Penny's wailing. The baby had lost the pacifier and no doubt was frightened by the quartet of booming shots fired not far from her face.

Ana wanted to console her child. She wanted to pull her from the pack and hold her tightly against her chest. She didn't have time.

She had no doubt the gunshots and the siren's wail from a baby would draw more attention. She kicked her heels into the horse and urged it into a trot. With the reins in one hand and the gun in the other, she couldn't reload. With the baby on her chest, the rifle wasn't an option. She had two shots left in the six-shooter. Ana coaxed the horse to speed up. She wanted out of Dallas. Nothing good would come of staying there. The wall was within reach.

She leaned forward and sang a lullaby to her inconsolable daughter. Ana felt tears forming in her eyes. Her voice warbled and cracked as she crooned.

As she found her way onto the interstate and the horse moved quickly north, she wondered if there were any good people left on either side of the wall.

CHAPTER THIRTY-TWO

OCTOBER 26, 2037, 5:40 AM
SCOURGE +5 YEARS
PALO DURO CANYON, TEXAS

Juliana Paagal turned off the satellite phone and set it next to the map atop the wooden desk inside her tent. She pumped her fist. "Yes," she said. "Everything is as planned."

She looked across the table at Baadal. His eyes were wide and his skin was kissed red from the tent as if he'd spent a week in the sun.

"So what does that mean?" he asked. "Are we winning?"

Paagal walked around the table, dragging her fingertips along the wood. She put her hands on his shoulders, squeezing gently, and pressed her lips to his. She lingered, inhaling his piquant scent of sweat and natural musk.

"Yes," she whispered and kissed him again. Baadal moved to put his hands on her hips, but she blocked his wrists with hers and stepped back. She moved away, walking back to her spot on the opposite side of the table.

"Dallas is in flames," she said gleefully. "Houston, as far as I know, is already under our control. San Antonio is turning. Austin is the only holdout."

She traced her finger along the map, drawing a circle around the former Texas capital. "The slogan there, you know, was 'Keep Austin Weird'," she said. "It still fits."

Baadal looked at the map. "So the cells did their jobs in every city?"

"It looks like it. Total surprise in every case. The posse bosses, captains, even the two generals never saw it coming."

"A lot of death."

"Collateral damage," Paagal reasoned. "Serious change cannot happen otherwise. There are always sacrifices made by the few that benefit the whole."

"I suppose."

Paagal ran her finger toward the lower right of the map and tapped it. "Houston has me a bit concerned, I'll admit," she said. "I haven't heard any updates since we took care of Harvey Logan. The team there assured me they were gaining control, but…"

Baadal's eyes danced around the room. "What about Lubbock?"

Paagal cocked her head like a bird, her eyes narrowed. "What about Lubbock?"

"That's their distribution hub, right?" he asked rhetorically. "Isn't that a critical part of the insurgency?"

"Not yet," Paagal said. "We need to contain as many cities as possible, draw the support of the oppressed, and then send large, well-equipped groups heading this way."

Paagal planted her hands on the large map atop the desk and leaned on them. The long muscles in her triceps flexed against the weight. "We'll have the retreating Cartel troops trapped. They'll have nowhere to go. They'll surrender or die."

"Then we shut down their distribution," said Baadal. "We choke off their illicit trade with those outside the territory."

Paagal threw her head back and cackled. "Shut it down?" Her eyes returned to Baadal's, flashing a hint of insanity. "We're not shutting it down, darling," she said. "We're taking it over."

Baadal's brow curled. "Wait. What?"

"Equi donati dentes non inspiciuntur."

Baadal folded his arms across his chest and pressed his lips together.

Paagal rolled her eyes. "Don't look a gift horse in the mouth," she said. "Why would we eliminate such easy income?"

"Because it's a violent, unethical trade," he said. "You're talking about selling and moving all kinds of drugs, providing an expensive black market for water and gasoline and food."

"And?"

Baadal stepped to the table. "And that's part of what kept us under the Cartel's thumb for so long," he argued. "We need a fair and open market like they have north of the wall. Otherwise we're no better than the Cartel. Maybe we're worse."

Paagal stepped back from the table. "Huh," she said, "I thought you were with me."

"I am," said Baadal. "I mean—"

"First," she said, "fear is what kept the Cartel in power, not a lucrative black market. Second, there's no fair and open market north of the wall. If there were, why would there be such demand for what the Cartel's been providing? Third, I'll take any characterization of our movement you offer as long as ours is the movement in power."

Baadal stood silently at the table. His eyes drifted downward, avoiding contact with the woman who, minutes earlier, he was anxious to bed.

Paagal took a deep breath and exhaled. "You seem…" She searched for the right word.

Baadal kept his unfocused gaze aimed at the table between them. "Disillusioned," he said.

She laughed. "Disillusioned," she said. "Isn't that the word that describes everyone and everything since the Scourge?"

He looked up at her and shook his head. "Your point?"

"Nothing is black and white," she said. "Nobody is all good or all evil. No group or movement or insurgency is entirely benevolent or exclusively malicious. I explained this to Marcus Battle. We live in a world where we must do what we must do to survive."

Baadal's gaze softened. He licked his lips and let his teeth drag across them.

"Some random virus mutated and killed two-thirds of the world's population," she said. "The only ones who lived have some genetic immunity to it. Good people died. Bad people lived. For the last five years, our world has been a confluence of chance and will. Those who take chances and have the will to survive flourish. Those who don't…" She shrugged.

"That sounds like you're trying to convince yourself," Baadal said, "like some moral rationalization."

"Hardly," Paagal scoffed. "You really are naïve, aren't you?"

"I—"

"That wasn't really a question," she said. "This is a harsh world, Baadal. It is Darwinian. Adapt or die. I'm adapting our cause, our movement, our insurgency, to the call of the times. We cannot be weak or wholly good. To serve the good, to make lives better for those who've suffered under the Cartel, we must harvest from the same soiled ideology they employed. We pick from it. We take the seeds that will nourish us. We ignore the rest."

"I'm not naïve," he said. "I've told you I'm not a good person. I know you're not either at your core. It's not about shades of morality. It's about becoming what we've sought to overthrow."

"You say potatoes," she said, elongating the "ayyy" sound. "I say po-tah-toes." Paagal ran her hands through her hair and sighed. "Either you'll stand here at my side or you won't. I don't have time for any more therapy session, Felipe. We have a war to win."

Felipe Baadal nodded. His eyes moved up and down her body as he assessed her soul. He spun without saying a word, grabbed his rifle, and pushed his way out into the morning. The sun would be up in less than two and a half hours. His men needed him on the rim.

CHAPTER THIRTY-THREE

OCTOBER 26, 2037, 6:20 AM
SCOURGE +5 YEARS
PALO DURO CANYON, TEXAS

General Roof fired the first shots. His SCAR 17 delivered as it was designed to and sprayed the Dwellers guarding the southeastern rim of the canyon with rimless, bottlenecked .308s, the same ammunition he'd used to hunt game before the Scourge. The Dwellers were smoking cigarettes. The orange glow at the end of the burning white column of paper was enough of a target.

One after another the deadly projectiles twisted toward their targets. Three of the Dwellers were dead before the fight began.

Roof advanced without fear. His long strides and deliberate steps toward the enemy had the look of a man who thought himself invincible.

By the time he was within thirty yards of the surviving Dwellers, his riding companions had dismounted and were targeting a secondary group approaching from the east. Roof directed half of them to stop the advancing Dwellers while he, Grat Dalton, and three other grunts took on the squad directly in front of them.

Roof looked east at the team he'd sent to protect their right flank. In the distance, where the canyon met the horizon, the sky was growing purple. Sunup was less than ninety minutes away. With the storm having passed, the moon overhead was enough to provide the vague image of movement in the dark. It didn't fully illuminate anything.

"Got one," Grat Dalton said from his position behind some low-profile mesquite. The tangled branches gave him enough cover in the dark. "Roof, I got one!"

Roof took a position behind a rotting stump. He lay prone on the ground and rested his elbows on the soft, crumbling wood. A thick root pushed against his ribs and made the position uncomfortable. He scanned the darkness for muzzle flashes. It had proven the best way to take down the enemy.

His finger rested on the trigger as he searched for a target. Grat cheered another hit, and Roof considered turning his aim to the overzealous grunt.

To his right, the sound of gunfire amplified. From the corner of his eye he could see the evolving firefight. He refocused at the edge of the rim and spotted the outline of a Dweller. He lost the slack and pulled the trigger. The outline jerked and disappeared.

Roof knew large platoons of Cartel grunts and their leaders would attack from the west within minutes, if they hadn't already begun their assault. If everything was as it should be, there would be simultaneous waves hitting the other parts of the rim within the hour. By sunrise, the entirety of the canyon's circumference would be under siege. He and his men would make their way down the lone, narrow entrance to the canyon floor. The end of the Dwellers was beginning.

A bullet skimmed the jagged decay on the surface of the trunk before zipping past Roof's head. A shower of splinters hit the side of his face, and his cheek stung as if peppered with needles. Roof winced but kept his eye on the remaining Dwellers ahead. He caught a shift of what he'd thought was a small boulder. He pivoted and leveled the rifle's barrel at the dark mass and pulled the trigger twice. The mass flattened with the first connection and shuddered with the second.

There was no more movement along the rim directly in front of Roof. He looked over his shoulder to his left. A pair of grunts were on one knee, out in the open, firing relentlessly into the dark.

Roof would have laughed had the reality of their ineptitude not been so remarkably sad. He thought back to a series of movies he'd watched in Syria during an R&R night in camp. The film's storyline had taken place a long time ago in a galaxy far, far away.

The bad guys had been these ridiculous white-armored clones called stormtroopers. They couldn't have hit the broadside of a barn with their laser rifles if they'd been leaning against it.

So many of the grunts who'd signed up to join the Cartel were like those stormtroopers. They'd apparently liked the idea of serving the evil empire. They just weren't that good at protecting it.

Roof's recollection vaporized as one of the grunts took a shot to the head. His neck snapped backward and he fell awkwardly into the grunt next to him. That grunt struggled to free himself from the weight of his dead comrade as incoming fire callously stopped his effort. He cried out in pain until another shot silenced him.

Roof tried to project the angle of the shots that had killed the grunts. There were too many muzzle flashes to count. Farther to his right, Grat Dalton was taking aim directly east. Beyond Dalton, grunts were retreating. One at a time, they'd fire off a shot or two and then run west.

Dalton rolled from his position at the mesquite and hurried to Roof. "There's too many of them over there," he said breathlessly. "Our guys are getting slaughtered. They're coming back this way."

No sooner had Roof pushed himself from the stump than the thunder of rifle and shotgun fire exploded in front of him. It was coming from the west.

He saw what looked like an endless stream of grunts marching his way. Armed with shotguns, some of them were wasting their ammunition, taking aim from well outside the weapon's limited range. The percussion of it was like the intimidation of a loudly beating drum. Some of the men were still perched on their horses as they rode toward the plucky Dwellers.

Roof grabbed Dalton by the scruff of his shirt and pulled him flat to the ground. They were caught in the crossfire when the two armies converged. Cries of pain and screams for help quickly joined the chorus of gunfire.

Roof elbowed Dalton and directed him to take aim on the horde of Dwellers pushing their way closer. A grunt stumbled past them and then arched his back wildly when he was shot. He fell face forward, landing next to Roof.

Roof looked at the man's eyes. They were full of the same icy fear he'd seen as he choked the life from Cyrus Skinner. Roof eyed the iron sights atop his rifle, found a target, and pulled the trigger. He exhaled through his nose and found another Dweller in his sights. Another pull. Another kill.

Dalton wasn't as confident as he'd been minutes earlier. There were no hoots or hollers with successful hits. Instead, he was emptying his weapon into the men and women trying to kill him.

Roof kept firing, one target at a time, as the reinforcements drew even with him and Grat. They set a line parallel to Roof, and he rose to his feet. He marched backward among the din of gunfire to find a hat-wearing boss.

He located one atop a palomino behind the front line of grunts. "You in charge?" he yelled up at the boss.

The boss wrapped the reins tighter around his right fist. "Yeah," he said. "What of it?"

"I'm General Roof."

The boss snickered and tipped back his hat, leaning over toward Roof. "Is that so?"

Roof grabbed the boss by the collar and yanked him off the horse. The man's foot tangled in the stirrup iron and he fell to the ground on his back. Roof let go and stood over him. "Yeah," he said to the wide-eyed boss. "That's so. Who are you?"

The boss scrambled away from Roof, angling himself to his feet. He picked up his hat and set it back on his head. He swallowed hard. "I didn't—"

Roof took a giant step toward the boss. "Who are you?"

"My name is—"

"I don't give a flying turd about your name," said Roof. "Where did you come from? How many men do you have? Are there more coming from your direction?"

"We come from Hereford, near the western wall," said the boss. "We was staged there a few weeks ago. We got a few hundred men, maybe thirty horses. Some of us got Brownings. Some of us got rifles."

"Hereford," Roof said. "Good. You're early. You got men from El Paso and Abilene, right?"

The boss nodded. "I'm from El Paso. Most of us are."

"You see any more companies coming this way? We should have more from Lubbock."

"I ain't seen—" The boss froze, his mouth agape. A trickle of blood streamed across his nose and over his lips. His brows arched with confusion and he dropped where he stood.

Roof instinctively ducked and turned on his heel. He raised his SCAR 17 to return fire, but a pull of the trigger did nothing. A second pull. Nothing. He tossed the weapon to the dirt and grabbed a long gun from a scabbard on the boss's saddle. He checked to make sure it was loaded and then marched back to the front line.

"Hold the line, men!" he called to those who could hear him. "Beat back these Dweller scum. Kill 'em and advance!"

Roof rubbed the back of his hand against his cheek, aggravating the porcupine of stump splinters dotting his face. He looked at the blood on his hand and licked it off. He ran his fingers along his cheek and plucked at the shards one at a time while he marched back to the dead boss's horse. Roof was oblivious to the bullets flying past him. He mounted the horse and raised his new rifle to his shoulder. Dwellers were dropping like flies. The tide was turning.

The Cartel pushed east along the rim, leaving a trail of bodies in the tsunami of their attack. Roof rode high on his horse, his chest puffed at the surprising relentlessness of his men. What they lacked in accuracy, they made up for with determination. When they'd cut a significant enough swath along the southern rim, he found another boss and put him in charge.

"I'm taking half the men and turning back," he told the boss. "We're heading to the floor." He offered tactical suggestions to the boss, knowing another company of grunts was to hit the southeastern rim within the hour.

Roof gathered his men and retreated west toward the funnel of a descent into the canyon. With more than one hundred men, he believed he had enough firepower to plow through whatever resistance met him at the entrance to the floor.

CHAPTER THIRTY-FOUR

OCTOBER 26, 2037, 7:00 AM
SCOURGE +5 YEARS
PALO DURO CANYON, TEXAS

The first shots struck the Dweller standing to Lola's right. He was perched on a narrow, rocky ledge that extended from the canyon wall. He clutched his chest with one hand and reached for Lola with the other. He lost his footing and fell twenty feet onto a jagged boulder, dying where he lay.

As gunfire erupted around her, Lola looked across the passage to Battle. He was on the opposite side, standing with Sawyer atop the smooth capstone of a tall hoodoo. She could barely make out his frame in the gray darkness. There were a hundred Dwellers lining both sides of the seven-hundred-foot descent to the canyon floor. Every fifty feet, a wall of a dozen Dwellers stretched from one side of the passage to the other. The passage snaked to the bottom of the canyon, opening its mouth wide to the floor. If an advancing army could navigate and fight its way to that opening, they could run roughshod over the Dwellers' encampments. Paagal had placed a paramount on protecting the single best entry to the canyon floor.

Near its entrance, fifty feet from the rim, she'd instructed Battle to hold his position. He'd chosen the hoodoo, a large rock seemingly balanced atop a narrower climbing formation and forged from millions of years of erosion, because it was what he thought might be the safest spot for Sawyer. Where the hoodoo met the canyon wall, there was an indentation, as if the hoodoo were a puzzle piece fit snug against its mate, providing some protection from the attacks near the rim.

Lola wanted to be with Sawyer on the hoodoo. Battle suggested otherwise. He knew the young boy would be too consumed with protecting his mother to focus on the enemy. He'd be at greater risk than if she were out of sight.

Lola argued, then relented when Battle offered her a spot where she could see her son from afar. In the dark, her son wasn't visible. The flashes of fire bursting along the rim above her were, however.

Resisting the urge to look over the ledge to see where the Dweller had fallen, she steadied the HK. It was impossible to know how many men were approaching. Instead of trying to find a target, she took a shot in the dark.

The rifle kicked against her shoulder and knocked her backward into the canyon wall. Two other Dwellers gave her sideways looks and returned to their sights. Lola rubbed her palm into the ache in her shoulder.

"C'mon, Aldo," she whispered to the rifle. "Work with me."

She flexed the shoulder, and this time drew the rifle tight, pressing it against the burgeoning bruise. She pulled the trigger again, the power of the Heckler & Koch vibrating thickly as she maintained pressure with her finger.

Although she had no idea if she was hitting anyone, she was empowered. With each thump against the bruise, a rush of anger-fueled adrenaline coursed through her body.

She emptied the magazine and, methodically, as Battle had showed her, removed it and loaded another into the German-made killing machine. Across the passage she spotted Sawyer on one knee, looking every bit the mercenary as he fired his weapon.

Battle was in front of him, also on his knee. He too was pressed to his sights, taking aim at the unseen enemy descending from above. She closed her eyes, said a quiet prayer, and ejected the second magazine.

***

Battle didn't like the odds. There was a tremendous amount of gunfire coming from above. He couldn't put a number on the enemy, but the volume of the weapons discharging was earsplitting.

Ahead of his position, he could hear the occasional cringe-inducing scream or wail from an injured grunt that pierced the air above the gunfire. It was the same from below as the line of Dwellers protecting the passage took heavy casualties.

Tactically, they were at a disadvantage. Battle believed the darkness, the elevation, and the lack of morality all favored the Cartel. The only thing the Dwellers had going for them was their intimate knowledge of the canyon's topography and a desire to live free. The latter was a powerfully motivating force. It didn't do much, however, against the bone-splintering shots from high-powered assault rifles fired at close range.

A Dweller lying prone at the front edge of the hoodoo took a hit. He cried out in pain and rolled over to reach for the wound in his side. When he did, a second shot killed him. He lay splayed across the flat rock, and his rifle fell from the perch.

Battle lowered his rifle and put his hand on Sawyer's bony shoulder. "Move to the wall," he said. "Stay low, go behind me, and press yourself flat into the indentation."

Sawyer glared at Battle. "No," he scoffed. "I'm not hiding. I'm fighting."

Battle gripped the boy's shoulder with a clawlike grip. "I'm not asking. Get yourself over there. If you want to keep fighting, you need to stay alive."

Sawyer's defiance recast into acquiescence and he lowered his weapon. Battle gave him a shove, and Sawyer stayed low, quickly moving to the relative protection of the rocky nook.

Battle held up his hand, urging Sawyer to stay put during the early flashpoint of the firefight. The boy nodded and Battle returned to targeting advancing grunts. He'd only caught a true glimpse of a couple of them. Their shadows and the reflection of the moon off the barrels of their weapons gave added guidance to his aim.

He emptied the thirty-round magazine, tossed it aside, and grabbed another from his pack. He jammed it into place and began again.

Battle cursed Paagal under his breath. She'd placed them at the most dangerously critical spot. Heavy casualties were a given along the passage. There was no retreat.

Battle looked over his shoulder at Sawyer. The boy was flat against the rock, bouncing on his toes. He kept repositioning his grip on his weapon, occasionally peeking around the front edge of the curve to get a look at the action.

He took a deep breath, puffed his cheeks, and exhaled through his nostrils. He waited for Sawyer to sneak another look around the corner, pivoted his weapon and aimed at the boy's head. He shifted imperceptibly to the right and pulled the trigger.

The bullet drilled into the rock, exploding debris two inches in front of Sawyer's face. He reflexively jerked backward, crouched down into a squatting position, and pressed his back against the deepest part of the rock.

"Stay there," Battle muttered. He scanned back to the front line of grunts.

***

Roof was in his saddle at the back of the company. They were at the entry to the narrow downward passage. He was sending the men in waves, ten at a time. As a man fell, another took his place. They were making incremental progress into the passage itself and had advanced maybe twenty-five feet.

Roof couldn't see the action from his vantage point. Even though the sun was beginning to emerge, the passage doglegged sharply to the right beyond the rim.

He picked at his cheek with his fingernail and dug out remnants of hair-width wood splinters. Soon, he'd join the fray.

Roof looked back to his right, toward the rising sun. The distinct forms of the canyon's irregular edges were taking shape in the predawn light. He envisioned the bloody battle that gained them control of the southeastern rim. A smile crept across his face even as he picked at the splinters buried under the surface of his skin.

He inched forward on the horse, closer to the entrance, and inhaled. The air was faintly acrid and tickled his nostrils. The mixture of the frosty morning, a slight breeze blowing toward him, and the hint of fireworks was strangely comforting.

His horse snorted and shook its head. As they neared the center of the fight, the noise grew louder and bounced off the canyon walls.

Roof had had enough. Despite his plan to stay astride his horse for much of the descent, he swung one leg over the saddle and hopped to the ground. His bum leg ached in the cold. His knee was stiff and radiated with a sharp pain when he landed on his feet.

He squatted and bounced on his heels to soften the angry joints and felt relief when he heard a pop crackle from his knee and his ankle. Roof sauntered forward. He carried the rifle in one hand by its fore stock. His horse whinnied behind him and retreated, galloping off to the west. It was running away from the battle, away from the dawn.

"Smart horse," he mumbled and turned back to the violent skirmish playing out in front of him. Roof trudged forward, stepping on or kicking aside the lifeless limbs of the fallen as he pressed closer to the meat of the fight.

At the entry to the passage, there was a cluster of grunts taking aim at the Dwellers hidden along the walls before the dogleg. They were the next wave to flood the passage. Roof joined them and shouldered his new rifle. Slowly the group pressed forward, shuffling down the gradual slope.

As they moved in a seemingly choreographed military dance along the descent, the walls on either side grew higher. The noise from the gunfire pounded Roof's ears. A constant high-pitched ring drowned out whatever other noise might try to compete with the sonic overload of so many weapons discharging at once.

The walls were exploding from the projectiles missing their human targets. Dust and pieces of twenty-million-year-old sediment rained down on the men while they fought. The slog forward was tedious. Men were falling all around Roof, but he maintained his forward drive and dismissed the possibility of being hit himself. He was the hunter and not the hunted.

Roof scanned the walls, looking for enemy combatants. He pivoted to the left as he rounded the dogleg. Hell unfolded around him.

A narrow plateau extended from the canyon wall some twenty feet above him. Access to the plateau came from an irregular, stair-like arrangement of irregularities that covered much of the wall. There were three or four Dwellers taking aim from atop the plateau.

To his right, against the opposite wall, was a hoodoo. He followed skyward the thin totem of a formation until his eyes met the wide perch balancing on top. There were what looked like ropes dangling from the perch, swaying in the breeze.

Roof cursed himself under his breath. This was a losing proposition. He looked ahead at the minefield of bodies littering the passage. Twenty yards ahead of him was what looked like a firing squad of Dwellers stretching from wall to wall.

He'd expected reinforcements by now. Additional teams should have lined the canyon rim to provide aerial cover. There was nobody there. He should have waited. He should have been patient and let the fight come to him at the passage.

Instead, he'd signaled for the first wave to advance and open fire. It was a mistake. He'd mistaken the forward movement of each wave around the dogleg as progress. Instead, each wave only replaced the one that had crashed ahead of it.

Grat Dalton appeared from out of nowhere. "General," he said, his eyes glowing white against the blood and dirt on his face, "we're getting slaughtered. Two-thirds of the men are dead. They're hitting us from all sides."

Roof bit his lower lip and then pointed the barrel of the rifle at both immediate threats. "Grab as many men as you can climb the wall to the plateau. I'm taking the next wave, and we're climbing the ropes to the top of that hoodoo. We take control of those positions and we'll turn the tide."

Dalton nodded and marched back into the fray to find survivors he could enlist. Roof marched past the dogleg to the entrance. Another wave was preparing to descend. He altered their plans.

***

Lola slapped another magazine into the bottom of her rifle, stinging her palm. She hit the bolt release and chambered a new round. She was drenched in sweat, her hair stuck to her face. She blew strands from her mouth and settled in for another volley against the encroaching Cartel.

She heard a scream directly behind her. It was a Dweller. He was one of four on the plateau with Lola. He was holding his left eye, blood spilling from between his fingers.

The other men glanced at him and then returned to their targets. Lola inched back toward the wounded man, crouched low, and drew him to the rocky ground with her. He was wailing, spit and drool spraying from his mouth.

"My eye!" he kept saying. "My eye!"

Lola laid down her weapon and wrapped an arm around his back. She rocked him as a mother would coddle an infant and tried to pull his hand from the wound. She figured it couldn't have been a direct hit; otherwise, he'd be dead.

His hand resisted hers, insisting it cover the injury. She coaxed it free and turned his face toward hers. She swallowed hard, pushing the bile back down her throat as she assessed the damage.

His eyeball was intact, but there was a lot of blood. It was streaming from the corner of the eye socket, where he'd sustained a glancing but damaging blow. From the corner of his lid to his temple, there was a gaping tear, as if the bullet had ripped past his eye by an inch but ripped open the adjacent skin along its path.

"Your eye is okay," Lola said. "Your eye is there. The wound is next to your eye. You'll be okay."

The man grabbed the wound again. "I can't see," he said. He pushed away from Lola and struggled to his feet. Against her protest, he stood up and backed away from her. "I can't see."

No sooner had he turned away from her did his head jerk awkwardly and a spray of blood exploded from the front of his head. He lurched, his muscles faltering, and collapsed onto the rock.

Lola shuddered and wiped the splatter from her face. She grabbed her rifle and crawled away from the dead man toward the edge of the plateau. She glanced downward at the wall and started to turn her attention toward the center of the passage when movement caught her eye.

Not fifteen feet from her was the first of a half dozen men climbing the rocky wall toward the plateau. Lola called to the remaining trio of compatriots for help.

Either none could hear her over the din of the fighting or none of them cared. Another wave of grunts was making its way closer to the position from the entrance. They were otherwise engaged.

Lola drew herself to one knee and leveled the HK. She pressed the butt against her shoulder and aimed down at the man closest to her. One pull. One kill. The man hitched and fell to the floor below.

Lola aimed at the next man in line and pulled the trigger. Nothing. She pulled again. Nothing. It was jammed. She pulled the bolt handle back, ejected the bad round, and chambered a fresh one.

By the time she'd taken aim, the man was at the plateau. He leapt forward as she pulled the trigger, burying the muzzle into his gut.

His full dying weight collapsed on top of her. She tried freeing herself, but couldn't. She was stuck on her back. She dropped her grip on the HK and used both hands to try to force the hulk from on top of her. The rattle of his lungs vibrated against her chest as he took his last rank breath. A damp warmth spread across her hips and trickled along her thighs.

She was surrounded by an envelope of yelling and a rapid exchange of close-range gunfire. Lola shifted her head so she could freely breathe and stopped her struggle. She lay still underneath the pressing weight with her eyes closed.

There was nothing she could do in the moment to stop whatever was happening. It was better that she save herself.

She took a deep breath and exhaled slowly through her nose. In and out. In and out. The thumping pulse in her neck slowed, her breathing normalized.

Grunts and calls for help punctured the staccato thwacking of the assault. Heavy boot steps pounded past her. Lola bit the inside of her cheek to keep from squealing or whimpering from the convulsive fear threatening to consume her.

And then it stopped.

The fighting continued below her. It echoed off the walls of the canyon, reverberating against the layers of rock that formed the deep gorge. But the sudden violence on the plateau was over.

Lola opened her eyes, still pinned underneath the most recent of her kills. Instead of looking straight up to the early morning west Texas sky, a pair of black eyes was staring back at her. A man with a long, thick beard and a ponytail draped over one shoulder bent over at his waist and narrowed his glare. His feet were spread, one on either side of the dead man atop her slender frame.

"I recognize you," he said, squatting onto the dead man, pushing the air from Lola's lungs. "You're the ginger I saw at the Jones." A smile spread across his face, stretching his beard. "That must mean Battle ain't too far from here."

CHAPTER THIRTY-FIVE

OCTOBER 26, 2037, 7:22 AM
SCOURGE +5 YEARS
LEWISVILLE, TEXAS

Breastfeeding on a moving horse was nearly the most awkward thing Ana had ever attempted. Given the depraved variety of life-saving activities in which she'd engaged since the Scourge, it didn't top the list.

The tug and pull of her nine-month-old's gums and teeth was worse than the aggravated saddle soreness along her thighs. She was raw on both accounts but couldn't stop. There was too much ground to cover and too little time.

Ana knew that once the Cartel fell, and it would, chaos would engulf the territory until the Dwellers dropped their own righteous hammer on the region. She needed to be well north of the wall by then. So she sacrificed her comfort for the sake of expediency and the health of her daughter.

The horse was making good time chugging north along Interstate 35 and showed no signs of exhaustion. Ana parsed the animal and coaxed it forward, pushing through Lewisville, a town not quite halfway to their destination south of the wall.

Lola had drifted into a daze as her child sucked and nibbled, when a flickering streetlamp caught her attention. It was the first working light she'd seen since Dallas. Adjacent to the light, stretching toward the orange glow arcing along the eastern horizon, was a wide utility easement. A succession of high-tension power transmitters guarded the land in an endless watch. Their main legs spread like duty-bound sentries. Above their waists, the conductor bundles drooped low, as did the overhead ground wires atop their upper beams.

North of the transmission towers and the strobing lamp were a half dozen boats askew on the side of the three-lane feeder road running parallel to the interstate. A couple of them were still attached to their trailers. The others looked as though they'd been tossed by wind. A couple of them were riddled with large holes.

Behind the boats was a long, single-story building. Along the front of its flat roofline was a ratty faded blue awning. Only the letters OATS remained of what Ana imagined was once the signage for a boat dealer.

Penny let go of her grip, signaling she was full, and Ana pulled her up against her shoulder. She alternately patted the child's back and rubbed her hand up and down along her spine.

Her gaze shifted to a squatty-looking brick and cream-colored building next to the boat dealership. It was a funeral home. That wasn't, however, what drew her attention. It was the group of people huddled around a long black hearse at the side of the building.

She hadn't known of anyone getting a proper funeral after the Scourge took hold. When it did, there were too many bodies to bury. After it was over, nobody had the money or inclination for an elaborate goodbye.

A pine box and a six-foot hole in a meadow or on someone's ranchland was a fine farewell as far as most people were concerned. They were relieved their loved ones wouldn't become roadside bird pickings or scraps for the coyotes.

Ana slowed the horse, adjusting her hold on Penny, and watched the collection of people watch her as she passed. They'd stopped moving as if caught with their hands in the cookie jar.

"You best keep moving," one of them called out. It was a woman's voice and it trembled with nerves. "Nothing to see here."

Ana turned the horse toward the group and trotted across the dirt. She wrapped the reins loosely around the saddle horn and reached for her wheel-gun. She laid it close to the saddle, hiding it as best she could, and kept her finger on the trigger.

"We said for you to skedaddle," said the woman, her voice a pitch higher. "Y-y-y-you ain't got no business here."

"I've got a baby," said Ana. "We're alone. We're tired. We're hungry." She counted the people frozen like wax figures around the hearse. There were five of them. When she got closer, she could hear the engine rumbling.

A man emerged from the driver's seat. That made six people. "The lady said you need to leave," he said. "This is private property. You're trespassing." He pulled a handgun from his waistband and flashed it at Ana.

"I'm not trying to trespass," said Ana, gently tugging on the looped reins. The horse slowed to a stop at the edge of the feeder road. They were ten feet from the hearse and its people. "I just—"

"You need to be on your way." The driver leveled the gun at Ana. "Understand?"

Ana eyed the driver, thinking he might shoot. He was twitchy and irritated. The others were wide-eyed and slack jawed. They were either scared to death or amazed at Ana's gumption. Either way, she could tell they were passengers. They had something to hide. She glanced at the back of the hearse. It had a Nebraska license plate. Above the plate, white lettering read Korisko Larkin Staskiewicz Funeral Home Omaha, NE

Ana looked at the front of the building. It read Dalton & Son. Her eyes met the driver's as he swallowed hard.

He waved the gun at her. "Understand?" he pressed.

Ana pressed her luck. "I understand you're headed past the wall."

The driver's brow furrowed. His mouth opened to speak, but he said nothing.

Ana sensed an opening. "I'm going there too," she said. "I could use a faster ride."

The passengers looked at each other, exchanging quick glances amongst themselves. The driver looked across the top of the hearse to the woman who'd first told Ana to beat it.

The woman shook her head. "We don't have room."

Ana studied the others. They dropped their eyes and looked at their feet. The driver stepped forward but lowered his gun.

"These people paid," he said. "They've got a ride 'cause they paid."

"I can pay," Ana said. "Any number of ways."

The inhospitable woman laughed condescendingly, offering Ana a complete lack of empathy. "We ain't got time for this, Taskar," she said to the driver.

Ana kept her focus on the driver. "Taskar?" she asked. "Is that Hindi?"

The driver's glare softened. "Yes," he said. "How do you—"

"You're a Dweller," she said. "That's your Dweller name."

"There ain't no such thing as Dwellers," snapped the woman. "The Cartel killed them off."

Ana laughed at the woman, mocking her. "Then who do you think he is?" She nodded toward the driver. "Dwellers are the only ones south of the wall who know a way across it."

"Well—"

"Why do you think the Cartel abandoned Lewisville?" Ana said. "They sent all of their men to fight the Dwellers in the canyon. There's a war that's already started."

None of the passengers said anything. Taskar moved closer. "You know about the war? How? You're not a Dweller."

"I worked for them," she said. "I'm part of the uprising, the insurrection, the resistance, whatever you want to call it."

"How can you pay?"

"I've got rations," Ana said. "I've got weapons. You could even have the horse."

"Taskar," snapped the woman, "we got to go. I don't care what this trollop got to say. We paid. We want out."

"I'll take your weapons and half your rations," he said. "I have no need for the horse. You can ride in the back with your child."

Ana nodded. "Perfect. Thank you," she said. She raised the pistol, spun it backwards, and extended her hand, offering it to him. She maneuvered Penny back into the carrier on her chest.

He approached her and took the gun, tucking it in the front of his high-water pants. He then offered her his free hand to help her from the horse.

"You gotta be kidding me," whined the woman. "This is ridiculous."

Taskar turned and sneered. "She's paying," he said. "It's my car. My rules."

Ana took his hand and dismounted. "You are a Dweller, then?"

Taskar shook his head. "I was. I left a year ago. I live north of the wall and make trips back here."

Ana started working on the saddle. "Why do you come back here?"

Taskar shrugged. "The money," he said. "There are no jobs north of the wall unless you work for the government. Those jobs are for people with connections. I have no connections."

"If you left a year ago, how did you know about the war?"

Taskar smirked. "They've been planning it for a lot longer than a year."

Ana nodded. She knew from her own involvement the war was part of the Dwellers' long-term plans. She stopped rifling through the saddlebags. "Is it better north of the wall?"

"As I said, it depends on who you are. A pretty woman like you?" he said. "You could be okay."

Ana didn't ask what he meant by that. She didn't want to know. Whatever the north held for her and Penny, it couldn't be worse than what the territory had been or what she assumed it would become.

"Help me with the saddle," she said. "We're taking it with us. You can take the rifle," she said. "It's yours now."

"We do need to go," he said. "Before things get out of hand more than they already are."

CHAPTER THIRTY-SIX

OCTOBER 26, 2037, 7:34 AM
SCOURGE +5 YEARS
PALO DURO CANYON, TEXAS

Battle turned in time to see the first of the grunts pulling himself onto the top of the hoodoo. He waited for the man's head to emerge and pulled the trigger.

"Get the ropes!" he yelled to the other Dweller still surviving atop the rock. "They're coming up the ropes!"

Sawyer bounded from the curve in the rock and met Battle at the edge of the hoodoo. "I'm helping."

Battle didn't argue. He needed the help. He cursed himself for not having thought about pulling up the ropes. It was another unsoldier-like blunder he'd committed in the last two weeks. All that preparation...

Battle lay down on his stomach, reached over the edge of the rock, and tugged on one of the ropes they'd affixed to a series of climbing anchors. Each rope was connected through a pair of carabiners that extended to a trip of metal anchors jammed into vertical cracks running along the face of the canyon wall adjacent to the top of the hoodoo.

The rope was taut as he tugged. Someone else was climbing it. Battle extended his torso farther over the edge and met the grunt's eyes with his. Battle pulled back and grabbed his rifle. He slid back to the edge on one knee and aimed the weapon straight down, bracing himself for the recoil, and applied pressure to the trigger. The unfortunate grunt ceased being a threat.

Battle dropped his weapon and began pulling the rope upward. Hand over hand, he looped it over his shoulder. Finished, he dropped the coil to the rock and moved to the second of four ropes.

***

Sawyer scurried to the edge and laid down his rifle. He studied how Battle positioned himself and mimicked him, leaned over, and grabbed the rope. He yanked it, but it didn't give. He looked over the side and saw the top of a man's head about halfway up the rope. Sawyer looked back at his weapon and then over at Battle, who was using his. He saw the kick of the weapon and knew he couldn't handle it. He'd lose his balance.

He looked over the edge again and the man was looking up at him. Sawyer's eyes narrowed and he focused on the man's face. It was familiar. He knew him.

Dalton!

Sawyer felt a rush of adrenaline. His heart beat against his chest. He backed away from the edge and freed his pack from his shoulders, rummaged through its contents, and pulled out a folding utility knife. He slid back to edge and grabbed the taut nylon rope with one hand while he began sawing with the other.

The rope was thick, its outer coating protective of the threaded, stretchable cords underneath the shell. Sawyer ran the smooth blade back and forth, his eyes darting between the rope and the climbing grunt, who'd hurried his pace.

Back and forth. Back and forth.

Dalton slid up the rope faster and faster. "Kid," he said, breathlessly, "I know you. You know me. Don't do this."

Back and forth. Back and forth.

Sawyer took his eye from the blade to look at Dalton and sliced his finger. He winced and tried to ignore the pulsing pain as he worked through the rope, blood trickling down the rope.

Back and forth. Back and forth.

He was halfway there.

Dalton grunted and shimmied closer to the top. His hands were no more than five feet away.

Back and forth. Back and forth.

The rope unwound and snapped looser. Dalton felt the give and yelled at Sawyer, "Stop it, kid. Stop it now!" His face grew dark and angry.

Sawyer started sawing at a new point in the weakened cord.

Back and forth. Back and forth.

His swipes at the rope were shorter and shorter and he worked the blade faster and faster across the fibers.

"I'm gonna reach you, kid," Dalton growled through his clenched jaw. "I'm gonna grab your throat and yank you over the edge." He shimmied up another foot and extended his reach.

Sawyer backed away from Dalton's outstretched hand but kept at his job.

And then it snapped.

Dalton reached at the moment the rope gave way. His fingernails clawed the back of Sawyer's hand as he fell, screaming for help until he hit the ground with a crack.

***

Battle reached Sawyer as the rope snapped. He watched the grunt, still holding the rope with one hand, fall backward, landing awkwardly on the ground below.

Battle pulled the boy from the edge with his free hand. "Good job," he said. "Now help me with the next one."

The other Dweller had coiled the third rope and was working on the fourth. Battle stood to the side, shouldered the rifle, and pulled the HK's trigger twice, knocking loose both the grunts trying to climb the remaining rope.

As he wound the last of the cord onto the rock, the Dweller seized, grabbed his side, and toppled over, tangled in the rope.

Battle moved to his side and checked the wound. It wasn't good. The Dweller had two large, leaking holes at his ribcage. The man was already coughing up blood.

Battle stood above him and tapped his trigger once. "As far as the East is from the West," he said, "so far has He removed our transgressions from us."

"Why did you do that?" Sawyer asked.

"He was dying," Battle said flatly. "I put him out of his misery." He put his hand on the boy's back and patted it. "It was the right thing to do."

"What now?"

"We keep fighting," Battle said. He looked over his shoulder and to the right. Some of the grunts had gotten past the first wall of Dwellers and were pushing ahead. The canyon was bathed in the yellow glow of sunrise, and his vision was much improved in the early daylight. He scanned the battlefield below and gave the plateau opposite the hoodoo a glance before assessing the strength of the next wave at the dogleg.

He caught something odd on the plateau that didn't register at first until he'd moved past it. He looked back. Standing atop the plateau was Lola. Directly behind her, holding a gun to her head, was a bearded, ponytailed man. It was Roof. He was staring directly at him as if he'd been patiently awaiting Battle's acknowledgement.

Roof's left arm was wrapped around Lola's chest, holding her tightly against him. Lola was gripping his arm with both hands.

Battle froze for a moment then turned to Sawyer. He pointed to the dogleg, trying to keep the boy from looking back to the plateau. "I need your help."

Sawyer's eyes brightened with a new responsibility and he nodded with enthusiasm.

Battle pointed his finger at Sawyer's chest. "Now listen, I'm going down there to get reinforcements up here. Once I've slid down the rope, you yank it back up."

Sawyer's excitement diminished, but he nodded his understanding. "Okay."

"Then you get over to that niche in the rock, make yourself as small as you can, and wait for me. You'll be safe up here. Nobody will be able to reach you."

Sawyer looked back at the rock and then to Battle with a dour look on his face. "How will you get back up here if there's no rope?"

Battle sighed. "We'll figure it out," he said. "I'll send you a signal."

"What kind of signal?"

"I don't know. You'll know it when you see it."

Sawyer nodded, seemingly placated by the vague response. The truth was, Battle had no idea how he'd get back up the hoodoo or what kind of signal he'd send if need be.

As it was, he had to navigate the fight on the canyon floor to cross the passage and climb his way to Lola. And Roof.

***

General Roof stared across the passage at the man who'd saved his life. He'd watched him kill a handful of grunts and callously drill a bullet into the head of a dying Dweller. He was the Marcus Battle he remembered. He was the Marcus Battle who'd staved off the Cartel for a half-decade and then survived the Jones as few men had.

He'd waited patiently for Battle to find his glare, using his superior strength to hold the woman in place. He didn't care about her. It didn't matter to him if she lived or died. She was a means to an end. Roof needed to deal with Battle face-to-face, and she was a serendipitous find to facilitate exactly that.

Roof scanned the rim. Even in the daylight he couldn't see the reinforcements he'd expected. Something had gone wrong. He looked to the dogleg and saw little push from incoming waves of men. Their offensive was failing.

"He's going to kill you," said Lola. "You're going to die here, and the Cartel is going to die with you."

Roof chuckled and used his arm to lift her feet off the ground. He arched his back, totally controlling her as she struggled against his arm. She dug her nails into his skin and dragged them downward.

"We're all going to die," he said and dropped her feet back to the rocky surface of the plateau. "It's a matter of when."

"Look at the passage," Lola taunted. "You're losing. You can't win. You didn't realize how strong the Dwellers' resistance would be, did you?"

Roof looked across the canyon. Battle was lowering himself into the passage on a rope. His legs were wrapped around the nylon and he used one hand to guide himself. He held a rifle in the other and had it pressed against his hip as he descended. Roof couldn't be sure, but he thought he saw Battle fire the weapon one handed as he dropped.

"You're losing," Lola repeated and jammed her elbow into Roof's solid gut.

He flinched but didn't lose his hold. "You're gonna have to be okay with staying here until your boyfriend arrives," said Roof. "Then you can go. Then you watch both of us die."

CHAPTER THIRTY-SEVEN

OCTOBER 26, 2037, 7:45 AM
SCOURGE +5 YEARS
PALO DURO CANYON, TEXAS

Juliana Paagal emerged from her tent into the chill of the early morning sunrise. She didn't feel the cold. She was warm with power.

At her ear was the satellite phone. Call after incoming call brought with it astonishing news. With rare exception, the Cartel was folding. What she expected to be a long, brutal war might be over by lunch.

"What about the north rim?" she asked. "What's their status?"

Her scouts had performed admirably. Throughout the night, across the territory, they'd alerted her of awaiting squads of advancing Cartel caravans.

They'd ambushed them where they were outnumbered, fought them hand to hand when they were evenly matched, and slaughtered the grunts and their bosses when Dwellers had the advantage.

Paagal thanked the caller and folded the sat phone's antenna. She slipped it into her pocket and turned to the operator. He'd kept her company since her security team died on the rim. They were walking to the tent enclave, ready to deliver good news to the elderly, the women, and the children who'd stayed out of the fray.

"We've timed this perfectly," she said to him. "Austin is beginning to acquiesce now. In a matter of hours, we will have control of everywhere behind the wall except Lubbock."

"Everywhere, huh?"

"One glitch," she admitted. "Something happened in Houston. Our cell successfully killed the general there. Then three of the leaders, the people who'd put the plan together, all died. We think the general's wife flipped on us."

"She's one woman," said the operator. "What does it matter?"

Paagal stopped and shoved the operator in the arm. "What does it matter?"

The operator shrugged as if the question were rhetorical.

"Battle is one man," she said. "Look at what he did. He created enough of a ripple in the water that it distracted the Cartel from the storm that was coming. If we find her, we can't let her live." She resumed walking toward the tent city. "Come to think of it," she added. "I don't think we should let Battle live either."

The operator stopped in his tracks as Paagal kept walking. She sensed he wasn't next to her and turned around. "What?"

"Why would you do that? He's helping us. You promised him safe passage beyond the wall."

"I don't trust him psychologically," said Paagal. "He's got issues."

The operator laughed incredulously and ran his fingers through his beard. "We've all got issues. We're living in a wasteland. The Scourge killed two out of every three people we knew. Cut him a break."

Paagal marched back to the operator, her mouth pursed with frustration. "I don't need your opinion, I need your obedience. I need everyone's obedience as we rebuild the territory into something better. Battle doesn't fit."

"He's not going to be here," said the operator. "He wants to live north of the wall, outside of the territory. He's no threat to you."

Paagal huffed and spun on her heel. "Enough," she said without turning around. "I need to speak with the invalids."

She walked with purpose toward the tent city, reluctantly considering what the operator was suggesting. Perhaps Battle wouldn't be a threat. Maybe he'd move across the wall and stay there. If he did, he'd be their problem. Instead of challenging the Dwellers' new order, he'd spend his days and nights exasperating those trying to maintain a tenuous sense of calm on a much larger scale.

Paagal had watched Battle work. He was an enigma. She'd seen him ruthlessly maim and kill. She'd seen him reveal remarkable empathy for that woman Lola and the boy Sawyer. She'd overheard him talking to himself, though the conversations sounded as though he believed the voices she concluded were in his head were, in his world, real and tangible.

Before the Scourge she'd treated patients who suffered from what were typically called auditory hallucinations. They were signs of psychosis and indicative of someone who had trouble distinguishing reality from fiction.

Battle, she was convinced, was teetering on the edge of schizoaffective disorder, if he hadn't already plunged headfirst into that surreality. He presented with so many of the symptoms beyond the hallucinations. He was moody, bordering on depression. He was a loner for years and was uncomfortable playing well with others.

She did consider the possibility that the loneliness begat the depression and the need for a connection with people, real or imagined. Maybe it wasn't psychosis. Perhaps it was a coping mechanism.

By the time she'd reached the first of the tents, Paagal made up her mind. It didn't matter why Battle was the way he was. She didn't care about the cause. She cared about the effect. He was a loose cannon, psychotic or not. He would not stay on the other side of the wall. The pull of his home was too great. He'd come back. She'd need to deal with him.

CHAPTER THIRTY-EIGHT

OCTOBER 26, 2037, 7:54 AM
SCOURGE +5 YEARS
SOUTH OF HICKORY CREEK, TEXAS

Ana had her nose pressed to the glass of the hearse's rear window. They were crossing a large lake. The sun reflected off the water, making it appear red in color.

Penny was swaddled in a pile of blankets next to her and had fallen back asleep. Ana rubbed the back of her head, gently thumbing the remaining fontanelle. Her baby, born of deceit and treachery, was perhaps the best child on the planet. She still napped twice a day for hours at a time, and when awake, she was as happy as a clam.

With each spin of the hearse's wheels, Ana was closer to freedom and farther away from her past lives.

Her breath formed, grew, and shrank against the cold glass. She pulled away and ran her finger through the condensation. She shifted to look toward the front of the vehicle. The hearse had a bench seat up front. There were four people squeezed onto the bench; the driver, a teenage girl, a teenage boy, and the dictatorial woman who didn't want Ana traveling with them. Behind the bench, to the right side, were a pair of facing jump seats that shared a foot well. A pair of young women, maybe in their early twenties, occupied the seats. The rest of the hearse was a laminate flatbed with recessed casket rollers every few feet.

"Who are you?" The whisper came from a young woman in the rear-facing jump seat. "What's your name?"

"Ana."

"I'm Becky. And your baby?"

"Penny."

The girl managed an insecure smile. "That's a pretty name," she said. "How old is she?"

"Nine months."

"Why are you running away?" asked the young woman.

The twenty-something facing her popped Becky on the knee. "That's rude."

"It's okay," said Ana. "I need a fresh start. I need a healthier environment for Penny."

The angry woman up front laughed from her belly. "There ain't no such thing," she said. "Not on either side of the wall."

Ana noticed the driver, Taskar, watching her in the rearview mirror. "Then why are you going there?" she asked the woman. "Why are you taking the risk if it's not better?"

"I didn't say it wasn't better," the woman said. "It ain't healthy. Taskar here was telling me about the way the world works up there. It's all about who you know. You know somebody, you got it good. You don't? You don't."

"So you know somebody?" Ana asked.

"I know lots of people," she said. "We got somewhere to stay. We got jobs lined up. We got official-looking papers."

"Papers?"

The woman laughed. "You ain't got your papers?"

Ana looked at the rearview mirror. "I didn't — "

The woman mocked Ana, whining as she spoke. "I didn't. I didn't."

"I can help," said Taskar. "Don't worry."

"Don't matter if you got papers or not, sweet thing," said the woman. "If you got nowhere to stay and no job, you might as well hop out of the car right now."

"Don't listen to her," whispered Becky. "She's always like this. She doesn't like strangers. It's not you."

"Damn right I don't like strangers," said the woman, overhearing the whisper. "Ain't nothing to like."

Ana turned back to the window and breathed onto the glass. They were moving at a good clip. The dotted white lane markings whizzed past, blurring into a single line from Taskar's speed. They'd be in Gainesville, south of the wall, in less than an hour.

CHAPTER THIRTY-NINE

OCTOBER 26, 2037, 8:00 AM
SCOURGE +5 YEARS
PALO DURO CANYON, TEXAS

Marcus Battle clung to the rocks, pressing himself as close to the wall as he could. He didn't like having his back to the fighting below him, even if it was diminishing and the Cartel's advance was in the midst of being thwarted.

He scaled the final jutting rock onto the plateau and pushed himself to his feet. The morning sun brought with it a whipping wind that swirled through the canyon and flapped against Battle's thin shirt. He stood with his rifle in his hands, the barrel pointed diagonally skyward.

Roof turned to face him, dragging Lola with him. He pushed the barrel of his handgun into her temple, forcing her to tilt her neck away from the pressure.

"I know who you are," Battle said, calling to Roof over the wind and now intermittent gunfire.

"Do you now?" said Roof, half of his face hidden behind Lola.

"You're Rufus Buck."

"The one and only," said Roof. "Good on you for figuring it out. Though, it's not like I was hiding it. I knew who you were when I saw you at the Jones. You didn't recognize me."

"You've changed."

"A lot has changed, Captain Battle."

"Major."

Roof laughed. "See what I mean?"

Lola's hair whipped across her face, and Battle could see the resolve in her eyes. She wasn't afraid.

Battle waved one of his hands, gesturing at Roof from toe to head. "So what's going on here?" he asked. "What is this?"

"I thought we should meet face-to-face again," Roof said. "Given that we've both saved each other's lives, I thought it appropriate."

Battle tensed. His hands tightened around the rifle. He spoke through clenched teeth. "How do you figure we saved each other's lives?"

"You got me out of Aleppo. I told Skinner not to lay a hand on you."

Battle's focused narrowed. He slid his finger onto the rifle's trigger.

"He's dead now," said Roof. "Skinner, that is. Got shot on his way here. I put him out of his misery, like you did with that Dweller across the way. We have a lot in common, you and me."

"Now you sound like the bad guy in an old James Bond movie," said Battle. "You can't rationalize what you've done."

"Nor can you."

"So, again," said Battle, looking for an opening. He needed only enough space to hit his target. Roof was smart enough not to provide it. "What is this?"

"We've saved each other's lives," said Roof. "Now we're going to end them. I'm going to let the little lady go here. You're gonna shoot me. I'm going to shoot you."

"Let her go, then," Battle said. "You've lost this war. You know it; I know it. You gain nothing by killing her."

Lola's eyes widened. She struggled against Roof's arm. "No, Marcus. No."

Roof laughed and then leaned into Lola's neck. "Marcus, is it?" he sneered and planted a big kiss on the side of her head.

Lola struggled against him. She kicked at his shins, clawed at his arm.

Roof growled. "Fine then," he said. "Be free."

He released his hold and shoved her forward. Lola stumbled. She fell onto her knees and slid, catching herself with her hands.

Roof raised his weapon. He aimed at Battle but stood his ground.

Battle pushed his left hand forward, drawing the barrel of the rifle toward Roof. His muscles tensed, anticipating both the recoil and the incoming fire.

In the instant before either of them let loose, however, Roof jerked to one side and then the other. He lost control of his weapon and dropped it. He turned his attention away from Battle and toward the hoodoo.

Battle followed Roof's gaze and saw Sawyer on one knee, his HK pressed to his shoulder, a series of muzzle flashes exploding from the weapon's barrel as he unloaded its magazine into Roof.

Roof's body limply danced in place until he collapsed onto his weapon. The last of the Cartel generals was dead.

Lola lifted herself from the rock and ran to Battle, burying her face in his chest.

Battle lowered the rifle and held it with one hand while he wrapped his other arm around Lola, holding the back of her head with his hand. He closed his eyes and felt the wind blow across his face. The gunfire had all but ceased. Behind him, farther into the passage, Dwellers were cheering their miraculously decisive victory.

Lola reached up and grabbed his face with both hands, pulling him toward her. "Thank you," she whispered through tears. "Thank you, Marcus."

Battle tried to swallow the hard knot in his throat. He smiled, then gently pressed his lips to her forehead. There wasn't time for more than that.

He looked across the canyon and found Sawyer. The boy had retreated to the safety of the curve in the rock. He was crouched low, as Battle had instructed.

CHAPTER FORTY

OCTOBER 26, 2037, 9:00 AM
SCOURGE +5 YEARS
GAINESVILLE, TEXAS

"I told you," repeated the sun-wrinkled waif guarding the gate, "you can't get through. You have to go to Wichita Falls. That's the only way out right now."

Taskar was leaning out of the driver's side window, his finger jabbing at the waif. "I paid good money to cross here," he said, pointing to the gate.

The gate opened to a wide no-man's-land that separated the territory from the wall. It was neutral land nobody controlled, and it was the most dangerous part of the crossing in both directions.

Taskar raised his voice in exasperation. "I do not have time to go to Wichita Falls."

Unfazed, the waif ran his finger across a deep line running the length of his forehead. "Make time," he said. "Nobody gets through. War is hell."

The obnoxious woman in the front leaned across the teens between her and Taskar. "There's nothing closer?" she asked as if she knew the waif was keeping a secret.

"Wichita Falls is it." The waif shrugged. "On the whole wall. West. North. East. All of the regular sneak-throughs are shut down. Somebody is trying to stop the rats from leaving the ship while it sinks."

Taskar cursed the waif and the gate and anyone else who could hear him. He slid the hearse into reverse, spinning the treadless tires on the asphalt. He shifted into drive without braking, and the wagon lurched into gear.

"Buckle up," he said, glaring at Ana in the rearview mirror. "We have another ninety miles to go."

Ana rolled her eyes. She had no seat belt. "Do you have enough gas?"

Taskar nodded and accelerated, turning right to head west on Highway 82. He took out his frustration on the vehicle's aging V6 engine.

"What happened back there?" asked the woman in the front. "Why couldn't we get across?"

Taskar pushed a button on the door to close his window. "It's the war," he said. "One side or the other is trying to funnel crossings to one location. Normally there are a dozen good spots."

The woman ran her hands through her short hair and grabbed it with her fists. "So we're screwed?"

Taskar looked across the bench seating at the woman. "I don't know. I'm not as familiar with Wichita Falls. I know the people on both sides of the sneak-through at Gainesville."

The woman slammed her hands on the dash on front of her. "You don't know? We paid you with everything we had south of the wall and you don't know?"

Taskar held up his hand. "Calm yourself," he said. "I'm being honest with you. I could be dishonest and tell you everything will be perfect. Would you rather that?"

"Yes," said Ana from the back of the hearse. "It's better if you give us hope."

Taskar squeezed the wheel with both hands, working them against the worn leather. "Okay," he said, "I am hopeful there is no problem. I am hopeful we will cross the sneak-through at Wichita Falls without incident."

"You paid to cross at Gainesville?" asked Ana.

"Yes."

"Is that payment good at Wichita Falls?"

"Probably not."

The woman in the front shot a look at Taskar, then Ana, and back at Taskar again. "Then what?"

"Then I'm hopeful."

CHAPTER FORTY-ONE

OCTOBER 26, 2037, 10:00 AM
SCOURGE +5 YEARS
PALO DURO CANYON, TEXAS

Paagal stood at the far edge of the tent city, her hands on her hips. She held her chin as would a queen. "You should leave immediately," she said to Battle. "I've had all of the wall sneak-throughs closed except for Wichita Falls. It's a five-hour journey by car."

Battle flexed his hands and crossed his arms. He tucked his hands under his pits. "We don't have a car," he said. He looked across the field of tent pitches. Dwellers were hugging each other, dancing without music.

"We can arrange for a caravan to deliver you to the wall. You'll be granted passage across the sneak-through. After that, on the northern side of the wall, you're on your own."

Battle widened his stance, spreading his feet shoulder-width apart. "Why are you in a hurry to get rid of us?"

A smile oozed across Paagal's face, illuminating her brown skin. "I'm not the one in a hurry, if I recall. You wanted to be north of the wall the moment you arrived here. Am I wrong?"

Battle shook his head. "No," he said. "I guess not. Still, it's strange. You've been the leader of the territory for a minute and your first official act is to help us north of the wall."

"I'm keeping my word," Paagal said. "Don't read anything into it."

Battle chuckled. "I might not have had you not just said that."

Paagal slinked closer to Battle. "Look, I have a lot to do. The fire is out, but there are hotspots that need my attention. Battles are ongoing in Houston and Austin. Lubbock will be smoldering for some time. I promised you safe passage north of the wall. I'm delivering it before other things become more pressing."

She extended her hand and Battle took it. "Thank you," he said. "Who is going with us?"

"Baadal will escort you," she said. "You'll have a driver who's made the trip many times. Plus I'll send a couple of sentries who've done reconnaissance along the wall. You'll be fine."

Battle stuffed his hands into his pockets and wove his way through the maze of tents until he'd reached his own. He stood there a moment and let the wind swirl around him. It was getting colder despite the sun rising higher above the rim to the east.

He drifted back to Syria, remembering the night that changed the course of the rest of his life. He envisioned the way Rufus Buck looked then, his electric razor haircut high and tight, his face angular and clean shaven. That vision morphed into the General Roof who'd just died: a man who wore a gray ponytail and a thick, wiry beard. He was easily forty pounds heavier than he'd been a lifetime earlier. He was unrecognizable.

Battle repeated that assessment in his head over and over until he began to wonder how unrecognizable he would be to Sylvia were she suddenly alive and standing across from her husband. Would she know him? Would Wesson instantly identify him as his father?

He chuckled to himself, vacantly staring off toward the eastern horizon. He didn't even know himself anymore. How would anyone else? Paagal had tried to weasel that admission from him more than once. He'd chosen not to give in to her psychological games.

Paagal was another one who was likely a different person than the one she had been prior to the Scourge. Then again, maybe not. Maybe she'd always been a manipulative power broker.

He replayed the conversation with Paagal in his mind. Something didn't sit right. Although he couldn't put his mental finger on it, she wasn't entirely forthcoming.

"You're back." Lola popped her head through the front vent of her tent. Her red hair was wild and tangled. Her eyes were framed by the dark circles underneath them.

Battle's pulse quickened at the sight of her. She was the prettiest she'd been. "Yeah," he said through a smile he tried to suppress, "and we need to get moving."

Lola pulled herself through the opening and moved next to Battle. "What do you mean?"

"Paagal's getting us an escort to the wall right now. We're leaving as soon as we gather our belongings."

Lola's eyes narrowed and she folded her arms across her chest. "That's weird, isn't it?" she asked. "We've been awake all night. We've been fighting. We've—"

Battle raised his hands in surrender and nodded. "I know, I know. I agree. It's weird."

"How are we getting there?"

"Car."

"Huh," she said. "Okay. I'll get our stuff together."

"How's Sawyer?"

"In shock, I think. He doesn't want to talk about it."

"Give him time," said Battle. "He'll open up."

"I don't know," Lola said. "I think he's seen too much. It's changed him."

Battle stepped toward Lola and wrapped his arms around her, placing one hand on the small of her back and the other on the back of her head, and pulled her close. She melted into his body.

"We've all changed," he said.

CHAPTER FORTY-TWO

OCTOBER 26, 2037, NOON
SCOURGE +5 YEARS
WICHITA FALLS, TEXAS

"It's been two hours," whined the woman in the front seat of the hearse. "We've been sitting in this car without the heat on for two hours."

Taskar was rapping his fingers on the top of the steering wheel. He didn't respond to the complaint.

Ana assumed there was nothing he could do about it. Otherwise, Taskar would have gladly sent them on their way. Instead, they were stuck in a parking lot, awaiting permission to pass through the gate. The lot was full of people waiting their turns. Apparently, Ana and her road-trip companions weren't the only ones who feared anarchy in the coming days.

The woman shifted in her seat, tightening the squeeze on the two unfortunate teens sitting between Taskar and her. "How long is this going to take?" she asked, her breath visible puffs of air that bloomed and dissipated in the cold air.

Taskar kept thumping his fingers, tapping out something that sounded like a jazz riff. He glanced over at the woman and shrugged, leaning back on the headrest.

The woman grunted. "I'm getting some answers," she said and opened her door. "This is ridiculous."

"I wouldn't do that," Taskar halfheartedly protested without taking his head from the rest or stopping his jam session. "It's not a good idea."

The woman cursed at Taskar, stepped from the hearse, and slammed shut the door. The two teens immediately slid over to give themselves more space.

"She shouldn't have done that," Taskar said. "It's dangerous here."

"I thought crossing the wall was secretive and publicly forbidden," said Ana. "If that's the case, why are there so many people openly defying the law?"

The front seat leather squeaked under Taskar's weight as he turned to face Ana. "It's not the law anymore," he said. "Or it soon won't be. Everyone who is here knows the Cartel is losing power. Plus, there's nothing illegal about entering the no-man's-land between the fences and the wall. It's just that nobody does it because it's a free-for-all."

"There are so many people," said Ana.

"A lot of these are Cartel," Taskar replied. "They're like the Nazis fleeing at the end of World War II."

"How can you tell?"

Taskar drew his finger across his forehead. "See the tan lines on their foreheads? Those are hat lines. These are bosses and captains who are running before Paagal and her people capture them."

It made sense that the feckless, cowardly leaders would flee and leave the underlings to fend for themselves. Ana hadn't seen any of the motorcycle-riding grunts she knew patrolled the border near the wall and figured they'd driven south to fight. She did, however, see endless desperation on the faces of those gathered in the lot and walking the streets nearby.

It reminded her of the television footage of the Syrian and Ukrainian refugee camps she'd seen in the months before the Scourge hit the United States. She hadn't thought about it in years, but there it was as fresh as if she'd watched it yesterday.

She positioned herself so she could see the woman through the front windshield. Becky, the young woman sitting in the jump seat facing her, had also turned around to watch.

While there weren't many vehicles in the lot, there were easily a couple of hundred people in various states of dress and levels of armed preparedness.

At the far end of the lot was an imposing eight-foot chain-link fence topped with rusting concertina wire and stretching hundreds of feet in both directions before connecting with buildings on either side. In the middle of the fence was a wide gate that slid open on rollers.

Every ten minutes or so a man with a rifle strapped to his shoulder would roll open the gate enough for the next person or small group of people to squeeze through. A pair of men with thick beards and cartoonishly large physiques prevented anyone else from trying to pass. All three of the men took their direction from a woman with a shaven head at the edge of the gate. She appeared to be the arbiter of who passed through and who was turned away.

In the two hours they'd sat awaiting their turn, she'd seen papers, weapons, and food exchange hands. She'd even seen bags of coins offered for passage. The woman would unclench the bags, pour the money into one hand and test its weight. The people she turned away didn't get back their offerings.

Another woman, also with a buzz cut, was circling the lot, taking names and assigning positions. She'd told Taskar he was next an hour earlier. He clearly wasn't. He'd known better than to press his luck and complain. Despite his warnings, the anxious woman from the front seat did not.

With her elbows locked and fists drawn tight, she marched to the gate. As she approached, one of the bearded men held up a hand to stop her. She kept moving until he drew his rifle to his shoulder. His face turned red as he barked an order at her and planted his feet firmly on the cracked asphalt.

Ana couldn't hear what the woman was saying or what the bearded man was telling her, but she could tell the conversation wasn't going as well as the woman would likely have wanted.

She kept pointing back at the hearse, jabbing at it with her finger while she complained. The guard glanced over at the hearse, keeping his weapon trained at the woman's chest.

The shaven-headed woman who'd lied to Taskar cautiously approached the exchange. She slid up beside the bearded guard and joined the conversation. Her approach, while supported with firm hand gestures, appeared more muted than the guard's.

Seemingly defeated, the woman from the front seat screamed something at the two decision makers and spat at their feet. She turned toward the hearse and started slowly back across the lot.

Behind her, the gate slid open, the warped wheels running their track as a guard pushed the chain-link barrier. The woman glanced over her shoulder and stopped walking. She gave a final look at the hearse, her tongue curled above her lip, and spun back to the gate.

Taskar grabbed the wheel and pulled himself forward in his seat toward the dash. "She's going to run for it," he said. "I can't believe her. She's going to run for it."

She did and she was fast. Her arms chugged, her heels kicking toward her behind as she sprinted to the opening. A group of a half-dozen men and women were slowly crossing into no-man's-land. Together they filled the space between the edge of the open gate and the fence post from which the guard pulled it. The woman from the front seat barreled her way through them, her arms swimming outward to clear her path as she bolted across the threshold.

She moved so quickly, she disappeared into the density of people on the other side of the gate before any of the guards reacted. One of them fired a pair of shots past the gate once the woman from the front seat had long since vanished. He got a tongue-lashing from a woman arbiter. She slapped her shaven head, pointing at him and then the gate.

Then the bald woman turned her attention to the hearse and began a march toward it and its remaining occupants. Taskar slammed his hands on the wheel and cursed the woman from the front seat.

"She left us," said one befuddled teen to the other. "I don't understand."

The bald woman rapped her knuckle on the driver's side window, and Taskar rolled it down. She stuck her head halfway into the car and eyeballed the seven remaining people inside the hearse.

She pointed toward the gate as it closed. "That," she said, "is going to cost you. You go to the back of the line. People are getting restless as it is. I can already sense a riot brewing. We're trying to control access, slow the exodus. We can't have anyone cutting in line."

"But she left us," said the confused teen. "She's our older sister. She took care of us."

"She doesn't anymore," said the bald woman flatly. "It's going to be another hour now."

"What's going to happen to her?" asked the teen, nodding toward the fence.

The bald woman scratched the stubble peppering her scalp. "In no-man's-land?" she asked, one eyebrow raised higher than the other. "Nothing good. She's a woman. She's alone. She's never making it across the wall. Now wait here. I'll be back in an hour. Or two. Or three. You're not the priority."

Taskar rolled up the window. "What she's saying is that we didn't give her enough of a payment. These folks from the Cartel have compensated her well. That's why they're the priority."

Ana leaned back against the tailgate, extending her legs into the flatbed next to the jump seats. She drew a bottle from her bag and eyeballed a tablespoon of formula, mixing it with the remaining water in one of her two canteens. She shook the contents.

Penny needed to eat. They'd be waiting a while. Ana figured she might as well do it while she had the time. No-man's-land wouldn't be the place to stop and feed her baby should the child suddenly get hungry.

CHAPTER FORTY-THREE

OCTOBER 26, 2037, 3:30 PM
SCOURGE +5 YEARS
WICHITA FALLS, TEXAS

"We're almost there," said Baadal. "Everyone should wake up now."

Battle hadn't slept the entirety of the long ride. His suspicious mind wouldn't let him. He'd kept one eye on the driver and the other on the passing scenery as their caravan sped southeast.

Paagal had provided a pair of Cartel SUVs Dweller scouts had confiscated west of the rim. They were full of gasoline, had spare canisters strapped to their roofs, and even had working heaters.

Baadal was in the front passenger's seat. Battle sat behind him. Lola sat behind the driver. She was asleep, her head leaning against the window and bobbing with the movement of the SUV. Sawyer was passed out on Battle's shoulder.

Highway 287 took them from the canyon through Memphis, Childress, and Vernon. All three of the towns were virtually abandoned. The road had cut through the center of the first two towns, revealing dilapidated buildings, tumbleweeds of trash, and traffic signals that didn't work.

In Vernon, they'd skirted the northern edge of town, but Battle had gotten the same sense from what little he saw. It was another ghost town in the vast territory of what was once Texas.

Battle wasn't born in Texas, but he'd gotten there as fast as he could. He loved its topography, its lack of state income tax, and its residents' rightful sense of provincialism.

He'd bemoaned what had happened. Regardless of what the Dwellers now did with their power, Texas would never be Texas again. People would forget the Alamo and the Battle of Goliad. He recited the Texas pledge in his head as they motored closer to Wichita Falls, trying to keep its words stuffed somewhere in his memory.

"Honor the Texas flag; I pledge allegiance to thee, Texas, one state under God, one and indivisible."

Battle had no allegiance to anything anymore. There was no country for which to fight, no state in which to take pride. All he had now were Lola and Sawyer.

He looked over at them. Neither awoke from Baadal's urging. He nudged Sawyer and the boy's eyes slowly blinked open. He reached across and gently squeezed Lola's leg. She put her hand on his, lacing her fingers between his, keeping her eyes closed.

"You should wake up," Baadal repeated. "We're getting close. Our driver is going to tell us what to expect."

The driver was a gruff man who'd not spoken the entirety of the long drive. He adjusted the rearview mirror and cleared his throat. His voice was deep and raspy, almost painful sounding. "This isn't going to be fun," he said. "This is the only open crossing point along the entirety of the wall. Expect to see fleeing Cartel. Expect to see dangerous loners and desperate families. And that's before you get into no-man's-land."

Sawyer rubbed his eyes. "What's no-man's-land?"

"It's the stretch of uncontrolled land between the Cartel's gates and the wall. It makes it harder to get access to the wall. That's how the Cartel wanted it. Now we're using it to stop too many people from leaving at once."

"Why let people leave at all?" Battle asked.

"Most of these people are Cartel or Cartel sympathizers," said the driver. "Paagal wants them to leave. But she wants it controlled. She wants to have an idea of who's leaving."

"That doesn't make any sense," said Battle. "None at all."

The driver shrugged. "It's what she wants."

The SUV slowed and turned left into a large parking lot. At the northern edge of the lot was a tall chain-link fence stretching between two buildings. There was a gate in the middle that sat on a set of wheels.

Between the SUV and the gate was a mess of people. Battle counted fifty men, women, and children. A behemoth of a man slid open the gate and a thin, broad-shouldered woman with a buzz cut waved through a party of four. The gate slid closed behind them.

"So she's funneling everyone through a single spot," said Battle. "That makes it easy for whoever is guarding the wall on the northern side to capture anyone who comes through. This isn't good."

The SUV slid into a parking spot marked with faded yellow lines, and the driver shifted into park. He left the engine running, and a second woman with a buzz cut made her way to the vehicle. She knocked on the window and the driver lowered it.

"Sneak-through?" she asked. "I need payment. Better it is, faster you go through."

The driver handed her a slip of paper. She unfolded it, read it, then eyeballed the passengers one at a time.

"I need to check this," she said and jogged through the assembled refugees to the bald woman by the gate.

"What was that?" asked Battle. "The paper?"

"A note from Paagal," he said. "It gives you clearance without payment."

"Who are those women?" asked Sawyer.

Baadal turned around. "They're priestesses."

Battle pulled himself forward in his seat, using Baadal's headrest. "What?"

"They're priestesses," Baadal repeated. "They work for Paagal. They help all new Dwellers assimilate. They give us our Hindi names. They guide us spiritually when we have trouble."

"Why didn't I see any of them in the canyon?" asked Battle. "In two weeks, I never saw one of these priestesses."

"They were sent away," said Baadal. "Paagal didn't want them in harm's way. They were deployed along the border to the safe houses we've long controlled."

"You learn something new every day," said Battle, plopping back against the leather seat. "A month ago I was the only person in the world, except when people came wandering onto my land."

Lola squeezed his fingers. Her eyes were still closed, but Battle knew she was listening to everything. He squeezed back.

"Then," Battle said, "there's a Cartel running every part of Texas. Except it isn't Texas anymore and the Cartel isn't in control of everything. Now we have Dwellers, who most people thought were extinct despite the fact they'd infiltrated every major town under Cartel control, and a group of bald, cultish priestesses kept in safe houses."

Baadal's eyebrows arched high on his forehead. He smiled. "That sounds accurate. Except most of those who joined the resistance against the Cartel didn't know they were working with Dwellers."

"This whole thing reads like a series of post-apocalyptic Western dime-store novels," said Battle. "It teeters on the edge of believability."

"A willing suspension of disbelief leads to a great deal of enjoyment in a barren word devoid of joy," said Baadal. "I often find myself daydreaming to escape the reality of what is plausible and what is not."

"Let me know how it ends," said Battle.

Baadal turned to face the front. He unbuckled his seat belt and shifted uncomfortably in his seat.

Battle looked out his window at a boy urinating on a fence post. A man who Battle presumed to be the boy's father stood beside him, doing the same until a guard poked the man in the back with his rifle. They both stopped midstream and shuffled off to join their group.

His attention shifted to a young woman with a six-shooter stuffed into the front of her rope-cinched pants. She couldn't have been more than seventeen. A boy, maybe the same age or a little younger, stood next to her. His pants stopped at his calves. His ankles and feet were black as soot. They were leaning against a hearse. Their faces were drawn with frowns. Neither of them appeared to have much hope.

The bald woman with their golden ticket started walking back to the SUV, the piece of paper flapping against her outstretched hand. She stopped at the hearse and spoke to the driver. The teenagers perked up. The doors to the hearse swung open. The seventeen-year-old girl pulled the back hatch ajar, and a young woman carrying a baby emerged from inside the hearse.

Battle counted six people, including the baby, standing next to the death wagon. They had packs and weapons. The young mother was holding the child over her shoulder, swaying as she stood there at the rear of the vehicle. The woman looked haggard, as if she'd experienced something beyond the pale, something far outside her narrowly defined comfort zone.

Battle'd seen the look before, on the faces of war-weary Syrians and Iranians whose homes and schools and businesses were smoldering piles of rubble and rebar. They walked aimlessly through their streets with no place to go and nothing else to do. They were ghosts, shells of what once had been whole people.

The young mother had that look as she vacantly rocked from side to side, her eyes fixed on some imaginary distant place.

The priestess arrived at the SUV's window. "You're with them," she said and pointed to the hearse. "Time to go."

***

Ana looked back at the pair of SUVs with the gasoline cans strapped to their roofs. She didn't like the idea of more strangers joining them on their already dangerous trip.

She stepped to Taskar. "Tell me why we have to leave your car. I thought you always drove your clients the length of their trips."

He nodded, his eyes glued to the shaven-headed woman. "I do," he said. "Things have changed. They're not letting vehicles cross. Only people on foot."

"So you're staying here?"

"I'm staying with my transportation. They'll open it up soon."

"How long can you hold out?"

Taskar pursed his lips in thought. "A few days," he said. A sly grin grew across his face. "I've half your rations now."

Ana thanked him and watched five people step from the first SUV. There was a thin red-haired woman, a boy who had to be her son, two men who were unmistakably Dwellers, and a tall, lean man with sad eyes. His unkempt hair was tousled atop his head. His face was tanned from the sun, save the feathered white lines that revealed the wrinkles in his forehead and at his temples.

He carried himself like a soldier, she thought. He had that confidence, despite his evident sorrow. He also carried an assault rifle.

All five of them slowly walked toward Ana and her group of disaffected teens and twenty-somethings. The man with the sad eyes spoke first.

"I'm Marcus Battle," he said and nodded at the woman at his side. "This is Lola, her son, Sawyer, and these are our escorts."

"I'm Baadal," offered the Dweller. The driver, however, said nothing.

Taskar spoke for the group, directing himself to Baadal. "I'm a fellow Dweller," he said. "But I am not making the journey. This is Ana and her daughter, Penny." He then introduced the rest of the party before excusing himself.

Ana took control. "We don't know you," she said. "You don't know us. For whatever reason, they want us crossing the wall together. We'll help you; you help us. Once we cross, do what you gotta do."

Battle nodded. "Fine," he said. "Whatever we find once we move past that gate, we're bound to be stronger as a group of ten."

Ana agreed. "Let's go."

***

The gate slid on ungreased wheels. They screeched and squealed their resistance along the track as the guard pushed the chain-link open. Battle took a deep breath and crossed the threshold.

He was side by side with the driver, the only one of the party to have crossed before. He'd told Battle his job was to get them into the sneak-through before turning around and heading back to the canyon. The other SUV pulled out of the lot and started back along the highway, retracing its route to the canyon.

Inside the gate was a row of six-foot-tall evergreen hedges. Even before they'd cut through a gap in the growth, Battle heard the chaos beyond it.

He picked through the hedge, helped Lola and Sawyer negotiate their way, and stepped into no-man's-land. One hundred yards in the distance beyond, he saw the wall for the first time.

It was thirty feet in height, maybe taller in spots, and stretched from east to west as far as he could see. It was made of Texas limestone, a mix of alabaster white and shades of rust.

From where he stood, he couldn't see a sneak-through. He did, however, see a large blackbird fly past him, using the wind to glide toward the towering wall until it drifted low enough to land atop it. The bird, Battle thought, was taunting him.

"Marcus" — Lola snapped Battle from his trance — "what now?"

"I don't know," Battle said and pointed at the driver. "We follow his lead."

Battle refocused on the world directly in front of him. He was standing in the middle of a sea of people. It was a mixture of a flea market, circus, and red-light district. Tents and corrugated aluminum structures crowded the dry grass prairie that constituted no-man's-land.

The wind carried with it the odor of burnt popcorn, ammonia, and grilled meat. It was immediately intoxicating, then quickly became nauseating. The odor was overwhelming and stung Battle's nostrils.

There was music, there were barkers selling their wares, and buried in the mix of sounds was screaming. Battle stepped over the stiffened body of a dead man nobody else seemed to notice. The man was on his side, one arm frozen awkwardly behind him. His neck appeared broken. His eyes were open, his swollen tongue hanging from his mouth. The crowd walked around the body, stepped over it, or on it as if it were part of the prairie.

Battle looked away from the body and spied a wiry, mangy woman working a group of men ahead of them. "Hold your packs in front of you," Battle suggested to his group. "Wrap your arms around it if you can. Hold your weapons in your hands."

The mangy woman snuck her bony fingers into an unsuspecting man's pockets and fished a knife from it. It was in one hand, the other, and then gone. She swiped a package of jerky from another man who seemed enamored with her endowments. He got too handsy with her and she stuck him in the side with the knife, jabbing it repeatedly in and out until the man dropped to his knees and she moved along.

In the distance, there was the rumble of motorcycle engines revving and accelerating. Battle couldn't see past the humanity pushing him westward.

The driver pointed to their right. "We need to make it north," he said. "Push this way."

Lola and Sawyer had their packs on their chests instead of their backs. They'd listened to Battle. He took Lola's hand, instructed her to take Sawyer's, and began forging his own path through the crowds.

He kept his eyes above the undulating crowd and focused on the driver. Baadal, he knew, was behind Sawyer. The others, the group from the hearse, were pushing their way northward in a path parallel to Battle. They were a step or two behind, but the young mother with a child in a pack on her chest wouldn't be denied. She shoved and pushed and shouldered her way past the people in her way.

***

Ana cursed her height. It wasn't a problem until she was mired in a mud pit of humanity that reeked of sweat and sauerkraut. Ana had never eaten the German delicacy, but had a good idea of its fermented odor from the people she elbowed past on her way north toward the wall.

She was trying to keep pace with the SUV driver and the man named Battle. They were bigger and stronger than she, but she imagined wrongly they hadn't killed as many people as she had in the previous twenty-four hours. Ana believed she was as tough as they were and could stay with them on a parallel line.

With Penny bouncing in the modified baby carrier, the teenage girl held on to Ana's rear waistband. Together, they and the three others formed an elephant chain that stayed together despite the torrent rushing around them on all sides.

"Over here," Battle called out. "This way."

She stopped moving and stood on her tiptoes. Through the heads and shoulders of others, she could see Battle pointing to what looked like a brick and stone outhouse.

Ana forged ahead, cutting a line across to an alleyway between a row of plywood stands. One of them proudly sold a variety of THC-laced products. The other was a gunsmith. The smith called after Ana.

"Give you a Colt with a handmade pearl handle for two minutes with you," he snarled. "You can have two if you bring the whole gang." He burst into laughter as Ana moved without acknowledging him.

Beyond the stands, she found the outhouse, flies swarming above it. Battle and the others were standing around it. They were in a small, almost hidden area behind the busiest parts of no-man's-land. They were away from the view of the swarm beyond the bazaar of stands and shanties.

Ana pointed at it and looked at the SUV driver. "What's this?"

"It's a sneak-through," he said. "You ready?"

Ana turned up her nose. "We're going in there?"

The SUV driver nodded and opened the door. Ana gagged from the putrid waft of stale air that spilled from the space.

The driver climbed into the outhouse, his feet pressed against the bottom of the interior walls while he moved past the hole in the center of a slimy limestone bench. Behind the seat, the driver lifted a leg and kicked the back wall with his heel.

A panel gave way, slamming into a space between the interior and exterior rear walls. He grabbed the top of the opening and then slid himself carefully into the hole.

He gagged and cleared his throat. "There's a ladder here," he said. "If you can make it past the stench, you'll be okay. Last one in closes the door behind them.

The driver disappeared down the hole. One by one, they skipped over the pot and positioned themselves on the ladder.

Ana let everyone go ahead of her. She switched Penny onto her back. It was her turn to make the descent. She took sips of air to avoid inhaling the abhorrence of the outhouse and found her footing. Penny put her tiny hands on Ana's ears, gently tugging on the lobes, as Ana stepped lower and lower into the abyss.

The worn grip of the vented, flat iron ladder rungs caught in the soles of her shoes with every downward step. She held the rails tightly with both hands and slowly loosened them when she slid lower.

With the child on her back, Ana moved deliberately. With each extension of her legs, she could feel the temperature dropping. It was dank and cold. The spring of goose bumps populating on her arms and legs sent a shudder throughout her body.

Ana looked up toward the shrinking sliver of light leaking through the gap between the access panel and the false wall. She guessed she had to be twenty feet below ground.

***

The dirt floor at the bottom of the ladder was soft, almost spongy in texture. It gave underneath Battle's weight with each step.

The sneak-through was a more sophisticated tunnel than he'd imagined. The driver explained it was a relic from the days of the Los Zetas and Gulf Cartel. They'd ruled most of the eastern Mexican drug routes along the Gulf and the northern paths into Texas.

When the United States started building the wall to contain the Cartel, the generals employed former Zetas to construct tunnels for them. The generals hadn't minded the wall. It kept the United States out of its business and prevented the vast majority of people under their rule from leaving.

They still needed smuggling routes beyond their territory. The tunnels were an easy way to make it happen.

The driver told them the tunnel would lead them past the wall and shy of the Red River. If they were lucky, there wouldn't be a patrol in the area when they emerged.

The corridor was dark, but Ana had a hand-cranked flashlight, which illuminated enough of a path for the group to see where they were going. She walked next to the driver. The baby bounced on her back in the dark, her little feet kicking and flexing as her mother lit their way.

They walked maybe fifty yards when they reached the end of the tunnel. There was another ladder.

"Let Baadal open the trapdoor up top and make sure it's all clear. Then the women and children go first," said the driver to Battle. "You and me go last."

Once Baadal had given them the okay, Battle helped the others, one by one, climb to the surface and disappear into a window of bright light some twenty-five feet above them.

Then the window disappeared. The tunnel went dark. Battle opened his mouth to ask the driver what had happened when he felt a thick punch to the back of his head.

***

Ana pulled herself from the tunnel and into the blinding light of the late afternoon. She closed her eyes and slowly reopened them as they adjusted. Before she could see, she heard the rush of water and a call for help. It was coming from the river. Ana recognized the voice.

As she neared the rain-swollen Red River, she saw the woman from the front seat. She was clinging to a large tree branch and fighting against the raging current.

For years, the river had run dry, a wide red clay berth on either side of its paltry trickle. In the years since the Scourge, it had found its moxie. Even a light rain would fill its banks. The repeated storms of the past week had turned it angry and vengeful.

Ana stepped to the southern bank and stopped. The woman was caught, only her neck and head were above the water.

The teenagers ran up behind Ana when they saw their sister struggling to survive. "You left us!" cried the girl. "You left us!"

The boy looked at the Dweller. "How did she even get there?"

The Dweller named Baadal joined Ana on the bank. "There are many sneak-throughs. She must have found one. You can't save her," he said, "and we can't stay here. We need to move along the bank until we find a natural dam of rocks to cross. If we stay here, the patrol will find us."

The red-haired woman was next to Ana. "I can go in after her," she said. "I'm not a strong swimmer, but I could hold onto the branch."

"Mom, no," said Sawyer. "You'll drown."

"Help me!" the woman gurgled. She was losing her grip on the branch. "I can't hold on much longer. Help me, please."

Ana began removing her pack. "Take Penny," she said to Lola. "Hold her for a minute. I can swim."

After a moment of protest, Lola slid the pack over her shoulders and held Penny against her chest.

The teenage boy grabbed Ana's arm. "She left us," he said. "You don't have to do this. She deserves whatever happens."

Ana took the boy's hand and gently moved it from her arm. "Nobody deserves any of this," she said. "Nobody." She took off her shoes, set them neatly on the bank, and stepped into the frigid, roiling water. She leaned on the branch with one hand and stepped deeper into the river. The icy rush took her breath away. It made her chest hurt the farther she moved from the bank. A few feet from land, the riverbed dropped sharply. Ana lost her footing and slipped under for a moment.

She found her balance against the rush of water and pushed herself to the surface. Shivering, she inched her way along the branch, careful not to put too much reliance on her footing.

"I'm almost there," she said to the woman. "You're going to be fine."

The woman wasn't speaking. The water was at her chin. Her lips were puckered, her eyes bugged with fear. She held the branch with one hand while the other one flailed and splashed wildly against the water.

Ana moved to within reach of the woman and offered her hand. "Let go and grab."

The woman shook her head. She was too afraid, too panicked. She dipped lower into the water until only her nose and eyes were visible. She was thoroughly entangled in the branch and had clearly lost her footing on the riverbed.

Ana inched closer. Still the woman wouldn't reach for her. Ana, losing sensation in her limbs and unable to stop her teeth from chattering, lost her patience. She let go of her branch and let the current carry her next to the drowning woman. As Ana tried to reestablish her grip, the woman lunged at her and climbed onto her back, forcing Ana under the surface. She struggled to free herself from the woman's grip, but she was facedown and couldn't grab hold of anything but the silty bottom of the Red River. She tried flipping over, but couldn't. Water rushed into her nose, choking her. She grasped at her back and neck, only managing to grasp water that rushed through her fingers.

Her lungs were empty and burned from lack of oxygen. Her eyes were losing focus. She fought the urge to take a breath.

The fire in her lungs radiated outward until suddenly it stopped. Her blurry vision faded into blackness. The weight atop her lifted. Her panic waned and became an overwhelming sense of calm.

Ana's last thought was of Penny. Instead of fear for the future, however, Ana died knowing her child was safe in the arms of another mother who also sought a better life.

***

Lola stood ankle deep in the Red River, calling out to Ana. She screamed at the woman to get off her, to let her free.

She cried out for the mother she'd just met, whose baby she held at her chest. For minutes, she stood in that rushing water, holding her balance as her feet sank deeper into the muck underneath the surface.

The woman didn't listen. Maybe she couldn't hear or comprehend what Lola was asking of her. Instead, she held Ana underwater long enough that Lola knew she couldn't hold her breath.

Despite her using Ana to try to save herself, the drowning woman lost her fight against the water too. She slipped beneath the surface, only then freeing Ana's lifeless body. It popped to the surface and then raced away with the current. Ana was gone.

Lola buried her hands in her face. She didn't know Ana. She didn't need to know her to mourn her loss. Ana, a young mother with a baby who couldn't be more than nine or ten months old, had risked her life for a woman who'd abandoned her family. She stood on the bank silently until Sawyer yelled for her from the sneak-through's exit.

"Mom," he called, "something's wrong. Where's Marcus?"

Lola didn't see him. She saw the teens and the pair of twenty-somethings. No Marcus.

"I don't know," she said. "Didn't he come up?"

She started moving to Sawyer before he could answer. Halfway there, Baadal stopped her.

"He's not coming with you," said the Dweller.

Lola looked at him sideways. "What are you talking about?"

"Paagal doesn't trust him," he said. "She likes you. You and Sawyer can continue on your way, or you can come back and live with us in the canyon. Actually, she said you could live wherever you want. Battle can't come, though. I'm doing what I'm told."

When Lola tried pushing her way past Baadal, he grabbed her arms and stopped her. He squeezed. His face turned sour and he bared his teeth.

"He's not coming," Baadal said. "And if you—"

With the baby strapped to her chest, Lola turned her body and drove her knee upward between his legs. Baadal's knees buckled and he let go of her arms to grab himself. Before he could, she kneed him again.

As he dropped to the dirt, the baby started crying. Lola planted one foot and then swung the other as if kicking a ball. The front edge of her foot met Baadal's face, snapping back his head, and he fell unconscious to the ground, blood pouring from his nose and mouth.

Penny's cries grew shrill and loud. Lola tried soothing her by blowing gently onto the back of her neck as she reached the sneak-through trapdoor. Sawyer was already there tugging on it.

He looked up at his mom as he struggled with the handle. "I can't open it," he said.

It was locked.

***

Battle was dazed and disoriented. He didn't remember losing consciousness, or regaining it for that matter. He was sitting on the floor of the tunnel, his back against the ladder, strapped to it. His legs and hands were bound. He smelled lighter fluid and realized he was sopping wet.

"This is courtesy of Paagal," said the driver. "She wants you dead." He aimed Ana's flashlight in Battle's face.

Battle squeezed his eyes shut and struggled against the bungee tightly wrapped around his wrists.

"She doesn't trust you. She thinks you're an instigator."

Battle chuckled. He sniffed and felt the burn of the lighter fluid in his nostrils. Behind him, on the ladder, was a sharp edge where the lowest rung had separated from the side rail. He started picking at it with the bungee.

The driver cupped his hand over his ears. "You hear that?" he asked. "That's a baby crying up there."

Battle looked straight up toward the trapdoor. The baby's cry was piercing. She was upset. It wasn't a hungry or sleepy baby cry. Something had happened up there.

Battle spat the fluid from his lips and glared at the driver. "What about Lola?" The bungee was tearing. He could feel it. "What about Sawyer? The others?"

"They'll be fine," he said. "Maybe. I don't know why that baby is crying like that. I had kids before the Scourge. That's an angry cry."

Battle felt part of the bungee snap. He kept working it against the rung's sharp, knifelike edge. "Why does Paagal want me dead? I'm leaving. I've already crossed the wall."

The driver turned off the flashlight and pulled a brass cigarette lighter from his pocket. He popped it open, flicked the file wheel, and lit an orange flame. In his other hand he gripped Battle's HK rifle.

"She doesn't think you'll stay here," said the driver. "She's afraid you'll come back. Better to elimin —"

Battle snapped the bungee and freed his hands. Before the driver could toss the lighter, Battle had rolled from the ladder into the dark. He pushed himself to his feet and, with his feet bound together, leapt onto the driver, tackling him to the ground and knocking the lighter from his hand.

The driver caught Battle in the gut with his knee and twisted partly out from under Battle's weight. It wasn't enough.

Battle caught the driver's head between his legs as the man tried to free himself. With his legs bound, Battle had him trapped.

He squeezed against the driver's neck and rolled with him, fending off punches to his side and back. Battle drew his body into a ball and used his hands to grab the driver at the front and back of his head. He gripped handfuls of hair and then wrenched his hands counterclockwise until he heard a rippling crackle announce the end of the driver's fight.

Battle released his grip and collapsed. He lay on his back, the driver's twisted neck and head still between his knees, trying to catch his breath.

Every inhalation was laced with the burn of the lighter fluid. He took shallower and shallower breaths until he could breathe through his nose.

He looked up at the light seeping through the trapdoor. The baby was still crying.

Battle sat up, pushed himself away from the driver, and untied the bungee at his calves and ankles.

Slowly, he climbed the ladder toward the top. Each step was painful. He was cramping in his side. Each breath stung. His eyes burned from the mixture of fluid and sweat that dripped into them during his brief fight.

He reached the top and flipped the latch. He opened it to find Sawyer, Lola, and the young mother's baby waiting for him. She had stopped crying and was sucking on a pacifier.

Lola helped him climb from the hole onto the dirt. Battle looked behind him and saw the wall mere feet away. It appeared so much larger than it had from a distance.

"Where is everybody?" he asked. "Where are the others?"

Tears streaming down her cheeks, Lola thumbed over her shoulder. "Baadal's over there. I don't think I killed him. I'm not sure."

"The others?" he asked. "From the hearse?"

"Ana is dead." Lola's voice cracked. Her eyes drifted to the river. "She drowned."

Sawyer put his hand on his mother's shoulder. "The other four left," he said. "They didn't want to wait for us while we tried to break back into the tunnel. They were afraid a patrol would find them."

Battle pointed east, past Lola and Sawyer. "Like that one?"

A black Jeep was headed for them, blue lights flashing as it bounded along the riverbank between the water and the wall. They were armed.

Lola looked back at Battle. The tears had stopped. "What do we do?" she asked. "We can't outrun them."

"We'll get caught," said Sawyer.

"We're not getting caught," said Battle. "Give me the baby and climb in." Battle motioned to the open trapdoor. "We're heading back."

"Heading back?" asked Lola, helping strap Penny to Battle's back. "Where?"

Battle smiled at her, took her face in both of his hands and kissed her on the lips. He pulled away and looked into her eyes. "Home, Lola. We're going home."

CHAPTER FORTY-FOUR

OCTOBER 29, 2037, 1:20 PM
SCOURGE +5 YEARS
EAST OF RISING STAR, TEXAS

The SUV was running on fumes when Battle decelerated into his driveway. It had only been a few weeks, but it felt as if he'd been gone for years.

He rolled down the windows to listen to the crush of the gravel underneath the tires. Next to him, with her window down, was Lola. She was holding Penny, who Battle had decided was maybe an angel from Heaven. No baby had ever been as even tempered and easygoing as she was on their three-day trip back from the wall.

They'd taken back roads through abandoned towns to avoid any run-ins with the Dwellers. It was best that way.

His momentary joy at arriving back on his land was tempered by seeing the blackened shell of the main house when he pulled around the front drive. Battle took a deep breath and exhaled slowly, pressing the brake and putting the SUV into park.

Lola put her hand on his leg. "I'm sorry," she said. "I'm so sorry. If I hadn't—"

Battle put his finger to her lips. "Don't," he said, shaking his head. He checked the rearview mirror. Sawyer was asleep, lying across the entirety of the backseat.

Battle lowered his voice to above a whisper. "All those years alone in that house, all I had were my guns, my movies, and my thoughts. I was going crazy. I didn't know it. I couldn't see it. But I was."

Lola choked back tears and raised her hand to Battle's cheek. "You're not crazy," she whispered. "You're my hero. You're my boy's hero. You're going to be this little girl's hero too."

"I'm no hero," Battle countered. "For five years I killed anyone who came on my land. That didn't take guts. I almost killed you."

"You didn't though," she said. "You saved me."

"You saved me," Battle said. "I've always believed that God only gave me what I could handle. In the end, he gave me you."

Battle shut off the engine and hopped out of the SUV. "I'm going to put this in the garage in a few," he said, shaking free of the emotion of the moment by changing the subject. "First, I want to make sure everything is good in the barn. If it is, we're golden."

He left his new family at the SUV and trudged the familiar path from the driveway to his barn. He opened the wide doors and slipped inside. The first thing he heard was the familiar hum of the freezers. He reached beside him and flipped on one of the switches. The overhead lights flickered and clinked to life. The solar cells were good. He'd check the gas backup generators later.

The wall-to-wall shelving opposite him was stocked with everything he'd left earlier in the month. There were clothes, toiletries, medicine, and plenty of food. He even had baby formula, which he'd purchased as protein supplement if they ever ran out of meat and couldn't hunt.

They could live in the barn, he thought. He'd take the seating out of the SUV to piece together some bedding for all of them. There was enough timber out back he'd be able to build some furniture with Sawyer's help.

They'd be okay.

He walked out of the barn, turned left at the edge of what used to be his house, and walked to the backyard. The garden was a mess. It needed tending. He might have to rip up what was left, cover it with black plastic sheeting to kill everything, and start fresh. He had seeds. It would be good to grow new crops.

He passed the garden and looked to the far end of the backyard, near the woods that crept close to the house. Lola was there, her back to him, swaying with Penny in her arms.

Battle stopped and listened.

"I need your help," she said to the headstones in the ground in front of her. "I want to love him. I want him to love me. I want us to be a family. I truly believe he wants that too."

Lola stopped swaying and carefully lowered herself to her knees. With one hand she wiped the black soot and ash from atop the headstones.

"I'm never going to replace you in his heart," she said. "But I need his mind now. I need you to help him see that."

She started whispering and Battle couldn't hear her. He started walking again.

"Hey," he said, startling Lola. "Sorry. Didn't mean to scare you."

"Hi," she said and pushed herself to her feet with one hand, holding Penny tightly in the other. "Just saying hello. I hope that's okay."

"It's good," he said. "It's okay. We're gonna be okay."

"What if Paagal comes looking for us?" she asked. "What if she finds us?"

"She won't find us," he said. "If by chance she does, I'll shoot first. I won't ask questions."

THE END

AVAILABLE FOR PRE-ORDER
THE NEXT BIG ADVENTURE

EXCERPT FROM SPACEMAN: A POST-APOCALYPTIC/DYSTOPIAN THRILLER

MISSION ELAPSED TIME:
72 DAYS, 3 HOURS, 5 MINUTES, 31 SECONDS

249 MILES ABOVE EARTH

The alarm sounded without warning.

It was shrill and echoed though the station until Clayton Shepard typed a series of commands into the computer to disarm it.

He ran his finger across the screen, not believing what was he was reading, what the alarm was warning. It was outside the bounds of what was reasonable or even possible.

WARNING: GEOMAGENTIC K-INDEX 9 OR GREATER EXPECTED
SPACE WEATHER MESSAGE CODE: WARK9<
SERIAL NUMBER: 476
ISSUE TIME: 2020 JAN 25 0225 UTC
VALID TO 2020 JAN 25 2359 UTC

He pressed a button that keyed the microphone nearest his mouth. "Houston," he said, "station on space-to-ground one. Are you seeing the alarm?"

"Station, this is Houston on space-to-ground one," the call replied. "We see it. We have a team looking at data. Stand by."

He rolled his eyes. "Are you kidding me?" Clayton said, keying the mic. "Houston, this is station on space-to-ground one. I don't think we have time for that. I'm asking we abort the EVA now."

He looked through the window to his left. Astronaut Ben Greenwood stopped his work, turned around to face Clayton through the mask on his helmet, and joined the conversation.

"Shepard," said Ben, "this is Greenwood station-to-station one. What alarm?" Greenwood's helmet reflected a fisheye view of The Cupola in which Shepard was monitoring the first spacewalk of their expedition.

Clayton read the alert again. A severe magnetic storm was coming. He swallowed and cleared his throat. "Greenwood, this is Shepard on station-to-station one. The onboard coronagraph is giving indications of large, transient disturbances on the Earth-facing side of the Sun."

"Shepard, this is Greenwood on station-to-station one. You mean solar flares?"

"Station," the radio call from mission control interrupted, "this is Houston on space-to-ground one. We've checked with SELB in Boulder. They confirm the alarm, as does Marshal in Huntsville. Loops are growing in intensity. There is a CME within striking distance. Our original assessment may have been incorrect."

The third member of the expedition, Cosmonaut Boris Voin, spoke through his mic. He was ten yards from Greenwood, tethered to the exterior of the station. "Shepard," he said, his English barbed with his native Russian accent, "this is Voin, station-to-station 1. Are we killing EVA?"

Shepard took a deep breath before answering. Two days earlier, they'd seen evidence of a coronal mass ejection, what they'd believed was a part of the corona tearing away from the Sun. After looking at the data, and considering the urgency of the spacewalk, Mission Control determined the reading was an anomaly. CMEs, as they were called, happened nearly every day. This one, they concluded, was no real threat. Despite the coronal halo visible around the sun forty-nine hours earlier, the numbers seemed so far beyond anything they'd ever seen they concluded there was a system malfunction and the sensor was offering incorrect data.

They were wrong.

Clayton keyed the mic. "Houston, this is station on station-to-ground one," he said, knowing the spacewalking astronauts could hear him. "It's my recommendation that we immediately kill the EVA."

"Station, this is Houston on station-to-ground one. We agree that out of an abundance of caution the best course of — "

The line went dead. The station went dark.

Clayton pressed the mic. "Houston," he said, a hint of panic in his voice, "this is station on station-to-ground one. Do you copy?"

No answer.

"Greenwood, this is Shepard one station-to-station one. Do you copy?"

Nothing.

Clayton tried Voin. He tried Shepard again. He switched to channels, two, three, and four. He tried the Russian channels. None of them replied. He wasn't even sure his radio was working.

"This cannot be happening."

Astronaut Clayton Shepard was ten weeks into his first mission in low Earth orbit when the impossible happened.

The CME experts thought couldn't exist carried with it sixteen billion tons of hot plasma and charged particles. It outraced the solar wind at an astonishing two million kilometers an hour, creating a blast wave ahead of its impact with the Earth and its orbiting satellites. The cloud, larger than any ever recorded, collided with the Earth's magnetic field and created an enormous surge.

High energy protons peaked at over two-hundred and fifty times the norm and slammed into the Earth where the effect was instantaneous. Electrical currents in the atmosphere and on the ground surged repeatedly at varying degrees.

Within ninety seconds of impact, chain reactions had begun to shut down power grids and damage oil and gas pipelines across the entirety of the planet. Satellites orbiting the Earth absorbed the electrical surge and those that had not shut down the high voltage on their transceivers were destroyed or significantly damaged.

Unlike solar flares, the CME had left the Sun slowly, gathering speed as it accelerated outward and away from the star's surface. It traveled nearly twice the speed of any previously recorded CME and carried with it sixty percent more material than the typical value of a CME cloud.

By the time it hit the ISS, the station was in the worst spot possible, racing above the Atlantic Ocean in a highly magnetic region of the planet called the South Atlantic Anomaly. It only worsened the impact on the station, which was radiation hardened to withstand minor event upsets. It couldn't handle anything like the invisible tsunami that had just surged and crashed over it.

Without knowing exactly what had happened, Shepard knew what had happened.

He steadied himself in the darkness of The Cupola, a dome shaped module with seven panoramic windows, and pressed his hands against the glass. It was almost five feet tall and a little more than nine feet across, but it felt like a coffin.

He looked to his right, out window three, and saw the Canadarm 2, the station's large robotic arm used to build parts of the station and to grab incoming cargo vehicles. Beyond the arm was his home planet.

From the underside of the station, the Cupola was the perfect spot from which to watch the Earth as the ISS moved at five miles per second around the globe. He was speeding past North America.

It was dark. The familiar spider webs of lights that marked large metropolitan areas across the continent were missing.

Like the ISS, the planet was virtually powerless.

"Jackie," he said aloud, looking toward the area he thought was Texas. A thick knot grew in his throat as he suppressed his emotion. "The kids." His lips quivered, his eyes welled, but Clayton Shepard, the mechanical engineer and astronaut, steadied himself. He'd have to worry about them later. His own survival and that of his crew were paramount.

Shepard gripped the sides of the laptop display directly in front of him. The screen was black. He thumped the spacebar with his thumb. He hit the power button as if he were trying to score a point on a video game.

Nothing worked.

To his right, facing the Canadarm2 underneath window three was a joystick. It controlled the arm. He jockeyed it back and forth and then slapped at it with his hand. Nothing. Not that he expected it.

Shepard spun one hundred and eighty degrees. Cosmonaut Boris Voin was still there. He was tangled in the tether than connected him to the ISS. Feet away was veteran Astronaut Ben Greenwood. Ben had his hands up in surrender. He couldn't know if they were dead or barely clinging to life.

Shepard took a deep breath and closed his eyes. "Tell me this is a dream," he said aloud. "This has got to be a dream."

He opened his eyes and reaffirmed what he already knew to be true. If he couldn't restore power, he was screwed.

ACKNOWLEDGEMENTS

Thanks to my wife and kids, who always have my six. They support me, my dreams, and the long hours required to produce stories I hope people will read and enjoy. I love them and couldn't imagine a world, post-apocalyptic or otherwise, without them.

Thanks to my editor, Felicia Sullivan. Her deft hand always finds the right way to turn a phrase. She is blunt. She is on point. I am thankful to work with her.

Pauline Nolet is a fabulous copy editor. She finds the things everyone else misses and makes the finished product as clean as it can be.

Hristo Kovatliev is a gem. My author friend Murray McDonald (go Google him and buy his books) recommended the gifted cover artist. He artfully crafted the covers for this series. I'm grateful.

Steve Kremer, Stephen Stewart, MD, and Mike Christian all provided valuable expertise in a variety of areas. Kremer helped polish an early edition of HOME and removed the weapons errors and typos. He's been patient and kind in teaching me about guns and HAM radios. Stewart aided with medical information, ensuring I wasn't off base. I'll be leaning on them again in my next series. Christian proofed the Syrian chapters in CANYON. He was fantastic with suggesting changes that made the critical scenes ring true. I appreciate all three of them.

I also am indebted to several authors who've guided my journey thus far or who are zealous in their promotion of my work: Steven Konkoly, Murray McDonald, A.R. Shaw, Franklin Horton, ML Banner, Jay Falconer, William H. Weber, Russell Blake, Lisa Brackmann, and Ian Graham.

Thanks to my parents, Sanders and Jeanne, my siblings, Penny and Steven, and my in-laws, Don and Linda, for constant encouragement and support.

Finally, thank you for picking up these books and giving them a shot. I hope you enjoyed them and can't wait to take you on the next adventure...

Printed in Great Britain
by Amazon